COLD QUIET COUNTRY

Clayton Lindemuth

M P Publishing Limited
12 Strathallan Crescent
Douglas
Isle of Man
IM2 4NR
British Isles

CIP DATA TO COME

Book Design by Maria Clare Smith

A CPI Catalogue for this title is available from the British Library

COLD QUIET COUNTRY

Clayton Lindemuth

MP Publishing
www.mppublishingusa.com

DEDICATION

Chapter One

Bittersmith, WY 1971

Got my eye on a purty waitress across the street named Jeanine; been telling myself for two years that one day I'd visit her on this desk.

Sonsabitches want to run me out? Sheriff Bittersmith, run out?

Only thing left to go in the box is my coffee mug. Soon as I dump the last cold swallow and run it under the sink, I'm going to prop my feet on the corner of my desk and wait for noon, walk over there for a wedge of cherry pie, see about Jeanine.

I'm grumbling out loud and Fenny watches from her desk. Women age twice as fast. Twenty woman-years ago, Fenny was something to look at. Now she's got corncob thighs and tits that spread like loose flapjack batter.

"What're you bitchin' about?" She smiles, and she's purty enough to bend over. Barely. "You got your health," she says.

"Aw, hell."

I rap a desktop that's as empty as a liar's stare. No time like the present. Grab my coffee cup.

"Where you going?" Fenny says.

Deputy Odum says, "We got coffee here."

"I'll be back in five minutes. Don't think you can move your shit in my office."

It's colder'n a witch's bippy outside, all snow and ice. Across the street, cattycorner, is the County Seat. Best hashed browns in the state, and the prettiest waitress serving them. I wait while old Mrs. Llewellyn drives past in her Mercury, still smelling like ninety-five octane gasoline 'cause she's never in the last six months had her carburetor adjusted. I wave, and she waves back. I toss my old coffee to snow piling on the road where the salt isn't keeping up and spend a minute with the broom outside the County Seat cleaning slush off my boots.

"What brings you back so soon, Sheriff?" Jeanine says.

"Need a refill." I rest my mug on the counter and look around. Late morning; nobody here. "Things not picking up yet?"

"Not for an hour, if then. We got the storm of the century coming in." She carries the coffee pot to my cup. "Something on your mind?"

"Couple of things."

She's an Irish brunette with skin the color of a pink rose and eyes like fireflies.

I look and she smiles.

"Couple things on my mind," I say. "Last day on the job."

"How's an institution like you get to retire?"

"Damn town council is how."

She carries the pot away but turns to keep eye contact.

"Had a vote last night," I say. "Back room. Brandy snifters and cigar smoke, you know. The public uninvited."

"Sounds rotten already."

"That's the story. I'm out."

"Terrible."

"Puts a man in an awkward situation."

"How's that?"

"I'll shoot you straight." There's noise in the kitchen. I lower my voice. "You started two years ago, and I've come here every morning. Every time I leave, it's been with the thought that one day we'd swan over to the station and get familiar with each other. You seem like a girl needs adventure, and I'm down to one last day wearing the badge—"

"What?"

"You asked what was on my mind."

"Familiar?"

"See, I know where you come from." Her lips aren't inviting now. I've seen it on other girls. "Elderberry has a sheriff, you know. Stevens. Good man. Good friend of mine."

"What'd you have in mind, Sheriff?"

"It'd be a shame for him to have to drive up here, weather like this, to fetch you home. Why, you'd end up in that jail across the street for a week, maybe, 'til the roads clear."

"You wouldn't."

"I'd be obliged. That's why I thought if you and I was to go over to the station, we might find a reason it don't make sense for me to call my friend Sheriff Stevens. Might find a way around some of the uglier aspects of the law."

"Two years," she says, shaking her head.

"Two years I wondered what'd bring a pretty thing like you up here. Keep you laying low, not partying about town like the other kids your age."

She looks at an oval clock above the kitchen window. "Just how familiar?"

"I dunno. Maybe a little head. Mornin' head is always nice."

She clenches her jaw.

"You wouldn't be able to do that," I say. "I'd put a pop-knot on your head, you did something like that."

"That it? Freedom for a blowjob?"

"Simple."

"You got people over there. Deputies."

"And Fenny. But you've never been there, so I wouldn't expect you to know there's no window in my office door."

"You're an asshole. Put me in jail."

"Think on it. Give it thirty seconds. You know the price of a good lawyer? You'll need some lawyerin' for sure. Grand theft auto's a big deal, great state of Wyoming."

Her jaw slides sideways. Tired. Predictable. Furrowed brows, then arched—but with squinty eyes. Mad as hell about being forced to buckle, but in the long run, things are going to be better if she takes the world—and her place—such as they are.

She turns her back and I count seconds. Fifteen, twenty. She faces me, says over her shoulder, "Eddy, I'm going outside for some air."

Eddy grunts.

She goes the long way around the counter, lifts a leather jacket from the rack at the far end, and precedes me out the door. Ass shakes like good stiff pudding. She takes the steps two at a time and strides across the street so mad she loses balance every other step. Old Mrs. Llewellyn is coming back the other way and slides partly sideways to stop, and I offer her another wave.

I hurry to pass Jeanine and she still beats me to the door, but pauses. "One time. If you ever come for me again…"

"Don't bother saying it. You'll scratch my eyes out."

"I'll castrate you."

"Promises. Let's get inside." I take her elbow. Guide her to my office. At the door I say to the deputies, "Miss Jeanine and I will be a minute. She's a potential witness."

I close the door.

"They know."

"Who the hell cares?"

I lean against my desk and she scans the office. Pulls a cushion from the couch against the far wall. Stands before me all perky and defiant.

"There? In front of the door? Sit on the couch."

"Plumbing works better standing. Getting old."

I unfix my drawers and pull out Big Nixon. She gapes. Gulps. Tosses the cushion at my feet and falls to her knees in front of me. She opens her mouth and leans, and I already feel that special scrotal tickle. Her breath.

"Let me be clear," Jeanine says. "I hope I give you a heart attack."

"I do too, sweetie."

* * *

The phone rings and Fenny answers. She clucks and chatters and I recheck my desk drawers for anything I've forgotten. Spot a paperclip and slide it across the drawer bottom. Can't get my fat fingers around it. Fenny clears her throat. She's at my door holding the receiver to her hip.

"Don't look so sour," I say. "They'll make you retire."

Fenny doesn't smile. The cord extends fifteen feet from her desk and swings against the garbage can. Her face is pale. Something urgent at hand. She presses the receiver to her breast and mouths, "Line one."

Fenny bird-steps away, smoothing her underpants line while jawin' into the phone. "Now Missus Haudesert, start from the beginning. The sheriff is on the line."

I press the phone to my ear. "Bittersmith."

"He's dead," she says. "Gale G'Wain run him through with a pitch fork."

I drop my feet from the desk. "Who's dead?"

"Burt is, you old fool. That whelp killed him this morning."

"Burt? What whelp?"

"That's right, and you got to get out here and do something about it."

"Burt's dead," I say. Breathing feels like pulling a hundred-pound bowstring. My face tingles and my mind is low-blood-pressure thin.

"Sheriff?"

I clench the edge of my desk. Cover the phone with my other hand. "Who's Gale G'Wain?"

Fenny's looking away.

"Sheriff?"

I uncover the phone. "Missus Haudesert, are you sure? About Burt?"

"Well, he ain't moved, and I don't expect there's a pint of blood left in him."

"I'm coming." I drop the phone in the tray.

Deputy Travis completes a form at his desk.

Deputy Odum peers in through my open door. "What's shakin', Sheriff?"

I have four deputies: Odum, Sager, Roosevelt, and Travis, a youngster whose father made an impression at the Lodge. Travis' daddy saw me in town, said Travis served with honor and distinction in the military police. He'd be coming home from the service and looking for work. Town Council anteed up the budget and the job was waiting when Travis got home. He's a solid boy and has the discipline. I'd sooner see him Sheriff than Odum, but he's only twenty-six years old.

"Fuck off, Odum." I check the load in my Smith & Wesson, snap the cylinder, and shovel the piece into my holster. Grab my coat from the rack.

Odum blocks the door. I shoulder past.

"Them roads is slippy," Fenny says. "And getting worse."

"Storm coming in." I can't think, so I ramble. "If it hits like the one in fifty-eight, like the weatherman said on the radio this morning, we won't have much time before Burt's snowed in for a week. Fenny, call the coroner and send him to Haudesert's. Odum, I want you at your desk, case I need you."

The door handle is ice, the wind outside brutal. Already a swirl of a drift forms at the west side of the steps. Like a fool, I've left my gloves in the Bronco. The snow on the steps is fluffy and the wood at the front of each plank is rounded. I grab the rail.

I scrape new ice from the windshield. Climb inside. The Bronco's heater blows warm air. I went for a cruise late in the morning and the engine is still cooling down. Fenny was right about the roads. A layer of white hides patches of black ice until skid marks expose them.

Haudesert lives south of Lake Wilbur. Lived.

I knew him—took an interest in him.

He was a wild man in his early years. A sheriff catches wind of things, sees all manner of idiocy. Years ago, he spent a night in my jail and I sat him down for a come-to-Jesus, and he quieted after our talk. But it was his wife and batch of rats that tamed his rabble rousing. He turned his energy to the Wyoming Militia and started running with a bunch of loons. I already got a gut that it killed him.

I take the empty roads slow. Word about the storm is all over and folks are staying home. There's not much that won't hold a day…long as you got a day. Goddamn town council held their vote last night behind closed doors. Edmund comes into the hallway with his hands buckled at his belly and says, "I hate to tell you," and I say, "Then keep your pie hole shut, Ed." He looks at the floor and I say, "How long have I got?"

"Tomorrow. They want you out tomorrow."

"For Odum?"

He nods.

"For goddamn Odum?"

"These boys think he's the bee's knees."

"He don't have the sense to pull his pecker out a hive o' hornets."

"You're seventy years old. You ought to enjoy your wanin' years."

And I said, "I'm seventy-two, and fuck my wanin' years, Ed. Fuck 'em. Fuck every one. I'm sheriff of this town. Town bears my name. I'm sheriff 'til the day I die."

I know the game Odum plays, that he can steal a man's job. He talks new ideas, as if keeping order is nothing but having cars with new radios and an armory stacked with sawed off shotguns. But the fact is, he got to the men who do the deciding.

Odum doesn't know how to get out among the people. Doesn't know how to take a personal interest in a ruffian like Burt Haudesert, lower his voice, lean in close, grab his eyes by the goddamn balls and say, "I'm going to give you some fatherly advice. You want to keep your momma from seeing your toe with a tag, keep your voice down in my town." Odum doesn't have the gravity to tell a man twice his size he's going to park a pile of hell on his front porch. He'd rather wait and face a big problem down the road than deal with a small one now. It's a lack of conviction. A sheriff has to own his town. Has to take things personal, and love the wayward son enough to set his ass straight.

Maybe that's why forced retirement feels like they cinched my balls in a leather strap and trussed me from a tree limb.

Haudesert's lane crosses a built-up section of wooded swamp formed where a crick's been backed up thirty years. Heavy rain came November—late—and ice sheets half the drive. I track slow on the snow. I'd planned to put on the tire chains on today, but to hell with it.

The two-story farmhouse stands on a bare knoll like a broke down castle keep atop a hill. A little farther and to the right is the barn where I'm betting Burt Haudesert breathed his last. The farm looks clean, but dreary. The air is so thick with snow that everything is gray, and the pall extends to the wood-smoke taste of the air.

It's been a long time since the town of Bittersmith saw a murder.

The Bronco slips and I downshift, ease along at an idle. Off the ice now, the rutted lane scrambles my guts. I stop on the slope to the barn door and pull the emergency brake. Let the engine run.

Fay Haudesert rushes from the house. "He took Gwen!"

I look inside the barn. Burt's boots point to the roof. I can't see the rest of him.

"Guinevere's gone!" Reaching me, she says, "Didn't anyone else come with you?"

"Who?"

Tears stream down her wind-chapped face. "You've got to find Gwen!"

"Did you see what happened?"

"It's plain."

"He's plain dead, but did you see it?"

"He's got the fork in his neck." She stands in the shelter of the Bronco and cups a hand over her eye. Snowflakes melt on the windshield as she looks across the field. Beyond is a band of forested hillside, and beyond that, the lake.

An eddy brings the taste of gasoline exhaust to my mouth.

"There was tracks that way, before it started blowing," she says.

"They're still there. I see 'em." I look at the purple storm clouds and then at the pair of prints headed across the field. Nodding back at the barn, I say, "You see who did this?"

"Who could it be but Gail G'Wain? Our hired hand."

"We'll see." I step inside the barn for a quick look and my stomach tumbles. Burt wears green corduroy and flannel, like he came out the house in a hurry. I imagine the scowl masking his face matches the one that fetched him without a coat. The pitchfork through his neck is narrow and Burt's neck is half as wide as his hips. Wider'n his head. Two tines go all the way through, the middle one piercing his voice box. His fingers are curled into fists, and blood is splotched all over the barn bay—not just the puddle where he bled out, but across the floor, on the joists, bales of hay, on the workbench. It's like a kid pumped a five-gallon bucket of red paint through a squirt gun. The drops are frozen.

Above him, off to the side, a truss hangs from a hemp rope. It's a two-by-four with thirty-penny nails pounded into the end for hanging deer. It swings in the breeze as each gust of wind sweeps through the bay door.

I wipe my eyes. They're wet from the cold. Fay Haudesert doesn't see, and I paint my face detached and solemn and turn to her.

"Where's your boys? Where's Cal and Jordan?"

"They ain't been around all morning." She turns her eyes to her husband. "But he's dead, and my little girl's out in that."

I look outside. The sky is mad as hell.

Chapter Two

Lord, I'm in trouble.

The blood in my boot is frozen and ice stiffens my corduroy pant leg. The lake ice is thick enough to support a truck but I think about being warm, and how I'd hate to drop through a thin spot and drown.

Snow falls and a good headwind keeps it in my eyes. It's been two, three miles, limping. I've got no coat and my calf is bare from where I cut away the corduroy. My skin is numb. My lungs burn. Ahead, a gray house sits at the lake edge, framed in the dusky storm. I'm in the middle of the lake and everything is flat to where trees border in the distance, and looking from my bloody boot to the far off swirl of snow and trees gives me vertigo.

I turn. No one on my trail. Yet.

There's no way this ends good.

It's been less than an hour since Guinevere was in my arms. Struggling, maybe. Eyes wide. There is something strange and fascinating about her hearing music when people are about to die. What she called the bullfrog notes. She heard the song for both of her grandparents years ago, and once for a man about to suffer a heart attack at the grocery.

While we fondled in the loft, did she hear music for me?

Is that why?

Each step is agony. My tracks are clean. The bleeding stopped when my blood became ice, but inside the muscles are chopped. The house draws near, as if it approaches me.

The house.

Falling snow obscures a drifted slope at the lake's edge. The wind has sheathed its fangs; snow falls straight down, like rain. I press my arm to my stomach and there's frozen blood there too. I blow my nose without plugging either side. Six hours ago I was inside her and warm and smelling her sweet breath and hair. Hearing telltale giggles. Too-loud giggles.

I near the bank and look things over. An inlet feeds from a draw in the woods off to the left; the streambed is evident under the drifts. The ice is thin at the edge. The first indication is a cracking sound and then there's a decrease in the ice's rigidity. Ten feet from the bank, I shatter through, slash forward, run on a sheet that plunges and slips, and I'm submerged and gagging…

It doesn't feel bad. The cold shock imposes a comfortable void between my thoughts and me. My leg doesn't hurt, though I'm walking on the lake bottom, chin barely above water, eyes peeled back and dancing freaked-out crazy-cold and maybe I'll stay. How long would it take to end? Two minutes? Thirty seconds? But I never stop moving. I rake snow and icicles, claw out on the bank, and the air is warm.

The two-story house looms, looking like thirty-year-old bird shit and absolutely still. The windows are dark. The chimney is a monument of cold stones.

I fight up the bank. Climb the steps. Hear my teeth chatter, but don't feel them. The door is locked and the knob sticks to my hand. I jerk away and leave a film of skin frozen to the brass. There's a rock on the porch, a doorstop. I cradle it between my palms and heave it through a window.

The glass is jagged. I push the doormat with my boot until it folds and then lift it, mash it against the standing shards. I duck through belly down, slip to the floor and huddle. Crawl as if drawing deeper into a cave. Darkness resolves into a fireplace, chairs, a sofa. The smell is damp ashes. I'm about to freeze to death.

If I get warm, the bleeding in my leg will resume. If I bandage my wound and survive the morning, men with guns will descend on this house.

I spot a box of matches on the hearth and slide the sleeve open. Matchsticks tumble in a pile. With inflexible fingers, I scrape one across the stone. It flares, and others beside it ignite. I cup my hands above. The color on my skin is red like Gwen's hair and freckles.

* * *

I met Gwen in the summer. She had a faraway, shattered look. A quick smile that said she knew more than her age entitled, said her flirting wasn't a tease but a promise of goods for the taking. I watched the dust at my feet. When you walk everywhere, you see your feet a lot. Hungry and unfed for two days—except what I scrounged from the forests and fields at night—I came upon the Haudesert farm knowing only that I smelled cow dung and saw fields of waist-high corn, and others of alfalfa.

Guinevere answered the door. Her eyes were startling and her hair was as red as mine. I didn't try to feel anything toward her, but in that very first moment I knew she had a pathway into me, if she wanted it. I didn't want to be her deliverer. Didn't even know she needed delivering. I saw her thoughtfulness and mistook it for empathy. In hindsight, she was edgy like a cat watching a caged bird. Her eyes flared and then narrowed. She was aware of biology and what it clamors for between men and women, and more so. Was eager to experiment with me. Perform.

That should have been my warning.

"Burt's in the barn," she said.

"Burt one of your brothers?"

"My father."

On the short walk to the barn I puzzled over her calling her father by his Christian name.

I found Burt Haudesert hammering steel around an anvil. He was dressed in a green flannel shirt and corduroys. Everything was one shade of green or another save his boots; the dust covering them caught a splash of sunlight that left them almost gold. I came alongside and he explained what he was doing without me asking: re-fabricating a busted hay wagon support that he'd asked Carl somebody to weld back together—Carl being a person who could weld but couldn't shape.

"I'm Gale G'Wain, and I'm looking for work."

"I'm Burt Haudesert, and I got work all around me," He studied my eyes, my clothes, my hands. "An unplanned labor shortage on account of Cal bein' so goddamn dense. There's tree stumps in that pasture with a higher IQ."

"Yes sir," I said, and stepped away.

"Stoned as a rock star, he gets up on that cross beam and tries to walk it with a shovel for balance. Busted half the bones in his body."

"That's something else, sir."

"You go inside the house, and if you ask Gwen real nice, she won't bite your head off," he said. "She'll scare you up something to eat."

I shook his hand and he winked at me and laughed. He read me right; I was grateful. But the feeling I got at his mention of Gwen should have sounded alarm bells in my head. His ease-making euphemisms about his baby girl. The tropes he put into play with a stranger. And if not that, if not him, the feeling I got as my mind followed through on those lascivious wanderings, as if Burt Haudesert had just granted permission to strip his daughter naked and enjoy her any vulgar way I wanted to—assured that she wouldn't bite my head off.

That should have been enough, but it wasn't.

I hadn't eaten anything but bitter, half-grown apples, two-inch carrots, and tiny shoots of corn ears since Mister Sharps cut me loose from the Youth Home, saying I was a precocious young man and the world would reward a boy of my bent. It was that time of year when summer isn't sure if it wants to come out and play but spring is sure it doesn't want to leave. Crops were growing slow and all the talk in the barbershops and seed stores was on the drought. How the almanac said it was this year for sure, and the best thing to do with seeds was to save them or grind them into flour, but don't plant them, because anything that grows will bake dry before it gets six inches off the ground. Farmers can be a superstitious, lot but their bellies force them to be pragmatists, so they spend their idle minutes framing every sort of omen in every shade of light, casting gloomy predictions of their own demise, and when the luxury of idle time disappears, they set about breaking their backs to ensure no axis of foul weather and nutrient deterioration or market glut or bad health will prevent them from feeding their babies and living as free men.

Burt Haudesert struck me as being like the men in the barber shops and seed stores. He stood in the barn hammering steel, and I got that he was as much a part of the earth as a cornstalk.

Just as stiff-backed and silly.

The front door opened before my foot hit the steps. Gwen stood with her arms folded below her bosom, plumping it. She had one leg forward, her ankle to the curve of her calf showing a lot of shape. Girls are spindles until they become women and there's nothing straight left. Gwen was a curvy country road. Red hair and freckle-faced, and freckles all the way down her arms. Her hair was up, and that made her look older. I allowed myself a good look as I came toward her and she retreated inside, still facing me, and backed against the counter.

With all the books I'd read and all the words I'd studied and all the miraculous fictions I'd imagined, the best I had for her was, "Burt says you'll find some lunch for me."

She studied me like she was taking the measure of a dolt and then swallowed slowly. "There's the refrigerator." She spun with a move that flared her dress, and left the room. Thirty seconds after she was gone, her calves were still burned to my eyes.

I filled a glass with water and sat at the table with the chair sideways so I could open the refrigerator door and study what was inside. I ended up slathering a couple slabs of fresh baked bread with butter and jam.

Burt put me to work forking compressed hay from the goat stalls. No one I knew raised goats, and I was unfamiliar with them, but the odor was just a new twist on the old rotten ammonia stink of composted urine and hay. I couldn't shovel very much before I had to run from the stall to gulp a few breaths of clean air. The goats didn't mind, because the smell was trapped; it was only digging a foot of hay that released its full power. I shoveled all afternoon for a belly full of food and a rip in my pants when I caught a nail sticking out of the wall.

I only had the one pair. Didn't have the money to buy another until two weeks ago, and that from working for the butcher Haynes. The whole time I worked for Burt it was mostly for food. I saved a few dollars and he allowed me to sleep in the barn and wash in the trough.

My first evening at the Haudesert place, Burt told me to get cleaned up, because even he—reeking of the barn and unaware of it—smelled goat stalls on me. I sat to dinner with his family, his wife Fay and his boy Jordan, and Guinevere. Burt's other son, Cal, had his supper brought to him in bed. The first month I was there I only saw him once, when Fay asked me to run him a glass of water because she was a mess with bread dough in her fingers and he was hollering for a drink.

Burt gave me a beer that night while we sat on the porch smoking stogies. He asked questions about politics. Had I done any thinking about natural rights? What did I think about the commies taking over the country? I listened and he explained what a reasonable man would believe about the subjects. As I tried not to puke from cigar smoke and beer, Burt announced he held rank in the Wyoming Militia. His boys were old enough to have made up their minds, and each of them were joining, and that's how I know that one way or the other when they see the way I left Burt, they'll be on their way to find me at this house. They're country boys with snowmobiles and friends. Heavy-artillery friends. They'll come for me. Them and every redneck militiaman they can find.

* * *

More paper. A wooden bin to the side of the hearth holds dry oak and cherry logs, already split. Many have long splinters barely attached and quickly fuel the blaze. I load the fireplace and huddle close, breathing smoke because it's hot and painful.

The chimney is open but the fire has yet to establish the right drafts through the house. Smoke hangs a foot below the ceiling. In the flickering light, ghosts almost lift up from the photos on the wall.

I fall to my behind and press stupid fingers to my belt. My leg wound seeps. Progress. With my belt undone, I look at my boots. Blow into clasped hands and then swing my arms. I fumble with the laces, pancake them between my fingers and pull. Toe the heels off and push until my boots clonk on the hardwood floor. Pull my shirt over my head and shake my hair. Ice flies. I'm naked on the floor, shaking, rapidly dying despite the inferno a few feet away. I crawl to the hearthstones and sit so close steam rises from my skin.

Heat scorches my face. Everywhere my flesh warms, it burns, and an image flashes through me—the hunched Buddhist who doused his robes in gasoline and lit them. A quiver originates in my spine and undulates through me until I am powerless. Violent action brings a measure of control that eludes my slower, studied motions. If I act quickly I might gain the precision to do ordinary things—like remove the carbine from above the mantle.

My thigh has a knife hole that goes in horizontal and flat, the direction a knife would take if it wanted to cut a leg clean off. The blade had dried blood and whitetail deer hairs stuck to it, and some maybe came off inside me.

Blood trickles toward my groin. I unfold my arms. The bulb at the tip of the rivulet plows over goosepimpled hair, and as I watch, another column joins, and another.

I've got to find clothes.

From the smell, this house has been empty for weeks. Pressing my wound, I limp to a desk holding a telephone. No dial tone. Perhaps this home's owner is on an extended visit with children or—again from the smell—grandchildren. Clearly, a woman has not been here for years, or she passed without leaving the faintest impression or barest scent. There's no lace around the curtains. No doilies under photographs, and none of the baubles that demand doilies, like little ceramic angels. No cinnamon or nutmeg smell.

I climb the stairs sideways. The floorboards groan at my presence. I deposit blood on each doorknob and drops on the floor. One room is an armory. Two gun cabinets, each full. Antlers adorn the walls, and a bear rug the floor.

At the end of the hall, a larger room retains a human smell. Old fabric and old things. Old man. I open the closet and drape a coat over my shoulders. As I throw pants and shirts to the bed, my leg bleeds freely. I passed the bathroom on the way.

My bare feet are tingly numb—a painful improvement. I open the bathroom medicine cabinet and see razors and hair pomade, combs and aftershave.

In a hallway medicinary I find Bag Balm, Mercurochrome, and peroxide. Gauze and tape and cotton bindings. I heap the items in my arms, return to the old man's bedroom, and toss everything on the bed. The curtains are drawn. I brush them open and light comes in so diffuse it leaves shadows undisturbed. On the bed, I throw the blanket over my unwounded leg.

I daub blood with gauze, but the wound flows too fast. There's no use for salve or peroxide. I press a fresh pad to the hole and add another on top, wrap them in place with a long bandage and tie the ends.

Did Gwen hear the frogs and music for this? Did her gift fail her in my case, or was it premature? Should I have drowned in the lake? Frozen before starting the fire?

With my leg wrapped as tight as I can bear, I open the bureau by the closet and shiver into a pair of old-man boxer shorts and a v-necked t-shirt. Pulling heavy winter socks on feet that can't move is like slipping a rubber on a cucumber. It doesn't cooperate—and the real question is why I know it's hard to put a rubber on a cucumber. That goes back to Guinevere too.

I don pants that fit slack about my waist but cinch good with a belt, and choose the heaviest wool sweater on the top shelf. It fits loosely, and I bunch the sleeves at my forearms. For the first time since I was warm with Guinevere in the loft, hours ago, I begin to feel as if this is my body and it might eventually get warm enough to follow instructions.

Moving back downstairs, I think about the carbine above the mantle. There are lots of other guns in the bedroom upstairs—newer guns, maybe—but the carbine has character. A scar on the stock looks like it came from a bayonet. Who knows if the man who carried it fell and a man with a different color coat lifted the carbine from his hands? Who knows if that happened a dozen times before it came to rest on this mantle, to be passed down from one man to his son and to his son, until I take it from the wall…

This morning in the loft, I wondered about Guinevere hearing music. She hears what she calls bullfrog music whenever someone that she's close to is about to die. Before Burt surprised us in the barn saying, "I know you're in there…" Long before that, she shushed me and said, "I hear bullfrogs," and her stare was like a needle sunk right into me. She had me in her hands, and all I wanted was to replace those hands with something twice as warm and seventy-seven times as slippery, but she said, "Wait," and I lay there with my behind hanging outside the coat, and it hasn't been warm since.

The bullfrog song might have been for Burt. But maybe the song came on double strong, and maybe the extra was for me. It's difficult to guess the way occult things work. What they put in the books is all made up, demons and spirits aside. I've heard of a cat that likes to go through the old folks home and lay on the lap of the next person to die, and I've heard of dogs that sniff out cancer. A girl hearing music before people die might be something the scientists will explain someday. I told her all that and she shook her head, said she knew when the visions had started, but not when they'd end.

The music must have been for me.

The fire has settled, and though it makes no sense, I pile on more logs. I feel better with movement. Unlock the front door. Step to the porch and look across the lake. The sun's climbed to a high angle. Wind blows over my tracks, and there is a chance I could stay here a while. With the blizzard they're calling for, it might be a couple days until a snowplow cleans the road. The only caveat is that Cal, Jordan, and their militia cohorts all ride snowmobiles.

I retreat inside and lock the door. Take in the gloomy sofa, chairs, mantle. More mounted heads of deer and bear. I pull the carbine from the rack, turn from the fire holding the rifle with both arms straight. The stock has been oiled for years, coat upon coat. I buff part with the wool of my sweater, and the walnut glows an orange luster warm as the flames.

I crack the lever, find a round in the breech. I close it, point to the ceiling, pull the trigger. The carbine leaps and the blast deafens me. Plaster rains through the smell of burnt powder.

With the carbine leaning against the fireplace, I kneel at the hearth and stretch my hands to the fire, rub them in the heat.

I sit where I won't fall into the flames. Cycle another round. The spent cartridge jingles across the floor as I cock the hammer and reverse the carbine. I press the muzzle to my clamped-shut teeth, and pry them open with cold metal that tastes of powder and carbon.

I squeeze my teeth against the barrel until the pain is all that holds my thoughts together. I reach to the trigger. Wiggle it.

My eyes flit from the couch to the roll-top desk, to the floor, to the window I smashed. The ceiling. Plaster grit still floating down lodges in my eye, and I blink—the irritation is a sudden respite from the ache in my teeth and all these crazy thoughts have juddered me right up to the edge.

I can't do this.

I've seen terrible things I don't understand, and I'm a fool. But for the moment, I live.

I shift the carbine away. The stock jars against the floor and the carbine explodes. A fireball envelops my face and eyes and the roar deafens.

I hold the carbine like a rabid porcupine. My eyebrows burn and my eyes are like someone threw red-hot sand grains into them. More plaster falls from the ceiling and it mists my hands and face.

Smoke floats from the barrel. Through it I see a small painting of Jesus Christ on the wall, the Lord with his hands together, looking at me, wavering ghostlike an inch above the canvas.

His head moves side to side, tut-tut.

Chapter Three

Gwen supposed it was her fault. Hadn't she been a little suggestive? Maybe aggressive for Burt's attention? And when she'd realized he intended to capitalize on her teasing willingness and do things that made biological, anatomical, barnyard sense, wasn't it her fault for having so much as proven her desirability?

Hadn't she almost—*almost*—wanted it? Before she knew what *it* was? Before she knew the visions the trauma would unleash?

She'd struggled that very first night with wordless questions, directionless anger, and pain down there, and her grandfather's face had arrived unbidden to her clamped, salty eyes. It wasn't a pose she'd seen in a photo or real life, not like a memory. His eyes were narrow and his grin was the kind a man assumes when he evaluates unknowns informed only by prejudice. The background to his face was azure, and his skin threw off a glow. She heard the throaty sounds of bullfrogs: oboes, brass. Somber instruments playing grave notes. A symphony composed by Mozart or Bach and performed by amphibians.

Grandfather hadn't seen her. He'd looked through her to something beyond, something he recognized but perhaps wasn't overjoyed to greet.

Gwen had no idea what the vision portended.

The image lasted a few seconds. A minute, at most. Gwen promptly layered the memory under a quilt of more ruinous, terrifying thoughts—her father—and slept.

"Morning," her mother had said.

"Good morning."

"You look like hell."

"Ginger slept on my face."

"Why do you let him in your room?"

"Where else is he going to sleep?"

"He's a cat. He can sleep in a damn tree. You're going to be late for school."

Gwen watched the floor.

"Oh, and your grandfather died last night. Funeral's Friday night."

"Oh, Mother! Are you okay?"

Fay smiled. "We'll be driving half the day to get there, so you tell 'em you won't be in school on Friday."

Gwen attended school that day, Thursday, and remained quiet. Her friend Liz Sunday sensed her unease, and when the winds of gossip carried the news that Gwen and Cal and Jordan's grandfather had died the night before, Liz patted Gwen's shoulder and defended her from less sensitive heathens who'd learned the old man had died in bed, and grew intoxicated on obvious punch lines.

Liz and Gwen were of the age when girls sometimes held hands. Guinevere found this comforting and was tempted after school to tell Liz about the evening before, sparing no detail from the pubic hair pinch to the vision of her grandfather. She didn't, and they rode the school bus home in the same seat, fewer than a dozen words passing between them.

Liz was a quiet girl, susceptible to long, vacant stares out the window, and obeisant glances at the floor. She suffered continual abuse, particularly from the boys, who taunted that her father was a communist.

None of this bothered Gwen. She appreciated silence.

Guinevere discovered her mother in the kitchen preparing deviled eggs while a ham roasted. Her sisters and in-laws could make the damned escalloped potatoes and bean casseroles. It was enough that she'd worked her fingers to the bone, slaving over a hot stove all day…yet she never seemed gayer than preparing food for her father's wake. Mother chattered like Gwen's aunts and uncles unburdened by too much Christmas brandy. How the weather couldn't be better for a good funeral. How the insects weren't bad, and her father did a fine job at picking the season of his exit, if not the year. It was convenient—if she dared say—that he'd be laid to rest on a Friday, and they could spend the night at her sister's house and not have to trouble with the drive home.

Friday morning, Gwen sat in the middle of the back seat between Cal and Jordan, who took turns pulling her hair and squeezing her legs above her knees. She yelled that they ought to leave her alone, and punched Cal, and found her father's eyes in the rearview mirror. He turned toward Fay as she clucked about how green the alfalfa was, and how blue the sky; but then his eyes found Guinevere's and held them. As if to say something. As if to throw her down on the hot car hood and wrap his fingers around her throat, to stifle her voice and drive himself inside her again. His eyes held an appetite, and worst of all, unlike the boys that noticed her sprouting breasts and rounding derriere at school, her father had the courage to hold her eyes as long as he wanted.

"Dad! Look!" Gwen screamed.

Burt swerved. Tires squealed. The car shook left and right.

In the approaching lane, a tractor-trailer barreled through a downhill turn, and in their path, a muscle car with a block on the hood attempted to pass. Burt split the distance between them. The truck roared by, inches outside their windows. The car passed to their right and kicked a plume of dirt from the shoulder and fishtailed back onto the pavement.

Burt pounded the ball of his fist to the steering wheel, and the car rocked. "God *damn*!" He punched the dash above the radio. "God *fuckin'* damn!"

"Burt…" her mother said, one hand on her chest, the other braced on the dash.

"Fuck!" Burt swerved to the side of the road at the top of the hill and three-point-turned. He sped after the muscle car.

Her mother's voice lifted in pitch. "We're going to be late for the funeral, Burt."

They raced down the hill.

"Burt? For so long I've wanted— don't do this to me, please? Burt?"

Chapter Four

I fetch field glasses from the Bronco's glove box, wipe the object lens with a flap of cloth from the seat cover. Climb out. A pair of tracks wander across the field. I can make them out for two hundred yards, then they fade into drifts and cornstalks. Somewhere beyond the fuzzy white, those tracks lead into the forest. I've hunted turkey in that stretch.

Hunted buck, too. Doctor Coates, rest in peace, and me used to meet at the far corner of the field where a tractor trail divides Haudesert and Sunday land. Coates died last month of cancer. He was dying for years and never let on. We hunted turkey in the spring, when the morning grass looked like green knives and the sky was so crisp a sneeze might break it. The only thing he said about the cancer was he'd sell his soul to see next spring's blue skies.

We hunted buck in the fall. We stood jawin' at the near side of the stream.

"I'll find a perch up the hill," he said.

He liked to wait on deer to wander by. I said I'd follow the crick a few hundred yards into the Sunday side and circle back, driving anything in front of me his direction. I reached for my tobacco and stopped. Three deer crashed through a wall of brush twenty yards off. They weren't ball-flappin' scared, but something got them moving fast enough to quit paying attention. Coates was closer, and I had to drop my rifle barrel to swing clear of him. Saw antlers flash against a backdrop of scrub. Aimed on the lead animal.

Out the corner of my eye I saw Doctor Coates wince. His ear was close to the muzzle. He gave a slight nod, and I fired.

"Hell!" he said, and pressed his hand to the side of his head. "Damn!"

"Got him." The buck stepped forward; his head swiveled to me and he fell.

"Shit!" Coates said.

He moved a few yards and stared at my rifle, as if to give it hell, and I said, "You coulda plugged your ear. I'd a waited."

"Mother of Christ, I'm deaf," he said.

"It'll come back. Let's take a look."

He lowered his hand and I slipped over the stream bank and followed a path of flat rocks to the opposite side. He shambled after me, grunting how he'd never hear again and if I wasn't the sheriff he'd murder me in cold blood. We'd been boon companions since the age of ten, and this little incident wouldn't change his estimation of me, whatever it was.

He's dead now, so any harm didn't last.

We stood at my kill and first thing I noticed was the missing antler. This buck was a spike, and not two inches at that.

"You shot a doe," he said.

I nudged the deer's pecker with my ot-six barrel. "What you call that?"

"The mother of all gizzies."

I drew my knife and sliced off his stink sacs, then split him from nads to sternum. Removed my coat, rolled my sleeves, and fished out his guts. You got to be careful not to split an intestine, and shit gets dicey around the anus. Puncture the bladder and you'll marinate the choicest cuts in deer piss—and a buck has some of the stinkinest piss in the woods. I cut an oval around his asshole, cinched it through to the inside, and my elbow nudged Coates.

"Excuse me," he said.

"What?"

"Just seeing what he had for breakfast," Coates said, digging in the pile for his stomach.

I reached inside the buck's chest cavity, split the diaphragm, and damned if his heart wasn't still pounding. Spookiest thing ever.

I told Coates.

"Let me see."

He reached inside and his face lit up. "Still going, but alas, I'm too late to save him."

"Rip it out," I say.

Coates shook his head. Stood to the side while I yanked out the lungs and heart. Caught a tick on my arm, squashed it between my knife and a rock. Coates wandered a few feet and pissed against an oak. Knowing I'd have five minutes, I dug out the buck's nuts, removed his pecker from the assembly, and hung his nads from a birch branch.

"What in God's name," Coates said.

I tied the deer's hind feet together with a hemp line and started dragging, but the terrain was choppy and we hadn't got any snow.

Coates stood by the deer's balls, looked from them to the guts and back, and finally said, "Some kind of Mafioso code?"

I heaved to get the buck over a log and finally hoisted it over my shoulder. Crossed the stream like that.

"You're the goddamn wop," I said.

"I'm English," he said.

"Guess you got your hearing back."

Old Coates, rest in peace. His house is empty, two, three miles from here, and if I was on the lam with a blizzard on my tail, it's where I'd go.

The crick spills into Lake Wilbur, and along the flats, patches of beech attract turkey that sit and peck apart nuts. Farther, deer bed in the pine. Ponderosa limbs break all but the coldest winds. The still air feels ten degrees warmer than twenty yards away, under bare oak or maple. The branches hold the snow, and even today, the cover will only be a few inches. If I didn't know there was an empty house waiting a short ways off, I'd head for the pine.

I tramp to the Bronco. Sit half in, half out, and grab the radio handset. "Fenny, scare up Roy Cooper. I need his dogs. And don't take any grief about the storm. There's a girl missing."

Fay Haudesert stands by my door.

"We'll need something of your daughter's for the blueticks to sniff," I say.

A car door slams and we turn. Snow and wind muffle sounds. It's Deputy Odum, and Deputy Sager follows. Odum approaches like it's caused him a moral crises to have disobeyed me. Walks past Fay Haudesert and crosses into the barn. Stands, hands on hips. Sager dips his head at Fay. Odum says, "Lord."

"Missus Haudesert, go inside the house and bring me one of your daughter's sweaters." I step out and close the door.

"Her name is Guinevere."

"I know her name is Guinevere." I squeeze her shoulder. She's a hard woman. I don't know if it's from throwing hay bales or whether she's just one of those women. She plods into the Bronco's tire tracks and slips along.

I watch Odum.

He kneels at Burt Haudesert; Sager faces away and unbuckles his drawers and re-tucks his shirt. Worse than a woman. Always pressed and shiny.

"What the fuck you doing, Odum?"

"Examining the crime scene."

"Did I tell you to come out here?"

"Wanted to see things for myself."

"I wanted you deployable. If there's any God at all, when you're sheriff, you'll hire a fuckin' bushel of Odums, every one as ambitious as you."

He watches me silently. There's something working underneath the surface. He isn't here because he wants to own the crime scene. No, this goes back to the Militia, the Lodge.

"You think you ought to look which way your killer went?" I say.

"I bet you're going to tell me."

"Took Haudesert's little girl with him." I face the barn door. "They're out there, in that."

"On foot?"

"There's tracks, for now." I pull a hanky from my pocket and wipe my nose. "I don't give a shit for the politics, you taking my job. We got a girl to find. So run the show if that's what you want. Tell me what to do, boss. We got to get a move on."

"Did the wife see the killer get away?"

"No. He's headed at the lake. You want to work the scene, or catch a murderer?"

"What are you thinking?"

"He's got a girl slowing him down. He's going to hole up somewhere, and there's only one place within a couple miles of here, that a-way."

"That farm. Coates's place."

"That's right. Empty the last month, and more guns inside than butter."

Odum stands. "What do we know about the killer?"

"Not a damn thing. But a man named Gale G'Wain took a young girl out across the field—"

"How young?"

"Too goddamn young. I'm going to keep Sager here. You head to Coates's and radio when you get there. Tell me what you see."

Odum stands at the Bronco, puts his hands on the hood while gazing into a gust that makes a million snowflakes into angry white hornets. Wind howls at the barn roof and a purple cloud blows past the sun. The land sparkles with whiteness and on the timber by the door, the blood drops glow like rubies.

Odum squints across the field and says, "Coates's place?"

"Been dead a month, and the whole county knows it. Gale G'Wain knows it."

He studies me.

"I'll check it out," Odum says. Looks away. "Tomorrow this is my scene. I want prints off the fork handle. Photos before the body is moved. You got to write down the widow's statement. You got to mind the rules, Bittersmith."

"That's Sheriff Bittersmith."

Odum looks again at Burt Haudesert; his eyes follow the length of the pitchfork handle. "How do we know it wasn't the wife that did him? She's plenty stout."

I point at a boot print in blood. "Yeah. Then she ran inside and took off her size elevens."

"All that proves is your boy was here when the blood was here."

"Goddamn it! We've got a girl out in that. Are you going, or am I? "

Odum shakes his head, heads back to his vehicle.

"And don't take Travis. I'm keeping him in reserve. Might need him out here."

I wipe my nose again. With the wind, the temperature has fallen. Air that was comfortable a moment ago has become brittle. Them kids out there got to wonder what'll become of them. With the right clothes, a man and woman can tramp around all day, and, if they're smart, build a shelter and a fire to keep alive at night. But I don't know if Gale G'Wain learned those skills. I don't know who the hell Gale G'Wain is. The name sounds foreign—like a medieval hero. Only thing I do know: today is my last with this badge.

"Look at this," Sager says. He's drifted to the loft ladder on the east side and stands above a girl's coat on the floor. Discarded, in a pile.

"Guinevere," I say. I nudge Sager aside and try the ladder's sturdiness. The rungs are smooth from a hundred years' boots, polished by a hundred years' oily hands. Slippy in the cold. One at a time, I climb. Eyes level with the loft, I go one rung higher, spot another coat spread out like a blanket on a nest of loose hay, with an imprint in the middle such as twain bodies would make. Isn't hard to imagine a boy and a girl nestled, groping…

When it came time for a sudden escape, the coat that covered them landed on the barn floor.

Frost lines the gaps in the wall timbers, and a gust blows a fountain of snow through. A loose board bangs in syncopated time. Something half buried in the hay gives me pause as I'm about to leave the love nest. Black and tangled—the first I think is a dead cat. I study it, and anger boils out of me.

"Sager, get on the radio and see if Fenny talked to Cooper yet. We need them dogs *now*!"

"What is it?"

I look over my shoulder. Missus Haudesert holds a red sweater. Sager eyeballs me.

"Sager, goddammit, move!" I climb down, find the barn floor. Fay Haudesert stands at the base of the ladder. "What'd you find?"

"A coat. Was Gwen wearing pants this morning? Or a dress?"

"Pants."

"Tell me what happened when you found Burt."

"Nothing. I came out and he was like that. I didn't touch nothin'. Just ran to the house and called."

"When did Burt leave the house this morning?"

"Around six, I s'pose. We had breakfast, and milking is always at six. Plus, he said he needed to look after Matilda."

"Who's Matilda?"

"Holstein going to drop a calf one of these days. I thought that was why he stayed in the barn after milking."

I fill in the blanks. In the barn, Gale and Gwen was fooling around. She removed her shoe and pulled one leg from her pants. Burt Haudesert heard his daughter's giggles, maybe moans.

"How old is Gwen?"

"Sixteen."

"And Gale?"

"Nineteen, twenty."

Three or four years. Ain't a man alive doesn't know his sixteen-year-old girl wants a man of her own. Hard to fathom a scene like this turning into a murder, and the weapon argues the events that unfolded in this barn weren't planned.

I know things about Burt Haudesert…a pair of dead men in his past. Dead men who had a lot of friends that knew Burt, and could've got in close. And Fay Haudesert's concern for her missing daughter over her dead husband? She's either constipation-tight or lying through her goddamn teeth.

"It wasn't any of them boys Burt's been runnin' with?"

"What do you mean?" She looks away.

"Them Militia boys."

"I don't know what you're talking about."

"Fay, I know this is tougher'n hog hide, but you got to level with me. Who else was out here today? What kind of argument did Burt have with the boys? Not seein' eye to eye…"

"They ain't been no one out here save that G'Wain boy, and too much of him."

I look to the loft. Think again. Burt Haudesert heard a giggle and decided to investigate. Snow was light, maybe, and he didn't see any footprints. He wouldn't have expected to hear his daughter in the barn. Or maybe Gale spoke too loud. Whichever way it worked, Burt confronted Gale and wound up stuck with a fork. Gale and Gwen left the barn in a hurry.

Fay Haudesert holds Guinevere's coat over one arm and a sweater over the other. She brushes hay from the coat with the sweater hand while tears spill over her face.

"She should have her coat, at least," she says.

Sager hollers from inside the Bronco, "Cooper's on the way."

"You might see this," Missus Haudesert says. She pulls a photo from under the sweater. A young man, awkward grin, hair blown over half his face.

I've seen the face but can't place it. "This Gale?"

She nods. "Several year ago. Face is thinner now. Longer, maybe, like yours. And he don't shave."

"Because he don't want to? Or don't need to?"

"Don't need to."

"He give this to Gwen?"

Another nod. "He was sweet on her from day one."

"You approve of him and her?"

"I never—"

"Was there ever words between Burt and Gale? Was Gale welcome?"

"There was words. But words won't find my Gwen."

"Dammit, be straight! What kind of words?"

"Two days ago, Gale asked for her hand."

"You saw it?"

"I saw *of* it."

"What the hell's that mean?"

"I saw what happened after he asked. I saw Burt go crazy like to kill him. Run him off with his tail 'tween his legs."

Twenty-year-old boy asks the father of a sixteen-year-old girl for permission to marry her.

"Was she…?"

"She *said* not."

"Did they fight? Did Burt and Gale fight?"

"Gale had his arms up and Burt was hittin' him. Mostly pushing him, saying, 'You get the hell off this farm, you goddamn pervert, and don't you dare come back here again!' He says 'I'll string you up, you hear…' and all the while pushing him and grabbing him by the shirt and dragging him from the house."

"What did Gale say?"

"He was red in the head like the dick on a dog, and mad enough to cry. You know how boys are. And I didn't hate him so much as feel bad for him."

I watch her.

"Because of the way he growed up, almost never knowing where the next meal was going to come from, or who was going to try and steal it from him. That boy had to be a fighter, and it ain't no wonder his morals was wrong."

"What do you mean?"

"Gale was an orphan. He was in the boys' school."

"Wrong is wrong, and everybody knows it."

"Did you? When you was a boy?"

"Where's Gale live?"

"I don't know. Maybe in town, but only these last two months. He never comes here by the road. It's always through the fields."

"What's he do for money?"

"Been working at the Haynes' Meat Market. Learning the trade."

I take her shoulders in my hands and squeeze. "I'm leaving Deputy Sager here. I want you to go inside the house. There's going to be activity—law enforcement activity. Coroner stuff. And I got Cooper coming out with the dogs. We'll get them kids' scent and hunt 'em down. It'll be better for you to wait in the house, with your mind on something else."

I get on the radio and tell Fenny to have Deputy Roosevelt check out Haynes' Meats. Then I come back to Fay. She's come to the hood of the Bronco.

"Where are you going?" she says.

"Out there." I take the red sweater from her arm and hold it like a dead baby. "To find Guinevere."

Chapter Five

The casket lid was open. The Haudesert family stood in the back by the door. Burt held his hands together at his crotch; Guinevere's brothers glanced from face to face. Gwen watched in silence. Her mother stood beside Burt, and Guinevere thought it odd; perhaps *she* should stand beside him, since he'd sought her bed.

It must have been the black dresses and suits and the smell of mothballs that changed her mother's look. Maybe the yellow lamp on the wall cutting a harsh shadow across her face. Fay turned to Gwen and held her gaze: a plain look that said nothing. Expressed no sorrow. No blame. No knowledge. But yet, something passed from mother to daughter, as if somewhere within the book of nature, or wherever it was written that men control the world, her mother had underlined a pertinent sentence and scrawled a note on the margin.

Ahead in the line, men and women filed past the coffin and offered condolences to Guinevere's grandmother, seated to the left. The woman was squat and round, arthritic and half-blind.

Drawn by a sorrowful snort, Guinevere looked to her right, where her aunt—mother's sister Ellen—clutched Fay's elbows and sobbed and pulled her closer. Again Guinevere's eyes crossed her mother's, and they were empty. Ellen's need of consolation was unrequited. "There, there," her mother said. "Shhh."

"I can't believe I'm crying for him."

"Shhh."

A hand on Gwen's lower back urged her forward. It was Burt. Cal and Jordan fell in behind her, and Gwen led them to the line.

She looked for faces she recognized. Aunts and uncles and cousins. Of those gathered, most faces were new; locals who had known her grandfather through his seventy years on the same plot of land, getting haircuts at a barbershop that had passed from father to son, the newest son there to pay his respects. The barber was a young man, meticulously groomed, and he followed Gwen with his eyes.

Guinevere glanced over her shoulder and cut out of line, circled her brothers and father and fell in beside Fay. She took her mother's hand, much like Liz Sunday had taken hers the day before. Fay tilted her head sweetly.

"We looked for you at the service," Aunt Ellen said to Fay. She wiped her eyes.

"We were delayed. Almost an accident on the way here. Was the service beautiful?"

"It was what I'd always hoped," Ellen said, and pressed her fingers to her eyes.

Gwen shuffled forward. The line approached the casket. Her other aunt, matriarch-in-waiting Meredith, had joined Grandmother beside the casket. Meredith's eyes were red and the bags below were swollen. Meredith raised her hand to hip level and wiggled her fingers at Fay, an unconvincing and almost unwelcoming welcome.

"She loved the son of a bitch," said Ellen.

"She never believed us."

The sisters continued as if Gwen was not near.

Aunt Ellen's tears had stopped falling. As the women passed the casket, Ellen kept her back to it and aimed her face to the back of the parlor. Guinevere imagined Ellen looking above the mourners' heads, as nervous speechmakers are taught to do. Gwen turned. Fay passed the wrinkled gray man in the coffin without looking and dragged her hand along the casket edge. Let her fingertips linger at the corner, as if savoring its smooth finish.

The line progressed. As her mother knelt quickly before Gwen's seated grandmother, Gwen studied her grandfather's face. It was the same as in her vision. The same hair and wrinkles. His eyes were closed and in her vision he'd studied the future, but it was the same face, only pasty with death makeup .

Months later, Gwen remembered her mother's face the morning she told Gwen that her grandfather was dead. Recalled the smoothness at the edges of her mother's mouth, the relaxed crow tracks at her eyes. Her father's death had washed away the harshness. As if his death had tied strings to her worries and floated them away.

His death freed her.

Guinevere had known the night of her vision that her grandfather had died. Fay's announcement merely confirmed what Gwen had intuited by having stood between her grandfather and the place he was going. That's how she came to think of it. She'd witnessed him on his path to meet his maker.

When Gwen considered Fay's response to his death, and illuminated her mother's face with the light of Gwen's own suffering at her father's…hands…she realized the face in the vision belonged to an irredeemable man—worried, yet not contrite, looking ahead to profound suffering.

Chapter Six

Seems the fire could blaze like the Hindenburg and not warm the rest of the house. I've emptied the bin beside the hearth and if there isn't more outside I'll end up burning the kitchen table and chairs. Moving around warms me. If I can get some wood and find food, maybe things will be okay.

The carbine is above the mantle, where I found it. Save the two holes in the ceiling and the carbon in the tube, it's like I didn't try to blow my head off a few minutes ago.

I spot a brass fireplace kit: shovel, broom, poker, and tongs. I thrust the poker into the fire, rest the tip on the reddest embers. For later.

Jesus still floats above the paint. His look says He's seen it all, and who ever painted Him was an expert at capturing nuance. Who ever painted that had to have actually seen Jesus, because I've never seen that look on a real person.

Well, maybe one: Mister Sharps, of the Youth Home.

There's a closet opposite the front door. On the other side of the wall is the kitchen and I'll explore that in a minute—that and maybe first I'll prowl about the roll top desk for any letters that will tell me whose hospitality I'm enjoying. Firewood comes first. I take a heavy winter parka, a hat, and leather work gloves with woolen inserts from the closet. They feel so good I could sit on the sofa and sweat, if it wasn't for fear of having no fire and nothing to burn.

The sun is high but the haze of falling snow filters the light. I circle the porch to the back of the house. Along the wall, drifts bury a few cords of firewood. I fill the bin with icy logs and limp out for another armload, and leave it on the porch, outside the door.

Inside the house I rest on the sofa and cold air from the busted window crosses my face. Drawing the curtains didn't cut the gusts. I hunt until I find a collapsed Kenmore clothes dryer box that still has shooting targets stapled on it. The old man has a bunch of thumbtacks in the first roll-top drawer. I tack the cardboard over the window. Draw the curtains again.

My clothes lie in a steaming clump at the hearth. Corduroy soaked in blood, and flannel streaked red across the front. I don't want them but they won't burn wet. There's no electricity, else I'd find that new Kenmore.

I hang the pants and shirt from different hooks on the mantle, like Christmas stockings in a Yuletide horror movie. The man who lived here had three children, from the hooks.

An orphan thinks about what it would be like to have a family, but only for so long, and then he thinks about how he prefers not having one, and if he did have one he'd tell them all to bug off because he likes solitude. But that's a lie. What really happens is he slowly understands the world is dark. Some people are born on third base and some are born in the dugout. Orphans are dumped outside the ballpark and won't ever get inside, unless they sneak around the fence and pretend they were there all along. You learn how to look like what you're not. Read about families and adopt the vernacular—and when you meet a stranger you sound normal, as if you've spent your life battling older brothers and pulling little sisters' pigtails.

I lived in the Youth Home in Monroe until last summer. They rented us out to farmers every harvest and used the money to feed us year around. Plus what they got from charities and philanthropists around the state. When I was nine a man named Dwight Moobender died. Though none of the boys had ever heard of him, we were happy to attend his funeral. Society people sat in the front row and forty ragamuffins cramped into the back. Moobender had left the Youth Home a Considerable Sum, a number that was never spoken aloud, but from the solemnity of the voices that uttered the words, must have been in the hundreds of trillions. Mister Sharps selected the least disheveled urchins from our group to pose with Widow Moobender, who had never borne children and looked like it was for a reason. I can't hear of Considerable Sums without remembering her taking me by the shoulders and repositioning me in front of her for the photo, me feeling like a rabbit being adjusted by a hawk.

Mister Sharps had preached before the ceremony about how important us making a good impression was to receiving our Considerable Sum. Seeing Moobender's pinch-faced wife, I understood. Over the following weeks we went from promises of seven course meals, Christmas presents, and warm winter clothes, to somber realities. After the funeral and the acclaim that attends philanthropists posing with starving children, Widow Moobender hired a lawyer. A judge decided Mister Moobender had been insane to leave money to orphans.

Sharps was a man in love with expediency, ramrod-stiff, but capable of flushing with empathy. Yet the two dispositions never surfaced at the same time. He kept a black paddle on the wall with eight drilled holes so the air could get out of the way—and many was the hellion who'd prayed for Mister Sharps to flush with empathy only to find him expedient with the paddle. When the Moobender money fell through, he seemed worse for it than us boys.

We boys continued to work the farms that fall. I was nine years old. I worked for a Monroe local named Schuckers but pronounced Sugars. He took five boys for two weeks of cutting corn. He had a device called a corn pole, nothing but a two-by-four that stood five feet tall from a tripod base. We'd cut corn stalks six inches from the ground with scythes and lean them against the corn pole, gradually surrounding it with a teepee of corn. When the corn shock was big enough Schuckers could barely get his arms around it, we'd tie it off with twine. He'd leave them standing in the field, and at the end of the harvest we'd stow the shocks in the barn. Later in the year he'd hire some of us back to shuck the corn and chop the stalks into hog feed.

Part of the arrangement was that he fed us while we were there, in addition to remuneration paid the Youth Home. Schuckers arrived one lunchtime carrying a metal bucket, and for five hungry boys that'd been working his fields since sunup, he'd brought ten hard-boiled eggs. We were sitting in a clump of shade by a small orchard. We'd been cutting his corn all morning and wouldn't see food again until six that night, and the oldest boy, Murph, asked Schuckers if he couldn't bring out a loaf of bread that we could all share.

Schuckers knocked Murph from his cross-legged seat.

"Say another damn word, you ungrateful shit! "

Every one of us leaned back.

Schuckers continued, "I'm helping you out and you gimme lip. No wonder your mothers dumped you in baskets. Each one 'em saw you'd be nothing but a bunch of whiners."

He saw something on my face he didn't like and towered over me with his foot reared back until I was about to tremble into pieces. "What do you think of that, Redpants?" He called me Redpants because every day I wore red corduroys that had fit me well when they were passed down to me but had shrunk since.

Schuckers kicked over the bucket of eggs. We'd only each taken one by that point. The other eggs spilled into the dirt and we ate them that way. No matter how skilled you are at taking the shell from an egg, if the shell is dirty, the egg will be too.

Toward afternoon, my belly was a knot. All of us boys were strung along the field, thinking the same thing. Words floated back and forth about all the food inside Schuckers' house, and the hungrier I got, the more I dreaded that one of use would be stupid enough to run inside and rob him. We kept working, and our progress took us closer and closer. I was closest.

Murph waved to me and I waved back. He waved again, underhanded, shooing me toward the house.

"He's in the barn. Run in there and get a loaf of bread or something!"

I looked from the house to the barn.

"We deserve better'n two eggs," Murph said.

I sprinted and stood on the porch before going inside. Breaking in was a matter of opening the screen. I hadn't seen Schuckers go inside the barn and didn't know how long he was likely to stay, but the longer I stood on the porch the more likely I was to get caught. I slipped inside and found my way through a narrow hallway to the kitchen. Schuckers hired us boys because he didn't have a wife and sons to do the farm work and we were cheaper than men, so I wasn't afraid of finding someone in the house. I listened and the only sound was a black fly that kept hitting the window.

Jars of noodles, jars with oats, and one with rice lined the counter. A breadbox next to the coffee pot almost spilled rolls and cinnamon bread. It was like a chef had been in the house cooking all the time. There were cookies inside a jar and the refrigerator had cheese and salami and bacon—the bacon cooked and cold inside Tupperware—and there was a full jug of milk and six-pack of Coca-Cola cans. I stood with the refrigerator air pouring over me, my stomach as tight as a ball of rubber bands, and I couldn't reach for any of it. I stood, and after minutes not being able to do anything, turned back.

It wasn't fear of Mister Sharps that kept me true. I knew if I was caught I'd be tied to a flagpole and flogged, but I didn't believe I'd be caught.

After watching from inside the screen door until I was sure Schuckers was still in the barn, I rejoined the boys.

"Where's the food? Why didn't you bring any back? What'd you eat in there?"

"Nothing," I said.

"Liar."

I didn't say anything to that. Schuckers was still in the barn and two minutes hadn't passed when Murph threw down his scythe and ran to the house. He was inside a long while. I watched the house and then kept the lookout in case Schuckers came out, but I didn't have any way to warn Murph that wouldn't give me away.

I ran into the house and didn't stop at the porch.

"Hey, you! Redpants!"

I raced down the hallway to the kitchen and it was empty. Off to the side was a coatroom with another door. I crossed into it. Through the window I saw Murph slinking back toward the field, arms full of spoils, waiting his opportunity to cross the open stretch and rejoin the others.

I didn't see the use in escape, since Schuckers had already seen me enter the house. At that tenderfoot age I didn't consider any natural advantage to being outside with an angry man rather than behind closed walls. I stood my ground at the corner of Schuckers' kitchen, hands open and up slightly, clearly empty. The screen door out front slammed. I swallowed.

Boot steps down the hallway. Schuckers was awful big or the house was awful small.

"What you doin', boy?"

"Nothin'."

"Uh-huh."

Schuckers strode to me, took my hand like it held something invisible that he could render visible by peering close, then tossed my hand aside. Agitated even more, he opened the refrigerator.

"Where's the salami meat? Where's my smoked cheddar? Hunh?"

He slammed the refrigerator door and glass jingled. He swooped to the cookie jar and held it upside down above the counter. Crumbs fell. He threw open the breadbox, and the cinnamon rolls were gone.

He glared at me.

"What?"

"Which one of you hoodlums was it?"

"Which hoodlum what?"

He nodded, dragged a chair from the table so its rear legs squawked, threw his leg over it, and said, "Sit."

I stood beside the table. Our eyes were level.

"Take a chair, Red. I know you didn't steal from me."

I pulled a chair and shifted sideways onto it, with my butt on the corner so I could run.

"Are you hungry, Red? Is that why you came inside?"

I shook my head.

"If I gave you some of that pie in the refrigerator or ice cream from the freezer, you wouldn't be interested in that?"

I swallowed and he said, "Ah! Let's work together, right? You get up and walk around this kitchen. Do it now. Stand up! Open the refrigerator!"

I stared and he nodded, urged me toward the refrigerator. I opened the door and the cool air looked like a person's breath in the winter.

"See anything you'd like? Take anything you want."

Inside was all manner of foods, and every one looked tastier than the last time I looked. I thought about Mister Sharps, about Murph, and about the rules. Dogs fight over a scrap of bone, and it doesn't matter which dog you give it to, the others will steal it. I never wanted to be like that. I'd rather be hungry. Though the refrigerator was chock full and all the smells made my mouth water, Schuckers had tied a deal to the food. I would have to sell out Murph.

I bolted.

Schuckers was on one side of the table; I leaped around the other. The back door stuck and Schuckers glanced my shoulder. The door popped open and the edge clonked his head and he fell back far enough for me to get through. I sprinted to the field, hiding among seven-foot stalks before Schuckers came cursing after me. I was going to get a beating—a deserved one—but it takes a just man to give a just beating.

It took until nightfall to hike back to the Youth Home. I went directly to Mister Sharps for my punishment. Mrs. Sharps answered the door and led me inside to his study. He made me stand in front of his desk and report what I'd done. I began my confession at the beginning.

"The other boys corroborate what you've said, so far," Mister Sharps said. "But you didn't mention why you ran back into the house."

"No reason."

Mister Sharps looked at his fingernails. "Gale, Murph came clean about the food he stole."

I kept with the story without a lapse from that point. I didn't leave out how good that cheese smelled, and how sweet those cookies looked with their chocolate morsels. The more I spoke, the sicker Mister Sharp looked. When I was done telling how I got away from Schuckers, and that I just now returned to the Youth Home after walking all those miles, Mister Sharp backed from his desk.

"You understand what you did was wrong?"

"Yes sir."

"How was it wrong?"

"I went into the house without Mister Schuckers being there. I was thinking about stealing from him."

"That's right. You went in to steal. You were hungry, yes?"

"Yes, sir."

Mister Sharps walked to the black paddle hanging from a nail on his wall.

"The world is slow to forgive even a hungry thief, Gale," he said. "Slow indeed." He pulled a book from a shelf and passed it to me. "I commend your integrity. Your restraint. But you entered the man's house, and that must be punished."

I nodded. So far he'd only walked to the paddle and left his arms at his side. I caught a ray of hope from his tone, but I had a whompin' due.

Mister Sharps lifted the paddle from its nail and said, "Hands on the desk."

I placed the book on the edge and braced against the side. He stood beside me so close I smelled tobacco smoke on his jacket. I waited and it didn't come, and then he whapped my backside like to drive that paddle straight through me. Though I was prepared to be a man, I bleated like a lamb.

"Have you learned your lesson from this affair?"

"Yes, sir." My behind was on fire.

"Then come with me."

I followed him out of his study. His house was a small thing—smaller than Schuckers', but tidy. Mrs. Sharps was a stern old bird who stared into the television as Mister Sharps marched me past her into his kitchen. I knew she knew I'd just been punished and the shame of it burned worse than my backside.

"I'm to understand all you had to eat today was your morning oatmeal and two eggs for lunch?"

"Yes, sir."

"Why don't you take a seat?"

"I didn't want to be bad," I said.

When the one who has the right and authority to punish you tells you to take a seat and receive his blessings—my eyes swam in water and my belly opened up and I was so grateful and hungry all I did was stand there with my face dripping until he put his hand on my shoulder.

"You're a good boy, Gale. You're a fine young man. Won't you sit for some supper?"

* * *

I never went to Schuckers' again. None of us did.

Now I'm in another man's kitchen looking at food that isn't mine, holding a candle I found in a cupboard and lit with a match from the hearth. I carry the tiny flame into a closet and behold shelves of soups and staples. If the man who owned the house was here, surely he wouldn't begrudge me a can of soup? A jar of venison? Some crackers to deaden the salinity? I pile interesting items on the counter. Jars of peaches and apples. Even a five-pound bag of rice.

I open the refrigerator and the stench is instant and breathtaking. Spoiled milk, vegetables, who knows what? I slam the door.

Before sampling my host's food, I pen a note on paper beside his telephone. "I ate a jar of venison and a jar of peaches."

I leave plenty of space to record additional items, and sign Gale G'Wain at the bottom.

Chapter Seven

Eight months and two days after her grandfather died, Guinevere Haudesert lay in bed. Her alarm clock ticked; it was a school night.

Floorboards groaned in the hallway.

The door handle clicked.

A yellow beam from the nightlight down the hall invaded through the door aperture. Burt's silhouette crossed it. The door closed silently, and her father's shadow melded into others. She smelled dried sweat—the scent of redness baked into his forearms and dirt below his fingernails. The most terrifying pungency was dried urine from his shorts.

His hand found her foot. Guinevere rolled sideways and squeezed her eyelids tight.

"This isn't right," Gwen said. She lay with her arm over the edge of her bed. Her fingers touched the hilt of a paring knife, tucked between mattresses. She'd chosen the knife not to kill, but to wound. While he was inside her, she capitulated.

"This is wrong," she said again.

He was silent. He was a hand on her shoulder, arm below her neck. He was a hand under her breast. He was an acrid smell. He was pain inside.

He shuddered as she sniffled. Withdrew and climbed from her.

"That's Daddy's special girl," he said.

She rolled from the mattress and clutched the knife. Standing deep in a shadow, she saw her father's waist in a bolt of moonlight; saw him stepping into and pulling up his underwear.

"What are you doing?" he said.

She trembled. "You better never come for me again."

"Yeah?" He stepped closer, still on the other side of the bed. "Or what?"

She pointed the blade at him.

He rounded the bed, snapped his boxers' elastic waistband. "You don't like what I've been giving you?" His voice was quiet like rocks. "Liked it enough when we started. Came on real strong. Now you changing your mind. That it?"

"I never liked it. Don't come any closer."

"Or?"

"I'll cut you."

"Cut me?" He stopped.

"I'll scream."

"I'll beat you silly."

He stepped into the shadow. She smelled his breath. "I have a knife," she whispered. She probed slowly, felt resistance. He grunted, slapped her hand and the knife vanished from it. He gripped her shoulders, drove her against the wall. Wrapped his hand over her throat. As the pressure grew, he brought his face close to her ear.

He exhaled, as if unsure how to express his fury in words.

She gagged. Struggled against his hand until faintness overtook her and she blacked out.

Guinevere awoke in her bed, tucked in, like it had all been a dream.

She curled into a ball and stared through dry eyes at a gray sliver of wall. This wasn't her father's second visit. It wasn't his tenth. She didn't count. Now, eight months and two days after her grandfather died, when she closed her eyes, Guinevere heard bassoons and oboes—bullfrog notes. The sounds so rich they might have had color. She could almost see them vibrate and wiggle like…sperm flagella on the films they showed in biology class.

The tones and harmonies whisked away her thoughts until an inevitable realization surprised her.

Whose face would she see? Burt?

She crossed her fingers then crossed her heart with crossed fingers. Before she could whisper an apologetic prayer, she saw her grandmother's face. Grandmother's eyelids were low, her jaw slack. She saw something she didn't like; her eyes canted toward the ground.

Guinevere reached into the vision but it was like reaching into a pool of water. Grandma was too far away—though so close.

"Grandma!" Gwen whispered. "Grandma!"

The old woman's gaze was solemn; her face was motionless. Guinevere lay still. Grandmother didn't move except to blink. Her watery eyes remained fixed, yet each moment carried her closer to death.

Gwen threw back her covers. Dropped her feet into slippers. Threw open her bedroom door and hurried to the hallway telephone. She pulled out the card tucked between wall and wall-plate, and held it to the soft green light of the handset. Too faint. She carried the card to the nightlight and dialed her grandmother's number.

The phone rang. Gwen counted one bleat after another, over and over, until at twenty she dropped phone into the receiver.

Her parents' bedroom door opened. "Who were you calling? You almost got yourself shot," her mother said.

"Grandma."

"Grandma? At midnight? What the hell for?"

Guinevere was silent.

"I asked a question."

"I had a bad feeling for her."

"So you wake her in the middle of the night?"

Burt joined her mother in the doorway. "What the hell?" He stood in his underwear and scratched his lumpy crotch.

Can't she smell me on him?

"Well?" her mother said. "What did she say?"

"She didn't say anything. She's dead."

Fay marched down the hall and swiped the handset from the wall. Dialed Grandma's number with her thumb. In her other hand, tucked partly under her arm, a handgun glinted in moonlight.

Mother waited several minutes with the phone to her ear. Gwen's feet grew cold and she stood with one set of toes resting atop the other, and traded off. She overheard the ringing in the handset. Her mother placed the phone in the receiver. "She's been a heavy sleeper all her life. Go back to bed."

"What if you're wrong? What if she needs help?"

"Go to bed," her mother said, trailing Gwen back the hallway.

Burt had already returned to the sheets and his snores drifted into the hall.

Chapter Eight

I open the Bronco's passenger door. Sager sits in the driver's seat. Looks sick. His face points at the floor; his elbows are braced on wide-set knees. The windshield is wet with melted snow, and flakes dissolve as they land, and it puts me in the mind of a snowball spittin' and sizzlin' on the flat of a wood stove.

"When Cooper comes, you send him out after me. Tell him I didn't figure to keep up with him and the dogs and went ahead. When coroner Fields gets here, show him the body and do as he says. And one more thing: I don't want Fay Haudesert in that barn."

Sager nods.

"You all right?"

"Breakfast ain't sitting too well."

"Yeah." I bust a clump of phlegm out of my throat. "Well, you got a job in the law. You'll have to deal with your breakfast."

I grab a furled balaclava and my gloves from the seat. Slap my holster. I kept a tin of jerked venison at the station and already had it loaded in the vehicle. A fistful of meat goes into my pocket. I pat my coat; pipe and tobacco are secure. On second thought, I remove them, pack a bowl and light it.

"Be careful out there," Sager says.

I slam the door.

Go inside the barn, step around the blood and return to the loft ladder. I climb it again, and reaching the top, get real slow and careful. Ease one leg over and half-lay on the loft, fingers stretched and searching for something to hang on to. Finally my weight is more on the loft than the ladder and I get on hands and knees and crawl to the spread-out coat and the object beside it. I reach, trembling. My eyes are filled with Guinevere running in a summer breeze, making bubbles. Guinevere tumbling on warm grass. Gwen gazing with curiosity at a buzzing insect.

I wish she'd worn a dress this morning.

I grab the object—Gwen's shoe—and put it into the wide, deep pocket close to the hem of my coat.

* * *

Looking across a field, the only way to guesstimate snow depth is by what it covers. Some places nothing sticks through, and the drifts could crest at six feet—and the storm is just getting started. Other places, corn stalks poke up, and the snow is ragged around them, clinging on the windward side, cupping on the lee, and it's like someone shoved a stick down through a giant white cobweb. Gwen, missing a shoe, walked through this with her lover, a boy a quarter-again as old as her. Twenty to sixteen.

Too big a difference in Burt Haudesert's book; too big in any father's book. Gale G'Wain run a pitchfork through him because of it, and by sundown, Gale G'Wain will answer for it. I won't have the luxury of working him over a few days before he goes to court, like in days past with vermin such as Smith Bixby or Marvin Waldock, a pair of characters that long ago learned you don't drift into Bittersmith and leave your worries behind.

I hope young Gale G'Wain enjoys all this scenery while he can.

Smith Bixby and Marvin Waldoff breezed into town and knocked over Jessup and Clare Mails. Left them stranded on the side of the road, thumbing their way into town like second-rate trash that didn't work their whole lives for what little they had. And them boys, racing across the state in Mails' F-150, thinking what they did in Bittersmith would fade like the plume of dust at their rear wheels.

I had something for them. Four days of something.

You strip a man naked and leave him in a cell with no lights or blankets or food, and show up at midnight to remind him the whole blessed world thinks he's a piece of shit with no future, and reinforce the notion with a little body-work, he'll make sure he steers clear of your town when he gets out. There's ways of doing it that leave no marks. Take the fleshy part of a man's hand between the thumb and finger, and squeeze the nerve 'til he's standing in a puddle. Take a broom handle and make him suck it, and tell him he better get it good and wet. Give him a minute to pick off any splinters so they don't give him problems for a month, every time he takes a shit. Then do what you've been promising, shove that goddamn thing so far you get shit on your knuckles. You'll break him into a thousand sniveling pieces, and he'll always remember the folks in your town ain't afraid to do right, distasteful or not. He damn sure won't hijack another car.

Gale G'Wain, you better damn hope you get away.

Not thirty feet from the tire tracks I debate what the boy was thinking when he took Gwen into all that snow. Where was he going? I've hunted these woods and though the trees give some protection from the wind, and a copse of ponderosa might seem snug compared to a field, the air is still twenty degrees. Unless Gale has some kind of lodge out there, they're lost. And every second I waste wondering what a boy in a dead panic was thinking, the smaller the chance Gwen will survive.

I cross the edge of the field and question the wisdom of a seventy-two year-old walking into a blizzard with a half-pound of jerky and day's worth of tobacco. Gwen keeps me going. The air is cold, but once a fella gets walkin' it could drop another twenty degrees and it won't bother him. A good heavy coat—and all of a sudden I realize Gwen's got no coat. I just turned away her mother and all I took was the sweater, and part of me is already thinking in the back of my head that it isn't going to matter, and I quiet that voice and turn back. Follow my steps to the tire tracks and then the widow's footprints to the house. Winded by tobacco smoke, I rap my corncob pipe on the porch post. The cherry falls and there isn't even a sizzle as it plunges into the snow.

Fay Haudesert opens the door, and her face is lit like she expects me to tell her something she hasn't heard.

"Let me take her coat," I say.

"Of course. I'll just pack a couple of things. Some food for her." Her eyes are fixed on my pocket and she steps to me.

"Just the coat," I say, and spot it draped over a chair.

"What's that?" she says. All at once she's up close, pulling her daughter's shoe lace from my pocket, and when she holds the shoe in her hands, it's like a wave of tears has nothing left to hold it from breaking loose. Her chin puckers.

"I'm going to find Gwen." I lift the girl's coat from the chair, and take her shoe from her mother's hands. Back out the door and close it before Fay Haudesert reveals any more of her horror.

I'm careful negotiating the steps. There's three, but no rail, and it's different going down than going up. On snow. The latest is an icy powder, not so much flakes as beads. I'm on the last step and the crunch of tires pulls my attention and I look to a sedan spinning up the driveway, fishtailing, plowing through a plot of unbroken snow. The motor races and the sound is distant though the car is only a dozen yards away.

My heel catches an ice patch and I drop six inches just like that, and slip on the packed snow of the path to the barn. I land on my ass and sit as Burt's mother, Margot Haudesert, explodes out of the car and hurries toward the Bronco.

"Margot! No!"

She spins. The wind blows her hair, still red, and she still doesn't wear a hat. Her dress is too thin; her legs show through even as it flaps about them, and it is easy to remember them in the summer, bare, with water streaming from her sodden hair. It's always easy to remember when she was Margot Swann.

She stares at me with a passion that is not love. She turns, closes the remaining distance to the barn.

Sager opens the Bronco door as Margot glides closer. He spreads his arms and steps toward her but she's not yet to the Bronco and races around the other side.

Fay Haudesert emerges from the house with a paper bag in hand, sees her mother-in-law and touches my shoulder as she passes me. My ass radiates pain through my back and legs, and there is no way to know, right now, what I'll feel like standing. I twist part way to my side and press against the steps; as I bend my stove-up back, my legs decide they're okay, and after twenty seconds of struggle, I'm on my feet. I take to the snow and break a new path.

Margot is in the barn and a caterwaul cuts through the wind. She's seen her only son.

The sound does something to Sager; he clutches his belly, wobbles a few steps and vomits over the edge of the dirt tractor ramp where the Bronco is parked.

Margot wails again. I stop halfway to the barn.

Is this what I want to do, while Gwen is lost without her coat? With frostbitten hands and feet? I pivot to the field and in no time the wind erases Margot Haudesert's sobs.

Chapter Nine

A boy had come to work at the farm. Gwen first thought he was a runaway from a poor household in some neighboring county, some mongrel who'd thumbed a hundred-mile ride and now hoped to find a place to work long enough to earn a meal. He was ragged. Gangly, and even more awkward in voice than body. He stood in the kitchen watching her with hunger in his stare, and said Burt had told him she'd put some food together for him so he could go to the barn and work it off. From his look, he needed the nourishment just to get back to the barn.

That night when Burt left Gwen's room, she rolled to her side and pulled her pillow against her breast. She saw Gale's clumsy smile. His clumsy innocence.

Neither Gwen nor her school friend Liz Sunday had shared the details of her travails with the other, yet each understood the bruises, tear-swollen cheeks, and bloodshot morning eyes. They were scrunched in the second seat of the school bus, leaning conspiratorially close. They'd ridden in the same seat for a year, always tucked below the high-backed tops, knees curled into the seatback in front. They'd held their voices low and painted hopeful pictures of escape. Such musings were irresistible. They'd fantasized about running away to Mexico, or Hollywood, or some random Iowa crossroads. Anywhere. They'd pretend to be sisters. They'd expropriate enough money from their fathers—except neither of their fathers likely had that much cash.

However, as late summer became fall and Gwen began noting little things—the way Gale's Adam's apple moved when he sang Amazing Grace, for instance—she dampened her runaway conversations with Liz. At the same time, Liz became more and more frantic to continue them. Her eyes seemed to be shrinking into black beads that disclosed nothing, ready to flash into any kind of wildness.

"I'll get away, someday," Liz said. "Tell me about this Gale G'Wain, again. What does he look like?"

"He's got red hair, like mine, and his joints are too big. But he works from sunup to down and never says anything but 'thank you' and 'that tasted real good, thank you.'"

"Does he like you?"

"I don't know if he likes anything but food."

Gwen closed her eyes for a moment. She didn't add that Gale attended church with the Haudeserts, when they went. Or that when singing, his sweet voice never stumbled in search of words, even when flipping pages in the hymnal. She didn't mention the way he seemed to pull the lyrics directly from the crucifix behind the pastor, from which his eyes never strayed. "He likes food," Gwen said. "Food and God."

"If you don't run away with him," Liz said, "I will."

* * *

The comment wore on Gwen for a month.

Burt sat at the supper table, brooding as if he looked upon Gale from under a rock. Gale didn't seem to notice, but instead studied dishes of potatoes and meatloaf. He took the place that had been Cal's. Jordan fell into the next chair.

Gwen watched. She imagined a smaller table, a smaller kitchen, with only her and Gale taking seats.

Normally Gwen would fill her father's plate and then proceed around the table. Instead, she hoisted Gale's, carried it back to the other side and filled it. Passing the plate to him, Gwen retracted it at the last moment. "You look like you could do with an extra piece of meatloaf."

She doubled his portion.

Below the table, Burt touched the bare skin of her leg. Gwen stepped sideways. Burt's face pointed toward Gale, and his lines were taut. Gwen lifted her father's plate and dropped a slab of meatloaf and a scoop of potatoes. A couple spoonfuls of carrots.

Burt's hand crawled higher. Gwen's mother had been washing dishes used in meal preparation, but the clatter and rattle had died several seconds ago. Gwen faced the sink. Her mother watched with humiliated eyes set above lips like a crack in concrete.

Gwen stepped away from Burt. Her mother leaned against the counter and looked off through the window.

"Time to eat, Fay," Burt said, without turning. "Come sit down."

"I've lost my appetite."

Gwen filled another plate and sat to the right of her mother's empty chair.

Burt bowed his head. "Good Lord, we thank you for this food. And do something about the price of corn, would ya?"

"Amen," Jordan said.

Gwen watched Gale. He waited for everyone else to lift a utensil before deciding on his fork, and upon Burt's first spoonful of mashed potatoes, shoveled a quarter slice of meatloaf into his mouth. Gwen watched his jaw work, the muscles at the hinge, the bobbing of his adam's apple. He was a queer boy, the way he mixed carrots and potatoes. Oblivious to all save what he ate, as if fearful it might leap from his plate and be forever lost.

Jordan cleared his throat, flicked his eyes to Burt. Gwen turned. Burt had been watching her. No one moved save Gale, who devoured his victuals with relentless concentration.

Glass shattered at the sink. Gwen twisted in her chair as Fay stalked away, crushing shards of a broken glass under her feet. She held one hand in the other and blood dripped from both. Burt turned back to the table, and a forkful of loaf that had been arrested in mid air continued to his mouth.

Gwen trailed her mother to the bathroom; found the door closed. She tapped.

"Ma?"

Nothing.

"Ma?"

"Go away."

"I'm opening the door. Ma?"

"Don't."

Guinevere tried the knob. It was locked. "Unlock the door so I can help you."

Silence.

"Please?"

"Let her tend herself," Burt said.

The lock clicked from inside and Gwen twisted the knob, peered around the corner. A trail of red drops led from the door to the sink. Fay stood with her hand in the basin, her face flushed and her eyes lined with water. Her shoulders shook but no sound issued.

Gwen closed the door, approached. Blood covered her mother's hand, the bottom of the bowl.

Gwen placed her palm on her mother's back. With her other hand, she twisted the faucet knob. "Run cold water on it."

"It's nothing." Mother wiped her cheek on her shoulder and kept her face angled away. Her hands shook. "It's a small cut. Just needs a Band-Aid."

Gwen steadied her mother's bleeding index finger under the water. "Does it sting?"

"A little."

"You see what he's doing, right? You see it, Mother?"

"I'll get this. Just a little old Band-Aid."

"Why did you hate Grandpa? Grandma?"

"Stop, Gwen. Please stop."

"Because of what he did to you? And because your mother knew, and did nothing?"

"Please..."

"How can you be so weak?"

"You don't know—"

Gwen released her mother's hand.

Mother stopped shaking, and Gwen found her eyes in the mirror. They dipped, and Mother said, "I've got this. Go back to supper."

* * *

Liz had been late to start school in the fall. This morning, weeks into the school year, she carried a new blankness, a dazed shock that eclipsed the wounds that had fed the girls' silent commiseration. After much hesitation, Gwen leaned across the aisle between their schoolroom desks, and tossed a note onto Liz's open textbook.

Liz read the note.

She looked down at her blouse, muffled a shriek with her hands, covered her bosom with her elbows, and ran from the room. Boys and girls twittered.

Gwen snatched the note off her desk and raced after Liz.

Mister Fitzsimons glanced up from his lectern. Alarm flashed across his face. “Girls!”

Gwen closed the door. She followed Liz into the restroom. Cornered Liz and pulled her hands from her chest. “How do we make them stop?” Gwen said.

“I don’t know.” Liz blinked away spaced-out tears.

Gwen gathered toilet paper into a ball. “Can you squeeze it out?”

“It’s going to stain,” Liz choked. Her face was red, her eyebrows dimpled. Mucus dripped from her nose and tears fell from her cheeks and she coughed.

“It won’t stain,” Gwen said. “It’s only…milk?” Gwen pressed the ball of toilet paper to Liz’s leftward wet spot and wiped. She tossed the paper to the trash and put her arm across Liz’s shoulder.

“Everybody saw,” Liz said.

“No one saw.”

“Mister Fitzsimons gawked at my boobs.”

“He’s a boob gawker. Yours, mine. Everything’s going to be fine. And if he says a word, I’ll kill him.”

Liz smiled, and it was repugnant, almost. Her face was red and her eyes bloodshot and far-off, and the white spots on her forehead were still there, and here was this silly simper on her face while the dark circles at her nipples expanded. She was interested in talk about killing. Dare Gwen go farther?

“I’ve killed two so far.”

Liz glanced beyond Gwen to the entrance. It was a door-less restroom, privacy provided by two ninety-degree turns. Voices easily echoed into the hallway. Liz canted her head sideways; her face betrayed credulity and candor. “Two? Tell me how.”

“Didn’t anyone tell you how to get them to stop leaking?”

Liz unbuttoned her blouse. "Look what they said to do." She pulled a flaccid, pale leaf from the cup of her bra. "Cabbage. The nurse said this would dry me up."

"Can't you press the milk out?"

"You're not supposed to. You make more."

The bell rang. In seconds, the restroom would swirl with girls crowding in front of the mirror. Waiting outside a stall.

Gwen took Liz's hands. Hurried her into a stall and swung the door as giggles and gossip rushed closer. She wrapped the half-undressed Liz in her arms and shushed her. Gwen waited for the light pressure of Liz's hands on her back, her side, anywhere. Liz let her arms hang. "You have to tell me how you did it," Liz whispered into Gwen's ear.

"I'll go to the nurse for some pads," Gwen said. "It'll be okay."

They waited three minutes until the traffic cleared. Gwen listened to the silence and rubbed Liz's shoulder, and when she was sure the restroom was empty and the next class had begun, she said, "I'll go now."

"You said you killed two people. I want to know."

The bell rang.

"The first was my grandfather. I was in bed. I saw his face, and heard music that sounded like dozens of singing bullfrogs. Grandfather looked past me like he saw the Devil. And I didn't do anything—"

"It was a dream?"

"No. I was awake. Wide awake."

"That's all?"

"The next morning my mother said he'd died overnight."

"You saw his face and heard music, and then he died." Liz pulled away. "You fucking lied."

"No! Listen. The next was my grandmother. It was the same thing; I was in bed and...and I was upset, a little, and I saw her."

"Why were you upset?"

"I can't talk about it. It's too complicated to say, here. It's…"

"Worse than this?" Liz cupped her shoulders and her breasts, still exposed on their cabbage leaves, swelled.

"Depends," Gwen said, "on who the father is."

"What?"

"I've got to go to the nurse. Stay here and I'll be right back."

Liz frowned, tilted her head.

Gwen unlocked the stall door and slipped through, quickly scanned the restroom, and rushed to Mrs. Reynolds, the school nurse.

Nurse Reynolds stood eight feet tall, was blade-of-grass slender, and wore her gray hair in a bun. Her face was all smile and spectacles, and from Gwen's posture, she immediately diagnosed the problem. She mouthed, "Pad?" and Gwen nodded.

As Reynolds turned, Gwen said, "Two, please."

Reynolds stopped.

"Another girl…"

In a moment Nurse Reynolds returned with a pair of maxi pads in a discretely flamboyant pink plastic bag. "Do you have more at home?"

"I'm fine. I just forgot. Thank you."

Moments later Gwen stood in the restroom. "Liz?"

The toilet flushed and after a second the stall door opened and Liz stood there, arms crossed at her bosom. Gwen slipped into the stall with her, gave her a pad, and opened the other. Liz applied each inside her bra, and threw the cabbage leaves to the floor behind the toilet. Liz buttoned her blouse. "I can't go to class like this."

"I'll go back and get our stuff. It's seventh period. We'll walk home."

Again Gwen set out. Fitzsimons had left the classroom door ajar. She looked inside and saw someone had secured her and Liz's purses and books by the window. She would have to walk in front of the study hall students. Juniors.

Gwen opened the door. Fitzsimons stood and hurried to her. "Is everything good with Liz? And you? What was the matter?"

"It was a…it was—"

"…A *female* matter?"

Gwen nodded. She peered closer at Fitzsimons, a man with what? An English name? He looked like a Russian Ichabod Crane. His hair was jet black and always needed cut, and his features were blunt like God had cut them out of granite and quit before rounding the angles. His chin was covered in a beard like Lenin wore, and if any man would be sensitive to a brooding gray girl with a communist father…

"Would you allow me to get our things?" Gwen said. "She's not well and I'm staying with her."

"Right over here."

He crossed the room and the juniors snickered. Gwen stood at the corner.

Fitzsimons returned with both purses and an armload of books.

"Thank you."

She threw both purse straps over her shoulder and filled her arms with texts and notebooks. She noted the concern in Fitzsimons' eyes as she backed away and fleetingly questioned whether his sweat would smell as disgusting as her father's. She looked at his hands, his clean fingernails, and spun the other direction not knowing if she would vomit or begin sobbing. She scampered down the hall, her soles barely rising from the linoleum. She ducked into the restroom yet again.

A pair of seniors huddled in the corner. Smoke curled from their cigarettes and a cloud lingered at the ceiling.

With Liz behind her, Gwen held the older girls' eyes. The blonde shifted sideways. "You ever get burned?" the blonde said, and dragged from her cigarette until the cherry glowed.

Gwen backed away.

"That's right, lezzie." The dark haired girl grabbed her crotch like a rutting boy.

Gwen navigated the two right angle turns and backed into the hallway. Liz grabbed her books from Gwen's arms and they hurried around the corner and sixty feet farther to their lockers, on opposite sides of the hallway.

"Okay," Gwen said. "Right out the front door."

Liz stared through her. "You need to tell me how you killed them."

* * *

They reached the street and turned left, toward town, and then crossed to the west side. After a quarter mile they'd pass Sheriff Bittersmith's station and then the Main Street businesses. On the concrete bridge that crossed Mill Creek, Gwen stopped and leaned over the side. A storm the night before had swollen Mill Creek's waters; the stream rushed with muddy runoff and overspilled its banks.

Liz came beside her and looked over the edge. "Think about being swept away," she said.

"It doesn't work like you think," Gwen said. "I can't just see someone and make him die."

"It would be nice if you could."

"The first was my grandfather. I saw him and heard funeral music, and the next day my mother said he was dead. Eight months later I saw my grandmother. I tried to warn her; I tried to reach into the picture; I said her name but she didn't know I was with her. She had her eyes fixed on the Devil, I think. She was looking down."

"What happened?"

"I went into the kitchen and called her on the phone. I let it ring for a few minutes, and when I gave up, my mother came out, and she tried calling, and Grandma never answered."

"She was already dead…"

"That's what I thought," Gwen said. "But she wasn't. Not when I called."

"What?"

"They found her on the floor, sprawled out, dead…she'd been crawling to the phone."

Chapter Ten

I climb the steps sideways, carrying a chunk of salted venison on a fork while it drips into a Mason jar. I want to be on my way before law enforcement follows my footprints from Burt Haudesert's blood to this front porch. More pressing is the likelihood a platoon of Wyoming Militia will storm the house riding thirty snowmobiles through the drifts, right across the lake.

It would be nice to know when the storm is going to be over, but unless I can find a radio and batteries, I won't know until I spot dripping icicles. There is such a thing as snow so deep a snowmobile will bog down, but until I know how the storm is shaping, I won't fathom how to survive any of it—the blizzard, the police, or the militiamen.

The room with the rifles overlooks the fields toward the road, about two hundred yards off.

I rub my bunched up wool sleeve against frost on the window. The road is hard to see, a gray line that traces all the way from left to right. I've been on that road, and seeing it and knowing the lake is behind me helps put my location in context. In fact, I passed by this place last summer working for Burt Haudesert.

The gun cabinets are locked, but the glass doors display their contents. I feel along the crown of the first, and then the second cabinet, and find a ring with a pair of keys.

I shot a lot of squirrel with Mister Sharps' twenty-two, and lining up the open sights and holding a steady bead is my strong suit. If a bullet comes out the other end, I'll hit what I'm pointing at. I choose the rifle with the longest barrel and examine the top of the breech for a stamp.

.30-06.

It's a bolt action, something I'm familiar with. Good for shooters, Mister Sharps said, because the bolt won't wiggle.

If that's what it takes, I said.

Two cabinet doors and three drawers sit below the rifles. I pull the top and find boxes of bullets. Fat boxes with shotgun shells. Long skinny boxes for rifles. I locate one that has .30-06 on the side, made by a company called Federal. There are smaller boxes and out of curiosity I open one. The bullets are the length of a .22 but plump as my pinky. They go to one of the pistols tucked between the rifle stocks.

I open the .30-06' s bolt and press rounds inside. It holds seven.

I came here for a radio, but firepower seems more pressing. Militia could be on the lake right now. They could be at the front door. I cross to a bedroom on the other side of the hallway and pull the curtain. The snow falls harder, and the sky, way off, broods as dark as any summer thunderstorm.

I return to the gunroom. There's another rifle almost as long as the .30-06. I pull it down and it reads .308. Better by eight-thousandths. I locate the box that goes with it.

In Westerns, good guys cache rifles by windows, as they won't have time to reload running from one blind to the next. Seems like sound policy. One by one I remove rifles, load them, and place them with their ammunition boxes next to different windows. Upstairs and downstairs. I read the manufacturers and calibers; everything starts with a three. Remingtons, Winchesters, and a strange war gun called a Krag-Jorgensen.

One fellow would be proud of my preparations: Burt Haudesert. I worked for him all of three months and he sat me on his porch twenty times, and said in slave countries they don't have guns, and through history, the first thing a despot does is take a man's firepower. Burt would sit and clean a rifle for an hour as the sun drew into the hills, until he was cleaning it by a yellow bulb over his head that flickered with moths. He'd talk to the rifle with a softer voice than he ever used on his wife. If he could see all the guns in this room, he wouldn't forgive me, but he might be misdirected long enough for me to make a break for it.

Of course, Burt Haudesert is dead.

It's the living chasing me…on account of Guinevere Haudesert.

In the beginning she was a tart. Burt worked me hard enough that some days the only time I saw her was when I sat down for supper. If she walked by and I was in a field or the barn or even on the porch with Burt, there was no way I'd look at her. I think she knew, and at some point Burt noticed I didn't see her.

But she took advantage of times alone with me. I didn't know what fabric she was weaving. I didn't know I played by one set of rules, and she played by none.

Burt sent me to work in the garden one morning. Told me there was a hand-pushed harrow in the shed out back the house, and he wanted each row dug up and the weeds pulled, since Gwen hadn't been living up to her chores. I did as he said and no more than twenty minutes passed before Guinevere came out of the house and stationed herself where I'd already roughed the ground. She crouched with her back to the fields and barn, and her knees were far enough apart that it only took one glance to see she was a full-grown woman and had forgotten her underpants that morning.

I reacted to that, and at the end of the row I didn't want to turn around, knowing she'd see, and I stood there examining the harrow's wheel, pretending it wasn't operating correctly. I pushed it a foot, and stooped, and jiggled it back and forth, and knocked a clump of mud from a spoke. But all I was seeing was a mat of red like something you'd find strawberries and mint leaves in. The more I thought about not thinking about her, the worse I got, until I dropped the harrow and walked out into the trees by the swamp where I could see her and be sure she wasn't coming my way.

When I came back she was still there and my problem was gone for the time being. I resolved I wouldn't even look at her until the garden was done. I started back toward her with the harrow and a little blue packet landed at my feet. I stopped.

"Pick it up," she said.

The devil got the better of me and I said, "You don't even know what that's for."

"I surely do, Gale G'Wain."

"Where'd you get it?"

"Not tellin'."

"You shouldn't have that. If your father saw—"

She sniggered. Stood, retrieved it. Walked the length of the garden to an area that I'd avoided, the cucumber patch. She sat cross-legged at the edge of the leaves and snapped a harvestable cuke from the vine. "You watching?" she said, and it was like she was chewing bubble gum while she wasn't. She ripped the package open and rolled the prophylactic over the end of the cucumber, and I watched because even though I'd seen them I'd never actually owned one. The way her hands moved was like the way you'll see ballroom dancers glide over a parquet floor.

"What do you think of that, cowboy?" she said.

My mouth was dry, and I had another problem in my pants.

"Now the cucumber won't get you pregnant," I said, and headed back to the woods.

* * *

The fire has taken the edge off the house. Only upstairs do I see my breath. In the living room the air is almost too hot, but I leave my sweater on.

My leg is going to be a problem. When the blade went in, I felt a jolt as it hit my femur. Pulling it out was difficult; it stuck in the bone like an ax in a knotty log. Every walking step intensifies a deep, skeletal ache, so much that I'd like to stretch on the sofa and watch the fireplace and its leaping orange ballet dancers. But if I allow my leg wound to become infected, my survival today will be for nothing. I'm not going to hike a thousand miles south on a rotten leg.

I've got to kill whatever bugs are growing in me.

I check a window on each side of the house and there's no indication I'll ever see another human being the rest of my life. If the storm keeps on, it'll bury the porch by dawn. Every minute makes it less likely Cal and Jordan will come, but these are not men who stop shy of their objective. I know from listening to Cal—Cal always took the lead over Jordan—revel in a story about tracking a gut-shot buck by lantern light, over fifteen miles of smaller and smaller spirals until he found it dead in a briar patch at dawn. The way he told the story it was adventure, but it was personal between him and the buck. It was about who was going to give up, and Cal was damned sure he wouldn't. And to show his cleverness, he liked to add a punch line at the end of the story, to make up for the fact that Jordan, Burt, and I had heard the tale a half-dozen times. He added that after he cleaned the buck, the only honest way to get it off the hill was the same way he'd come in, mile after mile around the hill, unwinding the corkscrew.

Cal and Jordan are coming for me.

I expropriate a can of Lysol from under the kitchen sink. Shake it and it's live. From the lower hutch cabinet, a bottle of 151 rum. I uncap it and sniff. Mister Sharps, at the Youth Home, watered down his whiskey. He said it was to make it less strong, but I suspect it was to stretch a bottle. This rum smells potent. I pour a drop on the sink ledge and reach a match from the cabinet with the candles. The rum flashes and flickers and it's an amazing sight, a flame that isn't attached to anything.

From the roll top desk I kife an ink pen and a roll of tape. A letter on the calendar pad is addressed to Doctor Wilbur Coates, and I surmise I'm wearing Doctor Coates's pants and boxer shorts and everything else, and digesting his venison and peaches.

I carry the items to the coffee table and drag the table to the hearth. Lastly, I return to Doctor Coates's bedroom, and gather the gauze and ointments and bandages on his bed.

The brass poker I put into the embers glows red. I sit on the hearth with my pants drawn to my knees. The heat from the fireplace rises and the cool stones remind me I'm not warm all the way through. I undo the knot, and round and round, unwrap the bindings. After a couple circuits the gauze becomes bloody and handling it without getting blood all over my clothes and hands becomes an exercise. I ball them up and toss them in the fire.

The wound is an inch and a quarter wide, and three inches deep to the bone.

I disassemble the ink pen, and when the guts are on the coffee table I chop the ballpoint mechanism from the end of the plastic tube, so that what remains has no ink. I pour some rum onto the plastic tube, then drink a tiny swallow from the bottle. I spit into the fire and figure it is better to feel the pain in my leg, and not in my mouth and throat too.

I press the ink pen tube into the hole in my leg. It slides and I'm numb until it gets close to the bone and sends a jolt of electricity through me that makes me almost empty my bladder. Instead, I shake the Lysol, and after a moment of thought, slip the white nozzle off the end. I tear a few lengths of tape and stick them to the table, then use one to affix the nozzle to the tube barely protruding from my leg. I cover it over and over until it's secure and there's no wiggling one and not the other, and then slip the tube from the spray can inside the nozzle, and before I have time to second-guess my way out of it, I mash the nozzle.

Lysol bursts through the clear tube and there is a second between seeing it go and feeling it hit the meat inside. I scream until I have no voice and Lysol foams out of my leg. I spray and spray and somewhere in all of it I find I'm sitting in a puddle of piss and my face is salty and my eyes inflamed. With no Lysol left I cast the can across the room and press the wound from the sides. Pink liquid squirts out, and panting and choking, I wipe it away with gauze. In one motion I throw the gauze into the fire and grab the brass poker and press it to my skin until the smell of charring smoking flesh finishes me.

* * *

After a day's farm work, sleep is sweet. Muscles ache, depending. If the work took a shovel or a pitchfork, there's likely skin missing on the inside of your thumb, and the muscle above your shoulder blade that you didn't know you had burns like a devil. Or if you were throwing bales from the field to the wagon all day, your forearms are chafed like you wrestled a kitten for sixteen hours, and the muscle ache starts at the back of your legs and goes all the way to the base of your skull.

And there are lesser pains. You pass a corner in the barn too close and a rusted nail slices your shoulder. Heck, you whittle a whistle from a shaft of elderberry and nick your finger. Say you drop to the ground to hitch a cart to a tractor and rap your knee on a stone. At night you'll lie there and wonder what you did that caused the bruise and it won't come to mind until three days later when you rap it again on the same spot doing the same exact thing.

Going to bed was as much respite as rest. Haudesert's loft became a sort of hospital. Other men might have done farm work without so many aches and injuries, and after a while I toughened up. But in the beginning I was sore all the time and bedding in a nest of hay, which I could clump up wherever I wanted, was the thing I looked forward to all day long.

After Gwen slipped the prophylactic on the cucumber, I steered clear of her. She was trouble. I hadn't grown up around girls at the Youth Home. Only time I saw them was in town, and all the boys would gape at anything shorter than a full-blown woman that smelled nice. Mister Sharps and the faculty didn't often take us into public. Even boys unschooled by actual experience wish for a pure harlot willing to get dirty at the first smile—but when a boy sees one acting out his most grotesque fantasies, he knows right off something's wrong. Gwen slipping that rubber on the cuke after disremembering her underwear signaled she knew what she was doing with her body—and worse, what it did to a boy's.

We boys at the Youth Home weren't fools. While the specific mechanics of a boy and girl consummating their interests were a mystery, and imagining how it would work was slightly absurd, we talked sometimes about how difficult it must be to find where you were supposed to go. You take plenty of lessons on the farm. I couldn't count the times I saw a stud miss a mare altogether, and he's bumping her and she's fit to giggle. We boys talked about that happening to us, and generally one of the older guys would say something smart about the last time he diddled Mrs. Smart she was so easy to find he could have drove a tractor in her. But that was when I was really young. Even older, though, the whole thing was an unknown. Most times I'd go to sleep trusting every other guy in the world figured it out, and I would too.

But how did Gwen already know? Her comprehension extended far beyond the syntax of two bodies, how they fit together. She didn't even need to demonstrate that knowledge, hers eclipsed it by such a margin. She knew the fundamentals. The biological mechanics. But she also knew how to attract, how to tease. She added fifteen years to her age by pouting her lips and making her brows dark like stormy skies. Daydreaming about her was like slipping off into town and finding a thirty-year-old woman—monstrously old, but magnificently schooled—who teases you to her cozy shack and devours you all day long. Thinking about Gwen was like thinking about an *older* girl, she seemed to know so much, and presented her complexity with such clarity and charm.

One night, after pitching bales from the field to the wagon and from the wagon to the loft, we sat to supper of dumplings and roasted chicken. There were carrots and potatoes and corn, and spices that seemed to come from heaven. Smelling them was enough to make a whole day's aches disappear.

"Guinevere did most of the cooking," Missus Haudesert said, and Burt nodded and beamed like his daughter was his prize, and Missus Haudesert caught his look and she didn't seem quite as happy as she had a second before.

Her look only lasted a few seconds, and I spent them shoveling dumpling and chicken into my mouth. I always wanted to get at least a piece of a carrot with each mouthful; something about the flavor of the carrots pulled the whole thing together for me. But then I realized there wasn't any talking going on and started watching the table politics around me. There was a signal being sent from Burt to Gwen, and Missus Haudesert seeing it, and Jordan, the cunning son, making sure he didn't.

Gwen was always in charge of herself when she was around me, but beside Burt, she was anxious as a one-eyed cat watching two rat holes. Tonight, tensions crackled. Jordan was sullen and Cal was in the other room, in bed, his body all broken up from having fallen from the hay loft a month before. Gwen smiled at Burt but couldn't sustain it in the face of her father's consuming focus. Missus Haudesert fixed her stare on Burt and put me in the mind of a dog that's growling that low, low growl, that means there's bound to be sixteen kinds of trouble, each different.

"You did real good with the supper, Gwen," I said.

Gwen's eyes flashed to me and they were glossy. Her glare was steady, as if to accuse and implore at the same time.

Burt nodded while he forked a clump of dumpling to his mouth, but he only looked away from Gwen long enough to cut another, then kept watching her. Missus Haudesert sniffed. Jordan watched his plate.

This was the first that I knew what everyone else knew.

After that, it got more obvious.

I went to bed troubled with questions. Sometimes evil is so entrenched you just go along with it. Burt Haudesert kept me from rifling garbage and begging for food. There was no easy life waiting for me if I just stood firm as an oak and said him having at his own daughter was wrong. I thought about ways to make Gwen's troubles less burdensome. There was certainly no ending them.

No longer was she the strawberry I wanted to consume and make mine forever. She was the half-used tart that was silently screaming. Maybe my self-interest colored how I saw her. Maybe she loved her father that way and my jealousy made me want to be her savior. I slept like my bed was nails.

Of course I dreamed of her. Torrid dreams that seemed more real for their vulgarity and coarseness, where I saw her doing those thirty-year-old woman things and imagined she did them to me.

About to explode, I woke.

Guinevere was nestled at my side, reaching across me, using her hand—and the realization that it was she and not a dream sent stars across my eyes and paroxysms through my back and legs. I gasped. The barn wall had a knothole you could chuck a football through and a bolt of moonlight caught half her face. She looked as if she expected power, but wasn't sure if she'd acquired it. Like Mrs. Sharps speaking on behalf of Mister Sharps, borrowing his authority because she had so little.

All that came to me later. At that moment I was in love and wanted to consume her, wanted to steal her entire body so I'd be sure to possess her soul. I needed her to be as frantic to consume me. I wanted to kiss her with my eyes open and see her eyes were open, and know she was just as frenetic and forlorn and bereft as I.

Her lips were lukewarm.

She pulled from me and snuggled her forehead to my cheek, and wrapped her arm across my chest. I was exposed and vulnerable, but she was uninterested. She shuddered. Her sobbing was quiet and she said, "Someday I'll hear the bullfrogs for *him*."

I didn't know about the music, and I didn't ask. I stroked her hair and told her she was a silly girl and I would love her forever and they were the easiest words to say.

We'd just wait out the evil.

* * *

Of everything I laid out on the coffee table—the gauze, cotton wraps, Mercurochrome—I failed to bring aspirin. I'm in a doctor's house: surely he has something more potent than aspirin. This is a war-style wound. Can a fellow get a bottle of morphine? My leg shouts and I look. Burn marks are squiggly like the red-hot brass I used for a brand. Lymph and blood percolate like I seared a steak but didn't cook it all the way through.

I paint Mercurochrome all the way around the fleshy part that is black and bloody, then wipe Bag Balm over it. The burn inside from the Lysol isn't going away, and the longer I sit the more I'm ready to vomit salted venison and peaches into the fireplace. I press a wrap to the sticky balm and unroll gauze around my thigh until the whole area is white and the bandages will hold. A couple strips of tape and I'm ready to return to the front lines, except I'm still sitting in a puddle. To the small degree the agony in my leg fades, the sting of sitting in piss for ten minutes replaces it.

I fight my way upstairs to the bathroom and discover the house has no water pressure. So I go to Doctor Coates' room and find another pair of underwear and carry them to the living room. I fill a bucket from under the kitchen sink with snow on the porch and put the bucket next to the fire, and in a few minutes, while I meditate on Guinevere, the snow melts and I sponge-clean my privates.

Finally dressed and warm again, I add a few logs to the fire and journey upstairs to the rifle room. Those pistols weigh on my mind. I'm trying to think like a soldier might, about repelling an attack, and it seems the more bullets I'm ready to offer my opponents and the more mobility I have while doing it, the better I can avoid being shot. And if in the end it comes down to a face-to-face at close range—well, a cowboy doesn't fetch a rifle to a duel.

The pistols' workings are internal and there's no way to puzzle them without breaking the weapon down. But one looks like the perfect gun, the one everyone sees when he thinks of a pistol. It is a revolver with a long barrel. The grips are white and the metal looks like silver bleu-cheese or horsehair pottery. I search for a marking that will tell me which box contains the right bullets.

Chapter Eleven

Tree roots had lifted the sidewalk panels. Gwen kept her gaze to her feet as she and Liz Sunday walked past the sheriff's station. Sunlight broke through the leaves and danced like butterflies on the grass and the cement sidewalk. Gwen kicked a bottle cap and watched it bounce over the curb.

"What are you girls doing away from school?"

Sheriff Bittersmith sat on a chair on the station porch and smoked a corncob pipe. His feet propped on the rail, he exhaled smoke through his nose. Eyed them up and down. He held the pipe at his mouth, dropped his feet to the floor, and leaned.

Gwen took Liz's arm. "We're going home, Sheriff."

"Home?"

"That's right."

"Not well, huh? School nurse have a look? Why didn't they call your father, girl?"

"He's not around."

"Well, hold on. Don't keep walking when I'm talkin' at you. So what's the problem, Liz? Liz Sunday?"

Liz nodded.

"Not well enough for school, but well enough to walk all the way home?"

"It isn't far."

"Come around the side lot and I'll take you home in the Bronco. That way you both won't miss school."

"Thank you, but I need to walk."

"Need to walk?"

"She can't sit very well. Very long," Gwen said.

"I can't sit. It's—"

"Then we won't stop for ice cream." Bittersmith took the handrail and descended the steps. Gwen and Liz backed away.

"Thank you, but we really have to keep moving," Gwen said.

Bittersmith stood at the bottom step and sucked on his pipe.

Gwen stumbled on a sidewalk panel.

"Easy," Bittersmith said. He smiled and nodded and nothing could have been plainer, Gwen thought, as she blushed in anger and embarrassment over losing her step, that his look was an appraisal and his nod was an invitation.

They walked with a harried pace until they reached Wilcox Avenue. At the traffic light, Gwen turned as if speaking to Liz, and sought Sheriff Bittersmith through the corner of her eye. He leaned on the rail and watched.

"Well?"

"The old pervert's still staring at us," Gwen said.

The light changed and traffic moved. Gwen and Liz crossed Wilcox. "You want to take the shortcut by Sheep Hill?" Liz said.

"The creek?"

"Uh-huh."

"It's a river. It's overflowing."

"It's better than being out here where everyone can see us. We don't have to walk in the water."

They followed Wilcox to a steel-frame bridge. Its blue paint had peeled, exposing rusted metal. Hundreds of love aphorisms and declarations vied for space on rare stretches of uncurled paint. Love Sucks. Joanne Remington sucks. You wish. Fuck you. Lou loves Michelle. Michelle gets around. No I don't.

They stood at the base of the bridge, Gwen scanning the names while Liz watched nothing at all, until an approaching car passed. They ducked around the column by the sidewalk and glissaded awkwardly down loose rocks to the trail beside Mill Creek. The overflowing creek's winding path would pass near both Gwen and Liz's homes two and three miles away.

The grass was dewy as if the sun had just risen. The sound of rushing water was hypnotic, and the humid air was dense and rich in a way that made Gwen drowsy. She yawned. A thicket of blackberry bushes spilled from the shade onto the trail, and Gwen stopped.

"They're not good this late in the season," Liz said. "Watch for stinkbugs."

Gwen plucked a berry from the bush. Dropped it into her mouth.

"Have you tried to see people?" Liz said. "You know? With the music?"

"One."

"Only one?" Liz led the way. The trail wound close to the creek. She misplaced her foot and slipped, barely catching a birch branch to stay upright. The muddy water carried an occasional leaf or small branch, but was mostly a roiling, churning torrent. The path narrowed, half of it below water. Gwen followed and collided with Liz, and they were awkwardly close, separated by books, looking through stringy hair tousles at each other.

"Who else should I try to kill?" Gwen said.

Liz backed a step from Gwen, and then another.

Gwen followed. They walked single file, ducking low-hanging branches, sidestepping tufts of wet grass, each foot closer to the roiling muddy water.

“Was he your first?” Gwen said.

Liz marched faster and Gwen allowed her a ten-pace lead. The creek tunneled through copses of vibrant green trees, walled by emerald shrubs so that every turn was a mystery and she couldn’t see more than a few steps ahead. The path finally separated from the creek bank. Liz passed out of sight and around a bend to the right.

Gwen said, “I didn’t mean anything. Of course he was your first.”

Liz didn’t answer and Gwen rounded the turn.

“Wha—!”

Liz stepped toward her, red-faced, eyes rimmed with water. “What is it with you?”

“What?”

“Why won’t you let up?” Liz stepped closer.

Gwen felt Liz’s breath warm across her face. “I don’t know—”

“Yes you do,” Liz said. “Just shut up. Stop asking.”

“I’m sorry.”

“No, you’re not. Why’s it so important? I got pregnant. It happens. It happens!”

“I know.”

“I didn’t do anything.”

“No.”

“I didn’t want him. I didn’t do anything. I didn’t DO anything!”

“What?”

“Nothing. Stop. Won’t you?”

“Okay.”

“No! Dammit,” Liz said, leaning forward. Her eyes flared and her mouth smiled confusion.

“What happened?”

Liz swallowed then cleared her throat and spat. “Never mind.”

Chapter Twelve

Now I pack a revolver. Doctor Coates was a southpaw; the holster hangs on my left hip. I haven't fired it, but I learned how it works with the chamber empty, and I'm satisfied that when I pull the hammer and squeeze the trigger with the cylinder full of bullets, it will fire. If it fails, I'll take it God made a mistake when the carbine misfired.

I stand on the porch not knowing the hour, feeling days have passed since this morning. Snow falls. It only looks aggressive when you let your eyes blur and take the whole panorama in at once, thousands of acres of sky, all filled with invading snowflakes, each one barely a wisp of water but combined with a billion brothers, enough to make life screech to a halt on half a continent.

Across the lake and a mile beyond the woods at the far shore, Fay Haudesert or Cal or Jordan has discovered Burt in the barn. Follow these footsteps off the porch and across the lake, and keep going through the woods along the side hill, across the Haudesert fields, and eventually they wind up at Burt Haudesert's barn. Eventually my boot prints smear Burt Haudesert's blood. These prints link me to a specific event that his kin are just now beginning to comprehend. These prints are real enough evidence for angry men. Cal and Jordan will follow them. The sheriff and his deputies will follow them.

They'll all arrive here and want to retaliate for something that is impossible to avenge. They'll want to lay blame, and they'll be unable to see that the person who deserves all the blame—and the person who deserves all the credit—is already dead. They'll find me and I'll either again receive unmerited grace, or they'll execute me.

Or I'll kill them. God puts teeth on a wolf cub, just like its mother.

I step inside the house. Leave the door closed but unlocked. Why bother when the window is covered by cardboard?

My eyes adjust from the snow glare after a minute. Dr. Coates' roll top desk beckons. I can't sit on the sofa and wait to die, and I can't bundle up and walk into the storm, trusting I'll survive the cold. Not when there's a fireplace and logs and food and guns here. But while I'm here I've got little to do save wait, and it becomes tiresome. I sit in the banker's chair, with wheels on the bottom and a leather cushion, and drag closer to the desktop. Letters in slots and papers scattered willy-nilly. Letters cast aside, opened with a clean slit the way people of culture do. And another letter, in the middle of the writing pad, penned but not signed. I steal a glance at it and look away. The portrait of Christ is above me.

Tape and white out and staple boxes and paper clips. A magnifying glass. Ink pens and pencils and a pencil sharpener that at first looks like a miniature coffee grinder, and at the bottom is the beveled razor. I thrust a pencil in it and twist, letting curls of wood fall to the floor. When it squeaks, I rest the pencil in the front drawer, careful of not bumping the point, and sharpen another. I'll do the whole drawer-full to avoid reading the half-penned letter in the middle of the desk, under my nose.

But didn't I come to the desk to read the letter? To learn a little of the story of the man whose hospitality I've commandeered?

Dear Jacob;

I received your invitation to chair the Bittersmith Chamber of Commerce's Christmas Festival with great excitement. Serving as the Chair in past seasons has proven the highlight of the dreary winter season.

It is with regret that I must decline your invitation, however. I find this year I am not of the soundest health, and am afraid the event would suffer from my unintended mismanagement. I have given my little remaining stamina to the church, and the urchins who attend Sunday school not knowing the gift that has been prepared for them. The gift that was prepared for all of us who regret having been born unknowing.

I've become a doddering fool, and

The text ends without another word, without a signature. I imagine a gray-haired giant of a man collapsing from on very desk, and tumbling to the floor.

Not knowing, and not yet regretting they were born that way?

I read the missive again, and its mystery is no clearer. I've had the basics of Protestant theology drilled into my head over twenty years of mandatory church services. I'm clear on the gift that's been prepared, but being born unknowing? Isn't that the point?

The only book on the desk is *Moby Dick*, and I know from past excursions that I can't read it. I take my Melville in shorter bursts. I carry the volume to the sofa anyway, and it sits on my lap while I watch the fire. There's a giant flame that the little ones feed. It keeps trying to climb into the chimney only to fall away over and over again. Minutes drift along, and I find I'm no longer interested and only watch through half-lidded eyes.

Through the day, Gwen and I kept our affair hidden. It would never have done to flaunt it or allow anyone to grow suspicious. I never looked at her. Even if she fawned on me I wouldn't give away the truth. I worried she appeared to have some childish infatuation, but at least I was sure it didn't look the other way around. I worried, but she was an actress and never slipped. In private, she stopped the teasing she had begun in the garden. No more rubbers on cucumbers.

In terms of prettiness, Gwen was fine-tuned. My instinct to help her might have clouded my feelings, but in quiet reflection I could imagine us spending a lifetime learning each other's secrets, and I knew she was special. You don't ever understand everything about a girl, but if you can strip away the fears that unbalance one side of the equation and the animal spirits that kowtow to the other, the real girl shines. Even before you witness her wrinkled brow and moving lips you know her prayers are sincere. You know her worthiness. In my soberest moments I knew Gwen was good.

Not that there were many opportunities to dote. Mostly I spent twelve or fourteen hours every day in the fields or the barn or the garden. Burt Haudesert only had so much equipment, and the rest of the work was done by hand, elbow, back, and knees.

A fall day came when Burt wanted me to help him slaughter hogs. Cal was barely getting around the farm with a cane, and Jordan had made it clear the night before how urgently he looked forward to turning over the section of cornfield farthest from town, some miles off. Burt sniggered and said if Jordan had a third hand he'd need a third pocket to put it in he was so damn useless. Rather sit on a tractor than mix with pigs.

Then he told me to be ready for blood and guts come sunrise.

"Slaughtering hogs," he said, "is an all-day event."

I didn't mind. I'd worked with a dozen farmers outside Monroe and if there's one thing consistent about farmers it's that they don't buy meat from the butcher. Harvesting animals is part of agriculture, and if you're apprenticed long enough, you'll see chickens with their tiny necks slit, and cattle, and hogs, and more steaming gut piles than you'd thought populated the earth, until you stop and think that every one of us has a mess of guts, and part of the game is to prevent them from winding up steaming on the ground. I nodded at Burt. "I better get my rest, then."

"Hold up a minute. I want to talk to you on the porch."

Gwen looked at me and I stared at the wall. Finally she said, "Gale?"

I looked.

"You don't want any apple dumplin's?"

"Didn't know you made any."

She fetched cereal bowls full of dumplin's and warm milk sprinkled with cinnamon and a touch of nutmeg—I asked later that night—and Burt and I retired to the front porch. The moon was out and the air was brisk.

"You staying warm at night?" Burt said.

"I just bury myself in hay."

I couldn't see too well, but it looked like he nodded. I spooned a bite of apple.

"I'll tell Missus Haudesert to give you a blanket."

He sounded unprepared to move the conversation where he wanted it to go. I was ready to jump up and run, or fight him, or defend myself. I didn't know which because I didn't know exactly what he knew. Guinevere had been out a half dozen times to the barn. Burt would have his way and she'd come out and cry on me. It made it hard to sit in the man's kitchen and eat his apple dumplin's. Made it hard to sit on his porch and thank him for offering to scare up a blanket.

"I'd appreciate that," I said.

"I'll just be out with it," Burt said. "I've talked with you at least a dozen times on this very porch about a man doin' his duty by his country, and you never let on any interest. The militia needs soldiers. Cal and Jordan are joining up, and you're a year older'n them."

I exhaled and downed a bite of dumplin'. "You think the militia would have my sort? I don't have much to offer. Don't even have my own rifle."

"You got your willingness to serve!" he said, and backed it up with a slap to my shoulder. "I speak from the highest authority, and I know they'd have you. We're fittin' to put on a recruitin' drive. Damned if it don't look like the End Times is nigh, commie shit going on, this country." He nodded toward his neighbor a mile away. "Give me the gold standard and a fair market price for a bushel of corn, and leave my goddamn guns alone."

"Yes, sir."

"Well, you've heard all that before. I'll take you to the next meet and get you enlisted, and you can go with me and the boys after that."

I chewed more dumplin's.

I thought about the militia that night, waiting on Gwen. I'd go, only to keep Burt happy. A man knows his principles, it don't matter what folk he consorts with. Some of it sounded interesting enough—who doesn't hate the commies? Who doesn't like the smell of a rifle and the punch line to a good country joke. Like Burt said, "The difference between men and women is that women want a hundred things from one man and men want one thing from a hundred women."

A fellow can listen to anything, even if it turns his stomach, so long as his principles get the final word.

Next morning Burt and I ate eggs and drank coffee. Burt looked rough and told Gwen to brew the coffee strong enough to float a railroad spike. Gwen had a bruise on her neck. She'd told me about it, snuggled up with me just six hours before. Told me how he always liked to cover her throat with his hand.

Things like that made me think in terms of finding a billy club and spreading his brains on the kitchen table. I got so mad when Gwen told me about it, she had to hold me back. No sane person can think about a girl enduring that sort of torment, but she was afraid of changing things, and it was easy to cling to the thought that someday he'd stop on his own if he loved her like he said. I told her love is what you do, not what you say, and I'd rather have no love than that of a god-forsaken pervert.

She was quiet.

I drank Burt Haudesert's coffee and ate his eggs. Sat at his table and grinned when he made smart-assed quips. We finished breakfast and headed to the pasture behind the barn. Burt had a dozen hogs, and he'd been fattening them on grain for a month. Before that they ran free over a couple acres of swamp closest the road, where they scavenged on tubers and acorns. It didn't hurt them so long as they went back on potato peels and grain for their last month.

I wound up working at a butcher shop later, only for a couple months, but long enough to know the way Burt slaughtered was different than the way a professional got it done. Burt liked the butchery of it, and that was different from a man who did it for a living.

Burt and I set up a tripod of four-inch oak poles with a pulley at the top and another on the ground with all the ropes attached beforehand. The pulley on the ground was fixed to a short two by four, and I saw right off that the intent was to suspend a hog by his hind legs. One leg of the tripod had a wheelbarrow-sized wheel affixed at the bottom, and that was a puzzle.

The success of the operation hinged on having the shortest time between killing the hog to getting him trussed and hanging with all that blood running out his neck.

Nearby, Burt had a fifty-five gallon drum set up on an iron platform. I spent the first half-hour filling it with buckets of water while Burt built and stoked a fire underneath. He dumped in a small bucket of hardwood ash and stirred it around. "Lye," he said, then set up a table on sawhorses and loaded it with tools of the trade. Bell scrapers for cleaning hair and scurf. A thermometer, a hacksaw. A .22 pistol. To the side was a blue plastic swimming pool.

Burt led me to the stalls and winked. "You got to pick the right hog to start with. You pick a gilt, she can't be in heat. Meat'll taste rank. And if you pick a barrow, you want him gelded. And healed from it. Leave nuts on a boar, meat'll be so rank a dog'll lick his ass to rid the taste. You're looking for a hog, maybe, two hundred-fifty pound. This girl's about right."

It was easy getting the first hog out by the tripod. Put a rope around her shoulders and kind of guide her along. Burt took the pistol and cocked it beside the table. "Draw an X between her eyes and ears, and aim for the middle."

He demonstrated with a grease pencil.

Pap!

Just like that, she stood there, dazed, half her brains scrambled. Blinked. Dropped to her knees and sighed.

"Now you stick her," Burt said. He slipped a six-inch knife from a sheath at his hip and shoved the hog to her side, grabbed a leg, felt for her breastbone, and thrust the blade into her neck. He sliced deep and long, severing everything in between, then did the same on the other side. "Bleeding out makes sure the meat ain't tainted," he said, and showed me his red hand.

We stood beside her a few minutes while she finished dying and the blood flow slowed to a dribble.

"Stick that thermometer in the vat, there. See what it says."

"Hundred-twenty."

"Shit."

"What?"

"Hundred-fifty's better. We'll give her an extra couple of minutes on the tripod." He knelt at her hind and slit her between hoof and hock. "Grab that truss."

I supplied it, and he worked the nails into the slits. Together we drew the rope through the pulleys and when the hog was suspended, he wrapped the rope around a notched tie-off on one of the tripod's legs. More blood flowed from the hog's neck. Again we waited. I looked to the house and then out at the field where Jordan was turning the soil for winter.

"Wish you was out there?"

"No."

"Come on. Grab a leg."

We each stooped to a different tripod leg, and the point of having a wheel on the third became apparent. We dragged the whole contraption real slow until the hog was next to the vat of hot water. Burt hoisted her higher and I pushed her over the tub as Burt lowered her in. He looked at his watch. "Four minutes. We don't want to cook her, do we?"

After the minutes counted off he raised her back legs a foot out of the water. "See if you can pull off any hair."

I did, and he raised her the rest of the way out. With the hog hanging and dripping water, he said, "This is the fun part. One of them. We got to get her on the table."

I bear-hugged her body but couldn't keep her from landing in the dirt. Burt unfixed her legs and joined me, and together we wrestled her to the makeshift table. He gave me a bell scraper and said, "Start at the feet. They cool the fastest. Hold it like so."

He demonstrated, holding the scraper like a chisel and dragging it across the hair. "Don't go so deep you take off the skin. Lot a lard under there we don't want to waste."

I took a tool and worked the legs. The hair was already cool, but under she was hot, and there was no escaping the fact this was an animal that a few minutes ago was looking forward to a happy day. We worked and worked. I got a blister on my hand. Finally the hog was mostly white, and I saw Burt scraping in a circular motion, digging out the worst of the scurf and dirt. I did it too, and he nodded. He took a bale hook and pulled off her toes and then rubbed her down with a bristle brush.

We hoisted her on the tripod again, wheeled her back a few yards, put the plastic swimming pool under her, and Burt split her open. He took off his overcoat and pulled what viscera hadn't already fallen to the pool, then got clean up inside her. Another mass of bright red fell out, her heart and lungs and all. A picture flashed in my head of him having his way with Gwen and I turned away.

"You sure you wouldn't rather be off in a field?"

"I'm sure."

"In a pig's eye!" He howled at that. "In a pig's eye!"

Burt let the hog hang while he brought over the truck from the driveway, and we wrapped her in burlap and carried her to the bed, and then Burt drove her to the barn. We hung her from a rafter and, covered in wet hair and sticky blood, went downstairs to the stalls for the next.

The second smelled blood soaking into the ground, feared what she knew, and coaxing her to the tripod, I wondered if even the most brazen man wouldn't feel like a liar saying 'come on, honey, come on, girl.' She was livestock, and killing swine is part of the way things are supposed to be, going back to the deepest reaches of history. But though there was no way she would understand my soothing words or the way I felt saying them, I felt guilt.

That's where Burt was different.

"C'mon, you stinky fuck," he said. "You're going to like this. Yes, ma'am." Again he winked. "You got to talk nice so they don't scare. Can't let 'em flush, or jostle about. That'll spoil the meat too."

* * *

Guinevere visited that night, and I had my new blanket spread over me. I lifted it and she crawled next to me and I closed the blanket over both of us. The hay was sloped like we were on a sofa with our legs stretched out. She put her head in the hollow of my shoulder and her arm across my stomach, and while she sniffled I told her the same soothing things I'd grown accustomed to telling her. Promises I knew I'd keep someday, but not which day.

"I'd like it if you'd marry me," I said. Her whimpers ceased and I said, "I'll take you away from here."

"Where?"

"Somewhere south, where the wind is always warm and the sky is blue, and you can stand on the top of a mountain, yodeling, bare naked, and no one will know."

"What if someone knew?" she said. We'd been through it before.

"He wouldn't care. He'd say, 'you yodel on your hill, and I'll yodel on mine.'"

And after the dialogue she would kiss my neck.

No more of the strawberry patch. Knowing what I did about her problems, I didn't want her that way. Well, I did and I didn't. When she wasn't with me I got pretty randy in my thinking, but when she snuggled up tight and clung to me like I was the only thing rooted in a shifting world, I didn't want her sex. I relished the softness of her breast, but mostly I enjoyed when she got her mind off her troubles and started talking about everyday things. How clouds can inspire dreams. How it'd be neat to taste sunshine. She demonstrated optimism that was incongruous with her situation, and I could listen to her for hours. She'd place her temple against mine and it was like thoughts would osmose between us if we only stayed there long enough trying.

Except that night she said, "Are you really going to marry me? And take me away? Because I think I'm coming to pieces."

"I will," I said.

I should have spirited her away with nothing but a blanket and a few pounds of salted hog meat.

Chapter Thirteen

Gwen leaned against the seat back and closed her eyes. She remembered the bullfrog song. Her mother loaded groceries into the trunk. Gwen recalled the pleasant man in the grocery who had commented that it was a fine day. She remembered him unbidden—saw his face against an azure field—and her heart trilled at the omen.

He would be dead in minutes.

Fay and Gwen had been working since before dawn; being Saturday, her mother had wanted to get all the pears canned. They'd spent the morning sweating jars and sterilizing lids, prepping cinnamon syrup, peeling and slicing pears by the thousands and tens of thousands, it seemed. Now, with a half-dozen paring knife cuts on her fingers and her cuticles stringy with torn skin, Gwen rested her eyes.

The face came to her suddenly, each line resolved, clear. Urgent. The cerulean background glowed and the man's countenance was unremarkable. He stared like the others had stared. Some part of him knew he was about to die.

Was he already clutching his heart or collapsing with an aneurism? Or was he still squeezing grapefruit? Had his end already begun, or did a subconscious part of him look death in the face?

The bullfrog music grew louder, strong and plaintive, like a ship's horn in the fog. Gwen looked out the car window to the storefront and saw him at the register inside, reaching into his wallet. She had taken too long to gather her faculties—too long, but she must try.

Gwen closed her eyes and shifted her frame of view. The azure background seemed limitless, and since she didn't actually turn, she had no sense of how far she'd spun. Until she came upon another face. This one was shaded, with an outsized proboscis, a gaping rictus, eyes like flat spots of cow dung. Its frown deepened, nostrils flared.

It saw her.

Gwen glared. Clamped her teeth and locked her gaze upon its eyes, and a chill spilled from the base of her skull to her spine.

Gwen's mother opened the driver's side door. Gwen opened her eyes. "Wait!"

Mother slipped behind the wheel, opened her purse for her keys.

"Wait what?"

"That man in the grocery—he's in trouble." Gwen reached for the door release.

Mother leaned close to the wheel and looked past Gwen. "What man? Get back inside!"

Gwen raced across the lot, felt the hard pavement through her flats. Ahead, an old woman returned a cart; Gwen jockeyed to the side but the distance was too short; she slowed behind the woman, who waited for the automatic door.

"Please, excuse me!" Gwen said.

"Hmmph!" The old woman jammed the cart into the door.

Gwen stepped back, looked through the glass at the man. His smile was the kind that might accompany a bouquet of flowers for a plump housewife. Gwen looked back at her mother, scowling beside the front fender.

The man stepped closer. The old woman reared back and drove the cart into the door, popping it open. She shoved through. The man approached on the other side, only a few feet away. He stopped pushing his cart. His eyes went pie pans and his mouth gaped. One hand slapped his chest. He fell backward, clutching the cart. He slumped against the wall and slid to the floor, tearing business cards and homemade ads from a corkboard. The cart wobbled sideways and toppled with him.

The old woman charged by. Unseeing, deaf. Gwen watched her stooped determination, her angry feet scuffing the floor.

Gwen fell to the man and took his hand. His face was ash and his hand cold.

Limp. His eyes smiled at the edges though his mouth was flat. His breaths were ragged and she closed her eyes and sought his face in the darkness, that she might do battle with the devil on the other side.

Nothing.

Gwen stood, slipped across the grocery store floor, around a corner to the service desk, which was empty, and yelled to a cashier, "A man's had a heart attack! Call help!"

She ran back to the man and ignored the ensuing confusion behind her. He would die. The Devil would get him, and nothing she did would help.

Gwen took the man's hand in both of hers. His face was wrinkled but not old. He was heavy-set, but not obese. Barely any flecks of gray hair. Taken too early. His bladder had released.

She closed her hands over his.

He wasn't breathing. His head slumped forward from the wall, and as he fell away, her anger swelled.

"What's happened?"

Gwen looked up. The cashier stood on legs parted as if to anchor a tug of war team. Gwen pushed the man the rest of the way to the floor and pulled his arm, dragging him away from the wall, flat on his back. "He's had a heart attack, I think. Call the ambulance!"

Gwen tried to remember the techniques. It had been a year since the school nurse instructed the entire class in the gymnasium. Press the person's chest somewhere—the sternum—above the sternum…But he wasn't breathing, and something had to be done—which came first?

"What do we do!" It was a woman with a baby in her arms.

Gwen squeezed her eyes closed, trying to remember the steps, and stared again into the face of the Devil taking this man from their side to his. His smile was toothy, like a dog showing fangs. And his flat, cow-shit eyes were hollows that led to blasting winds and frigid moonless nights.

Gwen opened her eyes.

She lifted the man's neck and elevated his chin. Pinched his nose. Covered his mouth with hers and exhaled into him, watched his chest swell from the corner of her eye. In her mind she heard laughter, and even with her eyes open saw the evil from which it sprung. She blew into the man again, watched his chest rise and fall, smelled his breath, the strange minty odor that faded into a residual coffee stink that in turn made her think of death and emptiness. Again she saw the Devil's face, leering, vested in her comic rescue. Gwen inhaled deeply and emptied her lungs into the man's mouth, again, and held hers against his, sustaining the pressure, so that his lungs wouldn't collapse. Finally she slipped to his side.

She saw her mother's shoes at the entrance, and other people's shoes, and Gwen pressed along the man's chest for his sternum, and finding the bottom, measured two fingers' width, and locked her right palm to the back of her left hand, interwove her fingers and bore down with all her weight. She rocked on her knees. Let up. Pressed again. Back and forth, forgetting to count. She wiggled across the waxed floor and pinched his nose, blew into his lungs, and allowed the air to trickle back out, and did it again. What was the count? The Devil grinned. Fuck you, he said, I win. And Gwen scooted to the man's side and locked her hands together and heaved her weight to his chest again and again.

"Gwen," her mother said.

"Sweetheart," another said.

Gwen closed her eyes and it was just she and the Devil. His mocking laughter rattled from one side of her mind to the other, and she looked through his flat eyes into darkness where the noise continued until echoes piled on his voice a thousand times over and it was an army of devils laughing at her. She heaved against the dead man's ribs. A hand touched her shoulder and she pushed it aside. Gwen moved to the man's face, lifted his neck, watched his blank eyes for the smallest twinkle of life. But his skin held the marks of her last touch, and not a muscle moved.

"Gwen, it's time to stop," her mother said.

"No!"

Gwen pinched his nose and blew into his mouth. She was dizzy and slowed to catch her breath before inhaling and blowing into his mouth again. She rested her head on his chest and again felt a hand on her shoulder. Firm, insistent.

"What!"

She looked up and her mother was still several feet away; no one was there, and the pressure continued though no one touched her. Heat spread through her shoulder. She pressed one hand to the other and lurched to the dead man's sternum, dropped her weight like a sack of feed, almost assisted by the dark hand on her shoulder, which now squeezed as if seeking that nerve that Cal and Jordan pinched to make her squeal. Still Gwen heaved.

"Go away, Devil!"

Him, or you.

She pressed the man's chest, slammed a three count against him, hurried to his head. She exhaled into his mouth again and again until the weight on her shoulder made her struggle to bear up against it. Each breath she fed the man was lighter, and each time she pounded his chest she was weaker. Flats and sneakers and heels circled her but she never looked higher than the peoples' knees so she wouldn't have to read the defeat on their faces.

"Get off me, Devil." she whispered. "You can't have everyone."

I'll have him, or you.

His laughter whipped through her like a cold winter gale.

Chapter Fourteen

Ain't a damn man the whole world over ever been seventy-two and had joints felt like two pieces of sandpaper, a back felt like a log split by a maul.

The sun is two-thirds to noon. Clouds blow in like a summer thunderstorm—but it's cold enough to freeze the balls off a billiard table. Seems the machinery of nature ought to run as slow as the machinery of man. It doesn't. Look at a crick bubbling under ice, or ice pellets blasted by a gust, and it's an illusion. Man at the center believing everything feels like I feel. There's nothing farther from the truth. All this belief that the world is thinking and feeling, and maybe empathic in misery, or delighted with reverie, is the worst kind of dreaming. Nothing out there gives a rat's rotten ass. I'm carrying a coat for a girl in the middle of a storm; she's got one foot bare and the other shoe full of snow and toes so numb she's forgotten she has them, or burning like as to catch flame. She's getting the full dose of nature right now. She knows there isn't a tree or a brook or a deer or fox that would spit to save her. She knows she's all she's got, and she's only sixteen. Girl that age is just getting ripe, and it makes me madder'n all hell.

The going is slow. Gale and Gwen's tracks are mostly filled. The wind screeches across the field driving snow and icy crystals, and any holes in the covering gets filled on the lee side first, so the footsteps I've been following have become peanut-shaped crescents. Spotting them now is no trouble, but they won't last long.

Half way to the woods I arrive at a mixed up jumble of tracks. They lost their gait. Gwen—judging from the print size—stumbled in a drift close to a windrow of trees, and Gale came to her. I study the impressions on the white canvas, and the footprints tell of a dance, him coming to her, bracing, lifting. They didn't roll around and fight, but putting myself in Gwen's mind, why would she? She'd just seen Gale murder her father.

Though I imagine when they were in the loft it was for love, no child will see her father killed—by her lover or any other—and feel nothing. She wouldn't run from the barn unwilling, and yet as I've plodded farther from the warmth of the Bronco, I've wondered with every step if I dare go much farther. This girl, with no coat, and snow in her feet, feeling the wind shred her clothes, tagging along behind the man who murdered her pappy—wouldn't she reach a moment where she'd stop and look back? Imagine the smell of baked bread? The taste of salt on beef? The warmth of her mother's arms? The agony in her mother's eye? And if she imagined these things, wouldn't she take a step closer to home, like this moon-shaped bowl indicates?

What prevented her from the next step and the next? Did she spin to Gale and race after him, or did he jerk her arm and drag her farther from home?

I peer deep into the forest ahead, searching tree trunks for motion. The bark is bold against the snow, and anyone passing through would be evident. I scan the tree line left to right and stop at a clearing midway up the hill. The easiest view draws the eye, though no stone-cold killer'd be stupid enough to traipse across an open section like that.

Though as I think on it, Gale killed Burt with a pitchfork, and that shows a madman's moxie.

At the bottom of the clearing, I see motion and my chest tightens. A flicker of black melding into a tree, emerging. It bounds away.

Deer.

Spooked?

I scan down the hill. Whatever set him running came from below. I look through the trees, downward, to the right, until I'm seeing dead ahead. Right where Gale and Gwen's tracks point.

A burst of wind cuts into my neck and ice stings my ear. I turn into it and stoop. Cast a sideways glance back to the house and barn, fuzzy with distance and the snow in between. Shift Guinevere's coat and sweater from my left arm to my right, and dig a piece of jerked venison from my pocket while watching the goings-on at the Haudesert farm.

The coroner beat Cooper to the scene. He pulls a case from his trunk. The gusts are gone. Standing here, I am suddenly warm and unbutton the top of my coat.

Up ahead there's a possibility that Gale and Gwen have rattled a deer loose from the underbrush. Cooper can catch up. I've got to keep on. There's only one more dead body I want to see today, and it damn well isn't Gwen's.

In forty years of lawing I've seen a lot of dead men and women, some more gruesome than Burt Haudesert. Bodies of geezers like me, pretending to be made of steel, face-in-the-soup dead. Bloated and black when a grandkid finds them. Or mangled in car accidents. Heroes wrap themselves around oak trees and their bodies come out like so many pounds of hamburger wrapped in blue jeans and t-shirts.

But of all the death and all the bodies, only two were the machination of an angry man. It was about the militia. This was eight years back.

Every state's got a gang of men with guns and tattered U.S. Constitutions stowed next to their dog-eared John Birch pamphlets. Bitching about government makes men happy, and in recent times, country folk have been fucking euphoric. Rumor was the boys in my neck of the woods were getting rowdy and ready to switch gears from talking to walking. I don't mind ten men at a hunting camp chucking bottles and blasting away. Any fella dumb enough to get drunk around a crew with guns half deserves a bullet. But I got a tip. One of the wives overheard talk of linking the local group with some radical faction out of Denver and marching with guns to Washington to take the country back from the jigs and the jews. A sheriff can't truck with that, but in a county of twenty thousand, everybody knows everybody, almost. At least the men who would be of age and frame of mind to join such a group knew everyone else who might be. I didn't have anyone to put inside. I kept my ear out, but no more tips came.

There was only fifty of them. They recruited primarily through the Masonic Lodge, though they were careful not to bring the Lodge into it. Of course, it's a different thing, what a group does in the Fourth of July parade versus what secret conversations goes on in the Blue Room. I wasn't privy, but I knew when the men who were part of the militia hushed at the Lodge, they weren't talking about saving widows and orphans or tuning Harley engines.

I joined the Lodge on Burt's invitation, thinking it was a thank-you for having set him on the right path all them years before. I'd turned down invitations for thirty years. Every secret brotherhood, and seems like there's more and more guilds, wants to claim the town's most prominent citizens on its rolls. I never joined one.

But Burt had a peculiar look in his eye, and I always had an interest in him, and so I went. Took my degrees, including the third, which was more memory work than I wanted, going over lines word after word, and only able to practice while I was with him. It gave me the chance to learn the way he thought. We'd sit at a picnic table, and he'd say the script from memory because it was against Lodge rules to ever have the secrets in print, and I'd repeat each ancient phrase and watch it hit Burt like religion. The catechisms came in two parts, a call and a response. He'd say the call and I'd stumble through the answer, and after each catechism we'd rest a bit and drink coffee and swat mosquitoes and I'd ask about his family. Gwen and the boys.

Sometimes I'd ask after his mother.

Lodge meetings were Tuesday nights at seven. I watched Burt with a critical eye, like a father, and listened to the others for Militia talk. If a group assembled at the rifle range to sight in for buck season, I made sure to arrive with my ought-six coming in high. When a group went fishing, I brought a case of beer. They were testing me, and I was testing them.

I placed each foot on the ground almost sideways, watching for twigs, and rolling across the leaves without a whisper. With a gurgling crick as a backdrop, an elephant could sneak up on two arguing men. I stood behind an oak so big it was prob'ly here when Jack La Ramie came through and lent his name in what, 1812?

"It's time," Steward Pounder said. "We can't wait forever. They're waiting on us to get our asses in gear."

And Burt said, "We wait and don't get involved. We're not about going someplace else. This's about stopping them goddamn commies from coming here. Takin' our houses and guns. Fuck Denver, and fuck Washington."

"Well, it's a goddamn good thing you ain't runnin' this outfit," Steward says.

"You don't understand anything."

"Just who the hell you think you're talking to?"

"Go fuck a goat. And don't think I'm going to let you get the boys riled up for someone else's fight."

"You ain't runnin' shit, no more."

"By God, I'll knock your ass into next week and kick it again on Tuesday."

Steward splashed upstream and Burt crossed to the other side of the crick and wandered downstream. My thought was to pull Burt aside later and begin extracting him from the group. Steward was crazy, but nowhere near the worst of the bunch. That honor belonged to his brother, Marshall, a giant man whose footsteps shook the forest and left an imprint like a dinosaur hoof. Had no luck as a hunter. Every animal a mile around felt him coming.

The situation for Burt was the kind you could see taking a good man and gradually turning him against his better judgment. Last thing I wanted was for him to wind up in a pissing contest with Steward and Marshall Pounder. Dicks like them wouldn't lose a pissing contest.

When two weeks later they were both dead, I had a suspect in mind.

Chapter Fifteen

It was late and Gwen couldn't sleep. She listened to the ghostly creaking of the house for any noise that might indicate her father slinking down the hallway. Fear was a weight that rested upon her, and thinking of her father called to mind her strange gift.

She'd often considered the implications of the man's death at the grocery—how it seemed to expand the rules that governed her visions. Her first, the one of her grandfather, had been immediately after her father...visited her. So had the second. But when she saw the man at the grocery, she had merely been trapped in a terrible rumination on the previous night's experience. Why hadn't the vision arrived the night before, while she wept in bed?

Gwen rolled sideways in bed and pulled up her knees. Her mind drifted. Sleep neared.

Maybe she had things backward. Her gift required an aggrieved state of mind, but also, a person's death had to be immanent—although each vision seemed to provide an earlier warning. Even if every criterion were met, someone had to be close to death, or she would have no one to see.

But there were people dying all the time, all over the town. All over the country. Her talent required proximity, she had to know the dying, even if only from a flash connection—like when the grocery man dropped four grapefruit and glanced up and met her eye.

Gwen flopped to her other side. At any sour-mooded moment, she might see the death-face of any person she had ever known. "Why?"

Him or you...

She blinked and stared into black shadows. There could be only one answer. She could affect the outcome.

* * *

Gwen knew Gale's window tap: three muted percussions with the round of his index finger, always barely audible, in case Burt was with her. But Gale had gone to work for the butcher Haynes, and the way they'd parted left little hope he'd be back. She'd told him to stay away.

So who had just tapped five times with fingernails?

Gwen approached the window from the side. Liz Sunday faced the glass. Her eyes were closed in a prolonged, tired blink. Faint moonlight gave her skin a weary pastiness reminiscent of dustbowl farmers frozen in black and white. But when she opened her eyes, her lips seemed drawn in scowl and her face became an edifice of desperation.

Gwen retreated to the edge of her bed. She collected her thoughts. Liz had never confessed the exact source of her problems, preferring to leave the father of her child a mystery while the deed eroded her grasp on sanity.

Now it seemed another of the frayed bands holding Liz together had snapped. How many remained?

Rapping sounded again, louder.

Gwen stood. Opened the window.

"Run away with me. Tonight."

"Shhh."

"Don't shush me. I have to get away."

Gwen opened her window all the way. "Shhh. I'm coming out." She grabbed a blanket from her bed, slipped into her shoes, and crawled through the window.

Gwen draped the blanket over her shoulders and led around to the front porch. If she could get Liz to whisper, they wouldn't have to go all the way to the barn—where being with Liz in the dark would be utterly sinister. Gwen sat in the chair that Burt preferred. Liz remained standing, holding a stuffed satchel by its strap. She dropped it.

"Sit down a minute," Gwen said.

"You didn't grab your things."

"I cant' run away just this second."

"You said you would."

"I did not. But why now? What's happened?"

Something in the darkness toward the driveway pulled Gwen's attention. A reflection. She looked into the shadows.

Gale, visiting from the butcher's?

"What?" Liz said.

"I—nothing."

"I knew I couldn't trust you. I was right." Liz snorted. "You know what I'm going through."

"You mean—"

"With my father. You know."

Gwen felt bile rise into her throat.

Liz stepped closer and hulked above Gwen. "I told him I'd run away if he ever touched me again. I told him I'd do worse than that." Liz hiccoughed. "That's why I asked you...about the music."

Liz swallowed. Caught her breath and shuddered as if from the chill. She cleared her throat. "I wanted to kill it," she said. "He sent me away to have my baby, and I hated that little fucker and I wanted to find a doctor who would cut it out. But when I saw him come out of me, and the doctor smacked him, and he cried, I wanted…to…keeeeeep—"

"Shhh. It's okay. Be quieter, if you can."

Between Liz's sobs, Gwen heard feet dragging on dirt. Pantlegs. Surely Gale would know to stay away.

Liz croaked, "They took him to an orphanage."

Gwen studied Liz's profile, parsed the hopeless shock evidenced in broad shadows, the bereft cant of her frown.

"Something will work out."

"You won't go with me to get my baby back?"

"Liz, this is crazy! How are you going to get him back? How would you take care of him? Maybe it's best that he's there."

"At the orphanage?"

Gwen didn't breathe for a moment. "The best person I know came from there."

"Gale?" Liz shook her head. "He's why you won't go."

"Don't you have family somewhere? There has to be someone who would—"

"I thought you were someone. But you're really quite a bitch. You know that?"

"That's terrible."

Liz stepped away, backed off the porch. "I'll do it myself. I'll get him back. And I'll make you sorry." She lifted her bag at the edge of the cement.

A cloud passed and the moon cast an eerie, dim glow across the landscape. Gwen gasped. A man wearing a straw hat and a greasy jacket stood behind Liz.

"Hey, baby," he said.

Liz spun. Scooped the strap of her bag and sidestepped.

"What you doing, Liz? Time to come home."

"No!"

He lunged and missed. "You airing family business all over, huh?"

"Mister Sunday?" Gwen said.

He looked at her. "Shut up. Get in your house, there."

"Mister Sunday, you better keep your voice down. You'll find my father doesn't appreciate men sneaking around after dark."

Liz stepped farther away. One foot behind the other, until a dozen feet separated them.

"That so? You'll find your neighbor doesn't right give a shit." Sunday turned and said, "Liz, we're going home."

But Liz had already disappeared.

The front door opened. Gwen spun. A hammer clicked. Burt stood in the aperture. His boxer shorts glowed. He pointed a rifle from his hips.

"That you, Sunday? You made a royal damn mistake comin' here after dark."

"This ain't got nothing to do with either of you." Sunday stepped backward, lifted his hands.

"Prowlin' after my girl, huh?"

"Liz was here," Gwen said.

"You and your kind is what's wrong with this country. But if I was to put a bullet in your in goddamned head, they'd say *I* was wrong."

Sunday backed another step into darkness. "Just here fetchin' my daughter home. Easy, Burt."

"All I see is my girl wearing a blanket."

Burt seemed provoked by his own voice. Gwen stepped closer, almost fearing he would turn the rifle on her, but somehow knowing he wouldn't. No one would die tonight. She was certain. She opened her mouth to speak and a blast flashed in the darkness. The sound crashed under the porch roof and the ringing shock of it seemed to hang there. Sunday shouted. Burt levered the rifle and another bullet clicked into place.

"Get out of here and don't ever come back! Go on!"

"Hey, goddammit! I'm here after my girl. My daughter run off!"

"I ought to take her in so she don't grow up red. Now get the fuck off my land, 'fore I bury you on it."

Sunday backpedaled and in a moment was gone. But from the darkness came a shout. "This ain't over, Haudesert! Not by a damn stretch!"

Burt kept the rifle trained ahead. Feet shuffled in the kitchen. Gwen heard whispers. Minutes passed in silence.

Burt said, "His girl was here?"

"Liz. She got away from him just before you came out."

"I don't want you around her." Burt stepped back inside the house and stopped. Cal and Jordan were behind him, each brandishing a rifle. Fay turned on the light over the sink. "No need to call up the militia, boys." Burt's voice carried a wink. He turned back to Gwen and nodded at the doorknob. "Noticed the door was locked. How'd you get outside?"

Gwen was silent.

"I'm going to nail that window shut." Burt ejected a shell from the rifle and left the breech open. The shell clattered on the floor. "You should have seen your sister's face," he said to Cal, and then looked at Jordan. Gwen watched in silence. "Eyes the size of a cross-cut log, and jumped three feet when I let out that shot. She thought that commie was going to meet his maker for sure. How 'bout that, Gwen?"

He was ribbing her. He was elated with having driven off a dreaded communist. He was strutting for his sons. This is how you defend the homestead.

"I didn't think he'd die." Gwen threaded a path between her father and brothers. She stopped in the hallway and faced Burt. "I would have known two hours ago."

Chapter Sixteen

I got the idea after watching Burt take joy in slaughtering hogs—the way he disrespected the carcasses. A dead pig is only so much meat, but it ought to be more than that in a decent man's mind, at least the man that watched it find it's mother's teat though its eyes were blind. The man that named it and fed it day in and out. It was a vessel that held something. Sure it was just a hog, but anything with eyes has something behind them. Sneering at a carcass illustrated the man's character.

Those times Burt asked if I wished I was out in the fields and I said no, I wasn't fibbing.

All that blood dripping into the ground and all those jeers and curses made me wonder how an artisan might kill an animal. Death finds us all, and there ought to be a special heaven reserved for those who deliver it with skill and respect, and I set my mind to discovering if the local butcher, Haynes, was a clean-hearted man.

At that time I didn't know his name. I had time on Saturday evenings and Sundays to myself and hitched into Bittersmith. One of Burt's militia buddies saw me at the end of the driveway with my thumb in the air and let me ride in the front seat with him. We never exchanged names, but he knew I worked for Burt, and he was forthright about how the militia could use young blood.

"Burt's taking me to a meeting," I said.

"That right?"

"It'll be interesting."

"Where you headed in town?" he said.

"The butcher."

"Haynes?"

I shrugged. "If that's his name."

The man spent the last five minutes of the ride telling me how property rights are the foundation of liberty and how it takes a patriotic man with a gun to defend freedom. He said he'd look for me at the next militia shindig and even said he'd vouch for me. He offered a pull of Beechnut. I never took to spit tobacco and said no thanks; he let me off at Haynes' Meats.

A *Sorry We're Closed* sign hung in the door. Through the window I saw lights in the back. I tried the knob; it was locked. I walked around to the rear and the smell of death overtook me. All at once it was like I was in quicksand of blood and whiz and rotting meat, flies swarming in heavy black thunderheads around gloomy cattle that looked at me without a shred of interest. They stared between two-inch brown-painted bars and nothing dispelled the knowledge their noses imparted: that this place they'd been ushered to was a place of death, and that their kind did the dying.

"You, boy! What you doing?"

I swung around. There was a door I hadn't seen leading to the back of the butcher shop.

"Nothing," I said.

"Nothing, hell. What you want?"

Lying only made me look like a liar and I had nothing to lose by the truth—it was just the surprise of being asked while I was studying the cattle's mournful eyes—

"Looking for Mister Haynes."

"Well you found him. What you want?"

"I want to work. Learn the trade."

He looked me over from my boots to my neck and it put me in the mind of the cover of an old Frederick Douglass book I'd read, where a slave stands on an auction block. Mister Haynes was a man accustomed to sizing up the worth of animals, so he could literally cut them to pieces, and having those cleaver eyes dissect me didn't leave me feeling all that worthy. He studied my face as if to burn its impression on his memory, and said, "You'll work for me on Monday."

"I appreciate that, but there's more to it," I said.

"What more?"

"I'm staying with Burt Haudesert in his barn loft, but I won't be welcome there if I come work for you, and I don't know about leaving him high and dry."

"You asked for work. You want work?"

"You have a loft I could stay in 'til I find my legs?"

"It'll eat some of your pay, but there's a shanty with a cot I could let you have."

We shook on it and he said, "You be here at sun up on Monday."

I didn't want to be late, so I said my goodbyes Sunday night. Burt wasn't pleased. He sat with his eyebrows looking like two fists grinding together.

Cal said, "I'm ready to work, if he's too faint."

Gwen watched with wide-open, blatant eyes and finally turned to her mashed potatoes like a good enough stare would make them disappear. She came to me most every night, slipping out her window, tomboy fashion, and I knew she'd find me that night.

I waited in the barn loft for her. She never came, and at one point I realized I'd been asleep and that the hour was late enough she wasn't going to come at all. I climbed down from the loft and stood atop the barn runway looking over the house and lawn and garden in the thin starlight. Everything was silent and the air felt like all it had to do was make up its mind and there'd be frost.

I circled behind the house and stole to Gwen's window. I reached to it, but before I tapped the glass, I heard a single, muffled sob, and paused. I was crouching below the sill; slowly I rose to where I had an angle to glimpse inside, and before I saw it was too dark to see anything, a grunt came through the glass.

Burt.

I knelt and palmed a rock the size it would take to brain him. I squeezed like to make it a diamond. I bit my lip to keep from crying out. If I'd had a gun I'd have gone inside and shot him; if I'd had a pitchfork, I'd have run it through his guts and taunted his dying face.

When Gwen had confessed about him almost strangling her, I'd told myself I'd kill him if he ever did it again, but this go-around I sat like a miserable coward squeezing a rock. There, on the ground getting ready to freeze. I leaned against the wall, careful, and listened.

There was no way every soul in that house couldn't hear them. No way they couldn't smell what was going on under their noses. But Cal and Jordan didn't care; Fay lacked the courage, and Guinevere suffered.

And I sat there.

Eventually the noise faded to nothing and I still sat out of regard for Gwen. How would she feel to have me there after what she'd faced? In the barn, earlier, I'd thought she might misunderstand my leaving as abandonment instead of what it was—a tactical step toward getting her away from her torturer. Now, outside her window, I didn't imagine she'd welcome the humiliation of me being there while her father was, and maybe that would overshadow what I was there to tell her—*I'll be back for you, I promise.*

My bottom fell asleep and my feet were almost numb. I moved sideways to get from under the window, and I heard a click and the window slid open. One leg followed another and she slipped out and I said, "Psst!"

She twisted, leaped back.

"It's me," I said.

She was in my arms sobbing, "What'd I do? What'd I do?"

"I'll come back for you," I said.

"No, you won't."

"Then I'll take you away tonight."

"I can't stand any more!"

"Then come with me."

"Where?"

"Butcher Haynes is giving me a shanty. We'll save."

"Save."

She pulled from me, crossed her arms low, not defensively. "You better go, Gale. You better go and never come back."

And what was I to say to that? She was out of her gourd, nuts.

"No," I said. "I'll take care of you."

She pushed me. Not hard, but steady, and then backed away. "Go."

Still, I stood.

She stepped into me, arms locked, and drove me back. My legs were numb and I lost my balance. I sat on the cold ground looking up at her, mostly a shadow. "Just go," she said.

I walked away, not believing, wondering. I was the only one that cared a whit for her, and me willing to work my guts out to keep her safe and sane seemed better than the alternative, being her daddy's plaything.

I arrived at Bittersmith more bewildered than when I'd left Haudesert's, and spent half the night pacing to stay warm in an alley that sheltered me from a breeze running up Main. I started back to Haudesert's a half-dozen times thinking I'd steal her away and she'd see things more clearly, later. But each time I started I stopped, always for a different reason. The last was petty insecurity. She'd been with her father and favored him. My mind couldn't reach far enough to grasp another possibility, and I resigned by dawn that I would someday revisit Gwen, but not before I was in a position of strength. When I had money in my pocket and I wouldn't be leading her deeper into desperation, I'd try again.

I was at Haynes's before dawn and sat on his doorstep. Haynes looked at me as he approached, and by the time he reached me the confusion writ on his face had disappeared and he said it would be a big day.

"Monday we slaughter. Thursday we slaughter. Where's your things?"

"What things?"

"Your stuff."

"I've got no stuff."

He fished a key from his pocket. He blinked a few times, and since I was still there he said, "Come inside."

Since working for Burt hadn't made me rich, and since taking care of Gwen would require dollars, I decided not to give away my labor for nothing. "What terms am I working under, sir?"

"We'll work something out."

"Can we do that now?"

He stood with the key in the lock and said, "You think we could make coffee?"

"Okay."

I followed him. He tidied a couple shelf items, barbeque sauce and mayonnaise jars, as he walked by, and at the back by the entrance to a darkened room, he took a giant coffee percolator from a small table and ducked into a closet.

"What you figure your time's worth?" he said.

Minimum wage was one sixty and a man can't take care of a woman on that—but a man can't demand more than he's worth and expect to have employment. "I'll work harder than anyone you ever saw. What's that worth to you?"

"I start my help at two bucks an hour, and you get scraps, and that saves the budget."

"Then I'll work even harder," I said, giddy like I hadn't been awake all night.

Haynes looked at the coffee pot. "What am I doing this for? I'll show you one time." He demonstrated disassembling the percolator and washing it. The faucet splashed to a floor-level concrete basin with a drain and built-up walls two inches high. Later, I'd see that just about every liquid you could imagine went down that drain, and I'd understand the smell that the water forced out of it.

By the time I'd seen Haynes stun a half-dozen cattle, slit their necks, and let them stand until they bled out and buckled, I'd had my answer about whether a professional killer did it any different. When a cow walks between ever-narrower steel bars until she stands over a drain and can't wiggle sideways and smells the blood that's only been hosed away a few minutes before, her eyes say she knows what's coming. She's been dreaming of it—wide-awake dreams—since she was standing outside. As if the shed full of salted cowhides baking in the sun didn't clue her in. There's no way to make death mechanical yet beautiful. It is always ugly, and those about to die see it.

* * *

I was sleeping in Haynes's shed when a clatter outside roused me. I had left a dozen metal shelves stacked precariously. I'd been stripping them with an electric drill and a wire wheel. The noise was a bolt of sobriety through an intricately detailed dream. I lay awake and beautifully warm in my cot between two wool blankets and with my winter coat on top of my upper half.

It was a strange time for Haynes to make a racket.

I held my wind-up alarm clock to the moonlight coming through the window. Two in the morning.

A thief?

I jumped into my pants and boots and grabbed a section of pipe leaning against the wall. I threw open the door and bursting outside, collided with a hooded figure. She gasped. She was shorter than me. Dark hair flowed from under the hood.

"Gale?"

Her voice was hoarse. Seductive.

"Let me in." She'd placed a travel bag beside the door. She was a runaway. I stepped back, and she swelled forward. I hung my coat on a nail and leaned the pipe back against the wall.

"Who are you?"

"Shhhh."

I looked past her to the silver night, saw nothing out of sorts. "Who are you?"

She slipped past me. "Does a girl need a name to come in out of the cold?" She collided with my cot and fell onto it. "Close the door. Come sit beside me."

I stepped outside, looked around. Across the dirt side street, dead leaves fluttered crisply on frozen wind. I went back inside and closed the door.

"What kind of trouble are you in?"

"All of them." She giggled, but her shrill voice was frosted with desperation. She mumbled something under her breath mixed with more giggles. "Every kind of trouble there is. Are you going to save me, Gale G'Wain? Because I can't go home."

"How do you know me?"

"Sit down. I'll tell you everything."

I sat at the other end of the cot, and tried to remain utterly upright. But the more I slumped, the more I recognized the danger of being supine. She pulled off her coat, and the glow of her white sweater revealed a chest like to find gold in.

I wanted to stop her, but I watched.

"You must be cold," she said. "Don't you want to get back under the blankets?"

"Look here. I don't know who you are or what you've got in mind, but you can't stay here. I asked if you're in trouble and you just giggle."

She leaned toward me. "You think I am trouble, is that it?"

"What's your name?"

"Liz."

"You assume much, Liz." I crossed the small floor and rested against the workbench. My hot plate knocked over a glass of water, and I stooped to unplug the plate from the outlet below the bench. I backed from under the shelf and bumped into Liz. She dragged her hand along my groin. I jumped and rattled the hotplate again. "What are you doing?"

I knew what she was doing.

I liked what she was doing and I hated myself for liking it. Gwen had convinced me we were through, and the only thing preventing me from bedding this crazy giggling fool was my fear. An ugly part of me rose up and I wanted to take her. I wanted to stake a claim upon her like no man had ever done. I seized her by the shoulders and she seemed startled by my decisiveness. I leaned to her and she thrust up her chin. I pushed my hands under her top and felt the warm softness of her back. She lost her balance and lurched against me. Her hand slipped between us. Down.

I was at Haynes's to make money to rescue Gwen, though she didn't believe it and didn't want it. What was Gwen to me when this girl was here right now? Just as desperate? Even more needy—

I pushed her away. She stopped breathing for a moment.

Gwen wasn't needy.

"You better go."

I loved Gwen and it wasn't just because I had been there and she had been there. It wasn't her enslavement. It was her goodness—something this runaway couldn't match. One glance into her pupils and I knew.

Liz sat with a startled frown, folded-in elbows and a diminutively slumped back. "If I go home, I'll get beat."

"Don't you have any family would take you in?"

She shook her head. Strained against her sweater. "I know how to make men happy."

"I don't want to be happy." I grabbed a flannel shirt and put it on, took my coat from the nail by the door "Where do you live?"

"Past Haudesert's."

I stopped buttoning my coat. "Oh." I soaked the new information. I was an orphan living in a slaughterhouse shed. Gangly knees and red hair. Any of a hundred town boys would have diddled Liz twice at every fuel stop from here to Mexico. "There's a lot of fellows who'd love to have you surprise them tonight. What did Gwen tell you about me?"

"She said you're a good boy. Nice."

"A good boy."

"That's right. And nice."

"That's all she said?"

"Not much more."

"What?"

"I couldn't tell you."

"Why?"

"It doesn't matter what she thinks. You…love her?"

"I love her."

"Too bad. She doesn't love anyone."

She giggled again. I wanted to hit her to make her stop. I had to get away from her cackling. I thought of Mister Sharps and the Youth Home. Maybe he would know what to do. "How old are you?"

"Sixteen. Plenty old to get familiar."

"I know someone at the Youth Home in Monroe. Maybe he would help."

"The Youth Home." Her eyes grew shiny in the half-light. "Gwen said you came from there."

"Gwen said too much, maybe. "

"You'll go with me?"

"I can't do that. I have to work. Maybe there's a deputy… no…Here, I'll give you money and you can ride a bus." I pulled a handful of singles from my front pants pocket. "Here, take it. I'll even write a note for Mister Sharps. He runs the Youth Home." In the half-light I wrote on a sheet of tablet paper, *Please help my friend Liz Sunday. She needs your help, if you can. Gale G 'Wain*. I folded the paper and handed it to her.

"You can spend the night in here if you like, since it's so cold out. I'd like to help you more. I would."

I left her in the shed and spent the night with the cows on death row.

In the morning she was gone.

* * *

I lived on hog side meat ends and hamburger and sausage, cooking on an electric grill, and washing it down with pork and beans. I was a regular stink machine, but I saved dollars and on Christmas Eve it was dark at five and I set out with boots and long underwear and a coat and hat and gloves. Set out like I was never coming back. I didn't want anyone to know I was out, and on rare occasions when car headlights flashed ahead, or when one of my rearward glances caught a vehicle approaching from behind, I ducked into the woods. Given the chance, I cut through fields to save time, though I wasn't happy about leaving tracks. In truth, I didn't know if when I got there I'd actually ask her. It was a lonely, frightening walk, the temperature far below freezing. Would her heart be as cold as the winter blackness? She'd told me to go and never come back. Did she mean it? Would I find her father in her room and overhear her gasp of pleasure instead of Burt's animal grunt?

Foolish fears, maybe. But real.

I waited at the edge of the swamp until long after dark. When her bedroom lights had been out a while I approached. I tapped on Gwen's window. She opened it and I passed her a box with a ring in it and waited for her to say something. She cried. She closed the window and reopened it and then slipped outside and wrapped her arms around my neck and said, "What's it mean?"

"It means I'm going to take you away from here."

"Now? Tonight?"

"We have to do it right," I said. "If I just take you away, we're on the lam. We'd have to leave in the dead of winter."

"What else is there?"

"I'm going to ask Burt for your hand."

"Don't you think you'd ought to ask me?"

I fell to my knee and took her hand. It was cold, and I sandwiched it in mine. "Guinevere Haudesert, I love you and want you to marry me. I love your freckles and I love when your eyebrows are mussed. I love watching you pray. And… so…what do you say?"

"What if my father says no?"

"He won't have a chance if you don't answer first."

"Yes!"

"Shhh."

"Yes." She kissed me on the cheek.

* * *

I wake to the frozen metal of a handgun against my temple. The barrel has been outside very recently. It is dead cold.

"Don't move," he says.

I am still. My leg is overwhelmingly uncomfortable, bent at a funny angle, and my neck is crooked. I open my eyes. The fire is embers and tiny blue wicks. The front door is open, and a gust blows ice grains across the floor.

"Where's the girl?" he says. "I know you killed her."

"I didn't kill anyone." My voice is husky, but if I clear my throat…

"Of course not."

The barrel leaves my head and he steps in front of me. Maybe his eyes haven't adjusted to the dark room. Maybe he doesn't see my hand is on the butt of a pistol in the shadow on the side of my leg.

"Who are you?" I say.

"Death, boy. Death. You ever hear of the Wyoming Militia?"

"I've heard." My hand closes around the pistol grip. My fingers slip deeper inside the holster and touch the trigger.

When I pull it the cylinder will rotate and click. I had it on an empty chamber. No matter how quick, the noise will alert him.

"You killed a leader in that organization. A friend."

"I didn't kill—"

"Shut up, boy!" He swings his pistol hand and catches the side of my head with his knuckles. My brain rings, and I see sparkles that aren't fire. "Shut up!"

He steps backward as he aims at me. I see shadows, his outstretched arm and the glint of metal. He swings his arm higher, points at my head. We're but a few feet apart.

My ears ring and my thoughts are murky from just waking, though the blow spurred my nerves. Yet in this moment of antagonism, a bullet hole in the ceiling reminds me this is not my hour. Having failed to blow my head off, I meet this man with a sense of calm that would have been impossible a day ago—calm I didn't have facing Guinevere's father this morning. If I wait for him to regain his faculties, I will live or I will die. I don't know what he'll choose. The longer I wait, the more opportunity I give him to deliver a final surprise.

Or I squeeze the trigger and take my chances.

"You killed a good man. Stand up."

"All right, Mister. Easy." I shift my leg and aim my knee at his right shoulder, pointing and lifting the gun. The trigger is tight; the cylinder rotates slowly within the holster.

"I said—"

The revolver explodes and a flame licks out the end of the holster. The man jerks two steps back and his hand falls to his side.

I draw the pistol free and point at him.

"You…killer…" he gurgles.

He drops to his knees and sprawls to the floor. He spits black blood. I kick the gun from his hand. Roll him by the shoulder and a silver star on his chest glints firelight.

"Who are you?" I say.

He wheezes with his arms wrapped around his chest.

"Who?"

"Deputy..."

He shakes and his breath is like a rasp on ironwood. And then it comes—the spasm. The death clench. I've seen it on a thousand animals.

He is gone. I stand in a puddle of his blood, press fingers to his neck. Silence has reconquered the house. I add wet logs to the fire. They sizzle. As minutes pass, a flicker of virgin flame invigorates the atmosphere. I have killed a deputy.

I drag him by his boots. He'll bother me if I leave him in the living room bleeding out. The fire casts long shadows across his face that turn his scowl into a demonic mask. Outside in the brightness his face reverts to a mere dead man surprised to greet his last moment. He leaves a red streak across the porch, and I drag him over the end and to the side of the house.

I could prop him like a law enforcement scarecrow, reminiscent of a head on a pike. I dismiss the thought, though the ones he might ward off will surely come.

I study a dotted line of tracks from the porch that trail down the steps and across an otherwise unbroken plain of whiteness. He left his patrol car on the road, two hundred yards away. I return to his corpse and remove the keys from his pocket.

Strange intimacy, rifling a dead man's pants.

I replace the spent shell in my pistol and head inside to resume the debate. Leave? Steal a patrol car and drive until the snow is so deep the car will go no farther and then seek new shelter? The prospect of living on the frontier in the winter, maybe inside a hollowed tree or a small cave, roasting game over a tiny hardwood fire, appeals. Grappling with the land and the natives made us who we are, and when I dream of being strong, it is the frontiersman's strength I see.

I don't want to be foolish. I'm under no illusion everything will be better if I remain at the house. Men who stalk, assault, and shoot are coming—men with killing skills. Others with badges will follow, and they won't come to hear my story. They'll come to end it.

Staying here is as clear a death verdict as a man would receive from a judge reading a jury's condemnation. If I hadn't already tried to carry out that sentence with the old carbine on the wall, perhaps I'd flee in the policeman's car.

I take a parka, hat, and gloves from the closet by the front door. The brim cuts the snow glare. The deputy strode with two strong legs; I have one. I exhaust myself trying to match him. Every fourth step is easy. The rest is trail-breaking. I fix my gaze to the left-most corner of the field, where additional cars would first appear, but there is no traffic.

I slip behind the wheel of the deputy's car. Look straight ahead and wonder what the dead man thought when he made the decision that ended his life. Ahead on the right are beech and white birch—a grove of ghostly trees that might have haunted a less intrepid deputy.

I knew when Guinevere and I ran from Burt Haudesert that I would be accused, and I didn't shrink from it. Honesty is a path through a minefield and if a man strays one step, one inch, he places everything he holds dear in jeopardy. But I have to believe virtue will steer me true.

Still warm, the engine turns over easily and the heater blows hot air. The deputy didn't sit for an hour in the car, equivocating once his mind was made up. He didn't ponder the unknown, the risks.

I slip the transmission to drive and press the gas.

I've driven before. I know the pedals and the shifter—it's just like a pickup on the farm, or Mister Sharps' car—though negotiating the snow is new. I tramp too hard and the tires spin, but it does no harm. The car rocks; I cut the wheel, ease off the gas, and float along listening to the crunch of snow.

The gas tank is almost full. If I caught a break long enough to get ahead of the storm, I could cross a county or two before emptying the tank. At least they'd have no idea where I'd gone.

The road turns and I greet it by easing the wheel left. The car slides straight—I bounce in a ditch and jerk the wheel, but a rut has me. Reverse. Forward. Tramp the gas and the car rocks back to the road and I yank the wheel right. I bust through a snow bank and the car jerks to a stop. I turn off the engine and leave the keys in it. The car has plowed sideways into a snowdrift and it takes me a minute to shove the door open. I pause to the faint sound of snow sizzling on the undercarriage.

I head into the woods.

* * *

I awoke on Christmas day with butterflies in my stomach. I lay on my cot, snug under a pile of wool blankets. I'd promised Gwen I'd be back to talk to Burt, and though I was anxious for it to be over, I was less so for it to begin. A small kerosene heater kept the shanty warm and cast a glow through blackened glass. The walls were cracked boards weathered gray on the outside. A previous occupant had stuffed rags in the knotholes and cracks. I watched the fiberglass ceiling insulation with Pink Panther cartoons on the paper. His smugness encouraged my pessimism.

How was I going to bring a bride here?

I'd saved almost every penny since working for Haynes and the money would keep Gwen warm and fed. Come spring we'd hoof overland, south, and I'd pick up whatever farm or butcher work presented. Getting Gwen out of Burt Haudesert's house was my priority, and when she'd said she couldn't take being there any longer, I took that to mean she'd prefer any situation to the one she was in.

But girls aren't called the fairer sex without reason—and from what I'd read, every woman is a cultured woman, and they all want frilly things that smell nice. Not wool blankets, a saggy cot, and a cold outhouse. She'd be a sport—but I didn't know if she'd be a champ.

While I wondered, an undercurrent of worry sloshed through me. When a crick is low, it's plain enough how the water eroded the bank, but when the water's high, a man can stand on the edge not knowing there's little under him. Below all my thinking was the miserable thought she'd only go with me to get away from him. Days before I asked her, I'd prayed and thought I'd heard back, but a man can never tell one hundred percent when God has spoken, and worse, it's oftentimes hard to parse His signals. I'd paid special attention when I asked Gwen to marry me, and when she failed to answer right off, she didn't ease my angst. One more thing to think about while I watched the Pink Panther on the ceiling.

We hadn't talked about many details on the night I proposed because we mostly hugged and tried to stay warm. She'd suggested going to the barn loft where we'd be out of the wind, but I knew if I went in there with her I'd want to do more than was right, and we'd made it this far without breaking too many rules. (Mister Sharps only talked birds and bees once. He'd said, "don't sit down to supper with a woman without saying grace...")

It seemed like I spent half the night walking to Haudesert's and the other half walking back. Christmas morning, trekking again, a different set of doubts filled me than the ones from the night before. What would her face look like if I swept her off her feet and carried her across the threshold—and instead of it being a nice place, I carried her inside a slaughterhouse shanty that smelled like scorched socks and a kerosene heater? I spent so much time worrying about not providing adequately for her that I never thought about what Burt would have to say.

I rapped the door. Through the window, I could see Burt and Fay arguing. I turned away, but Burt saw me, and after he said something final, Fay went into the living room and Burt came to the door. I hadn't seen Gwen yet, and somehow it seemed wrong to ask him without double checking that she hadn't lost her nerve, but I couldn't hardly ask him to chat with Gwen, so when he put his hand on my shoulder and pulled me into the kitchen, like he'd forgotten his disappointment from two months earlier, I stumbled inside and tried to meet his eye.

This was the man who was raping Gwen.

Cal looked in from the other room. He wasn't on a cane anymore. His brows were low, and when he nodded it was as good as calling out, "Hello, traitor."

"What do you need?" Burt said. "Finally here about the militia?"

"Good morning," I said.

"You walk from town?"

"Yes, sir."

"Well?"

I breathed deep. "Mister Haudesert, I love Guinevere and I want to marry her. I want your blessing."

He was standing beside me, side by side and at an angle. He stepped back like he'd lost his balance and his face had that confused, betrayed look I'd seen on a few hogs' faces, right after he'd scrambled their brains with a twenty-two bullet.

"You what?"

"Guinevere and I want to get married. I've got a good wage in town, and I'll take care of her. I came for your blessing."

"My blessing."

Cal stood in the entrance to the living room, now with his arms crossed and his head moving side to side like I had some kind of gall, and I wished he wasn't there because I felt like the guy going unarmed to parley with the enemy camp. Behind Cal, Guinevere leaned against the far wall. She pulled from her pocket the ring I'd given her and slipped it on her finger. She crossed her arms almost like to show it off, but I couldn't decipher the cant of her lips. Whether she was glad I was there or if she thought the ring came from the tooth fairy.

Burt launched his fist at my face, and next thing, I was on the floor looking up at my arms and legs, like a junebug when you flip him over. Burt didn't say a word. He swung his leg back and I rolled and scampered, and he tried to kick me anyway.

When you fight, there's a switch that if it goes one way, all a man thinks about is getting away, and he doesn't care about shame or saving face. If the switch goes the other way, he's ready to die for his cause.

It went the second way for me.

Burt glanced his boot against my ribs. I caught his leg and hung on, rolled and pulled. He bounced on his behind. Table silver clanged.

I looked in his face, and instead of the man who gave me work and a place to sleep, I saw the man who'd slipped his pecker in my girl. The one who was supposed to defend her from all assaults, defend her mind and body and soul until she was old enough to deliver to the world a finely finished young woman. I saw the man charged by *God Almighty* with the most precious task ever given to any man of any generation—and he was the one who snuck into her room and covered her mouth with his stinking hand. The switch went the second way and I didn't think about anything save breaking his neck.

I scrambled to my knees and swung my fist at Burt's eye, but he moved too quick and my knuckles went by his hair. He grunted and somehow after that first missed punch I stopped throwing singles and instead fired barrages, salvos. Fay Haudesert shouted something and I knew Cal was coming, but I didn't stop.

Burt grunted.

I felt his blood on my hands. I was berserk and he was panicked. I felt strength in my back and force in my arms and shoulders. I wailed on him faster and faster. I shrieked. Each time my fist connected I felt the world getting a little better. I felt Gwen healing. My knuckles hit bone and teeth. My knees drove air from his lungs, and all I wanted was to hit him so hard his lungs would never again have need of air. I wanted to hit him until his bones gave away and I was pounding the soft flesh within.

Guinevere rushed from the wall and screamed, and I didn't know any more until I came to. Burt had my boot. I was outside, and he was dragging me through the snow. Gwen shouted for Burt to stop and Cal pulled her back inside the house.

Chapter Seventeen

Gwen huddled in bed and her anger focused in a single place—the spot between her legs where she was soaked, where she burned, where skin was raw. If she could cut that part of her out and never have to feel this confusion again...If she could drive from her mind the self-loathing, for daring to stand up to him when he wasn't there, only to crumble into slutty obeisance when he snuck to her room. If she could stash a gun by the bed and make sure that the next time he invaded her, a bullet invaded him...

Her eyes closed, opened; she couldn't tell. It was dark, and the covers were over her head. The vision came like a memory; soon Gale would take her away. What had started as a plan had become something more; her visits to him in the barn had begun as calculated seduction, but became succor. Her sanity.

He had proposed last night, and asked her father this morning. Tonight he would come for her. If he was alive, he would come for her. He had to be alive. She would have known. She would have seen him.

And now that he was about to take her away, she saw his face. His brooding eyes looked hurt, even when buoyed by a smile. His hair, not a sunny red, but deep and muddy like the clay in an exposed stream bank. His cheeks burned like they had in the fall, when he spent his time in the fields.

Even as she saw him, it was like he was outside, framed by a cold blue sky…

She heard an oboe. A bullfrog note. A slow, earthen tune; it vibrated through her like an approaching train. Higher notes, faster notes tethered to the ground by that low bullfrog rumble.

Gale was going to die.

Gwen jerked upright in bed and looked out the frosted window to the silvery gray outside, the snow and cold. He was alive now, she knew. Alive for the moment. The history of her visions proved her ability was growing. She'd explored each vision with more confidence. Gale might be close to death, but he might not. It could be hours. Was it too much to hope it could be days? Long enough to do something about it?

Gwen brought her hands to her eyes and pressed until she saw stars. When the colors were dizzying and the pressure brought pain, she slammed her fists to the bed. She stared at the ceiling. Tears welled. Soon her temples and ears were wet.

Him or you, the Devil had said about the man at the grocery, as if there was a deal to be had.

She'd stifled growing rage at Burt by honing the knowledge that someday she'd escape. Someday she'd be away from the constant threat, protected by Gale's arms and by his ownership. She'd be his, and hence, no other's. Every time her father had visited her, she consoled herself with thoughts of freedom.

But without Gale?

How would he take his last breath? Would he die violently, at her father's hand? Would it be an accident at night in the cold, on his way to see her? Or after their escape, tomorrow, thumbing for a ride along the road?

She couldn't wait for the window tap.

Gwen threw on her clothes and tossed her coat through the window. Outside, she put it on and paced at the back of the house. Finally she waited at the corner, staring out over a bare field of six-inch cornstalks.

When Gale arrived she clutched him; they went to the barn and huddled together.

Him or you, the Devil had said.

"You don't seem yourself," Gale said.

They'd been nestled a long while, silent. She kept her head pressed to his chest, listening to his heartbeat. His body smelled young, in spite of the sweat and work. His flesh was alive in a way that Burt's was not, almost in defiance of all things that had met their peak and begun the slow trail back to dust.

From experience, she knew defiance seldom worked out.

Chapter Eighteen

I turn a circle where I lost Gale G'Wain's trail. The only part of the sky that isn't gray or purple is a sliver out west, but it'll disappear soon. Snow falls so heavy you'd have to poke a hole to take a piss. Standing here depletes me more than work. It's ball-frost cold. I wear long johns six months of the year, and it's no accident I have them on now. A film of white blows across the field, and seeing up or down is like adding water to a half-full glass and trying to remember which part was which. From low on my back to the base of my neck, a shiver starts and won't let go.

To keep moving, I step away from the woods, and after twenty paces, turn right ninety degrees and march perpendicular to the way I came. Stooped, I watch whiteness that long ago lost any markings. Unblemished save the prints I leave. After fifty paces, I've not found the kids' trail. I about-face and re-examine the same terrain. Reaching my former trail, I cross it and continue fifty paces beyond.

They're lost.

"Sheriff!"

The voice arrives against the wind. I turn, each step in the foot-deep snow a minor obstacle. It's Cooper, with one bluetick hound straining on a leash. He's a hundred yards from me, on a tangent for a forest that has become darker with proximity and stands forbiddingly gloomy. "Are you good?" he calls.

I wave him forward. Why slow for an old man when there's a girl? I fix on a pale stump at the forest while Cooper progresses to the field.

Step over step. Old legs. Old feet. Old man. Old father. Grandfather. My princess is going to die too.

I lift my foot. Throw it down. Lift the next. Throw it. And I taste snow, feel it in my eyes, feel pain in my arm, and wonder what happened that I'm sprawled like a dead snow angel.

* * *

Had a conversation with Burt about the Pounder boys. Of course, coroner called it a suicide pact, and it was well and good. But I wanted to be sure there wouldn't be any more. I know the history of organizations that want to change the world.

Sidekicks get shot.

I protected Burt; damn right I protected him. What sense would it make to drag him through a court and make him prove the two of them came after him and not the other way around? The bodies were dead without marks. I couldn't have proved they were murdered, to begin with. Not a bruise on the neck. Not a frown on their faces.

Nothing like the snarl on Burt's face back at the barn. Pitchfork through him—that's a murder. Steward and Marshall Pounder? Neither suffered a pinhole.

* * *

I wrestle my clothes until they permit me to sit and flog the snow until it allows me to stand. My thoughts are lean, like the air at the top of a mountain. The throb in my arm lessens as the wooziness in my head fades. Gwen is my one constant notion.

I follow Cooper's tracks and pull my pipe and tobacco. Light a bowl and the smoke tastes like smoke. Gives me strength.

Man can't shit blood for too long before his insides disintegrate and he's shitting himself. That's a proverb.

The going is easier following Cooper's trail, though the drifts at the edge of the field are deep and taxing. Out of the worst of the wind, the going is treacherous; I catch my heel on a log. Snow gives way to a film of ice; the whole thing's slippery as snot on a glass doorknob.

The quiet rallies me. Through twenty feet of jaggers, my heart keeps pounding and reaching the silence of the ponderosa I know I'll see this ordeal through. Tobacco smoke does something good to my nerves.

These ponderosa stand fifty feet, higher. Their trunks are three and four feet in diameter. In the winter, still air feels warm. An illusion. But outside the wind, and stepping in snow only a couple inches deep, and finally out of the never-ending glare, I'll permit it.

Cooper has picked up his pace and I can't see him. The terrain is flat, punctuated by knolls, until after two hundred yards, where Mill Crick is. I want to find a log and sit, but the dog bays and Coop shuffles after him like they've found something.

Gale and Gwen turned along the side of the crick where the water flows too fast to ice over, and followed upstream fifty yards to a brook and walked across there. I cross, and claw up the bank on the other side. My back aches from landing on the steps, and whatever happened in the field when I made a snow angel has left me weak like I went to bed without supper and set out without breakfast.

Black cherry grows along the stream. Beech displaces pine. The trail veers aside and veers again, and at the corner, I spot a white paper birch and follow snowed-in tracks to it. The curly, papery bark's been stripped here and there. Enough to start a fire.

Coop's dog lets out a long howl, lonely as a dark night. I hurry, and my heart rumbles.

I sniff, but there's no smoke in these woods, not close by. I tell myself that by now, Odum's arrived at the Coates place and found Gale and Gwen inside, thawing out in front of a fire made of birch bark and Coates's kitchen table.

The hound is silent. Coop's dropped from view.

Lungs heaving, I advance. My legs have weights attached. I pull a fleck of dried venison from my pocket and chew it, not knowing what I'll see when I crest the next knoll.

* * *

It had to have been Burt. The exchange I overheard on the first day of trout season those eight years ago was about the leadership of the militia. Men form militias because some ideals are worth dying for. If they're worth dying for, they're noble enough to kill for, and once a man commits to the first, he's obligated to the second. Enemies are for killing.

Steward and Marshall Pounder lived in the house their mother raised them in. Neither married. They did their share of carousing; I'd see one of their trucks parked at the Bear Claw Inn off Route Thirteen every night. Except for rubbing elbows at the Masonic Lodge, I didn't have anything to do with them.

The Pounder boys were in the junk business. They converted their momma's house—six acres of lawn and a garage set off to the side—into a junkyard. They added a new garage wing onto the old one and blacktopped an acre of lawn. They lined vehicles three and four deep the length of the woods. Cars between the windrows of spruce. Cars on top of cars. Trucks. Ferried parts and scraps from one side of the yard to the other on the bed of a World War II ducenhalf.

They were in the parts business. The shade tree mechanic business. I suspected a couple more businesses, most of them having to do with the junkyard dogs they bred or the out-of-state drifters that wandered by.

During the fishing expedition up at Elk Run, when I overheard Steward and Burt, neither one of the brothers tossed so much as a "hello" my direction. It was prickly, and afterwards I wondered if there was dissent at the lodge about my membership.

Before a man learns his first catechism, the lodge brothers vote on his application. Each mason stands in a line passing a wooden box shaped like a baby carriage, open on the front top. He reaches inside, and votes with a white or black bead. A single black bead disqualifies a man from receiving the rites.

If Steward and Marshall had a problem with bringing the sheriff into their midst, it would have been easy to prevent. I learned later that neither was present. The Worshipful Master—Burt Haudesert—held the vote while the brothers were away on business in Denver.

They employed a work-release prisoner out of Monroe. Brady something or other, serving five years for robbing a grocery store and doing it with a gun. Long hair on the sides and bald on top. So skinny he had to stand up twice to make a shadow, and tall enough to hunt geese with a rake. Had the right mix of thoughtfulness and contrition, and always seemed more interested in how your day was going than how bad was his. Someone society could get something out of, after he paid his debt.

It was only a few months 'til his release. The county warden let him catch a bus and work all day under Steward's watch, and so long as Brady was back by six p.m., no one much cared what he did. Brady made the phone call from Pounders' garage phone.

This was shortly after I hired Odum. We drove out and found Brady sitting on the blacktop with his arms wrapped around his knees. He led us to the garage, which was closed up.

The Pounder boys had a reputation for building exotic derby cars for the county fair. They built machines all year long and sold them. Every autumn, Steward and Marshall took to the dirt track and half the competition drove cars they'd built. Had a trademark look. Eight chrome exhaust pipes straight up through the hood, belching flames. A sixteen-gallon beer keg where the back seat should have been, used as a gasoline tank. They only used Chevies, and preferred station wagons.

Brady cracked the side door and a cloud of stink spilled out. Exhaust fumes and the beginning of bloat—the whisper of death before the smell gets rank. I told Brady to open all three garage doors and the air began to clear. A station wagon occupied the middle bay. Inside, two men faced the far wall—one of them so big the car tilted to the passenger side. Marshall Pounder. I walked to the driver window, which was rolled partways down. They'd buckled themselves in. Their eyes stared at a pinup calendar on the wall above the workbench.

"Open it up," I said.

Brady lifted the latch on the driver side. It was stuck. Brady fumbled, looked back at me. "Should I be doin' this? I mean, is this a crime scene?"

"Don't know that yet, Brady. What do you think?"

"It don't look good."

"No, it don't." I shouldered him aside and lifted the latch. The heavy door croaked on its hinges. Steward sat with his hands on his lap, crossed like an undertaker'd seen him last.

I hunkered down and looked inside. Marshall was the same, though his belly didn't leave as much lap.

I reached around the steering wheel to the column. The keys were in the ignition, left in the "on" position. I left them.

"Get the print case," I said.

Odum lollygagged across the lot to the Bronco.

"Whaddaya suppose happened?" Brady said.

"Both these boys died."

Brady snorted.

"This don't look like a Pounder derby car. What was they building?"

"I dunno," Brady said. "They keep me working in the yard, bustin' parts loose."

"Well, you seen 'em build cars."

He nodded, looked at the wagon. "For one, the brothers always strip a car first. Get rid of everything they won't want later. Pull the seats, radio, glass, upholstery, everything. They rebuild it the way they want. Reinforcement welds. A roll bar. A big-ass V-8. The regular stuff."

"So a demo car doesn't have any glass."

"Not a bit." He looked at the windows.

"What about headlights."

"No, sir. Nothing. Too dangerous. You don't want chunks of glass flyin' at you in the arena."

"Pop the hood." I circled to the front. "Don't stand there lookin' at me. Pop the goddamn hood."

Brady wiped his hand on his pant leg and reached inside. The latch snapped, and I lifted the hood. "Come around here for me."

Brady stood beside me.

"You know any station wagons come with a five oh-two?"

"No, sir. No, I don't. But I ain't a car man—"

"No, you ain't a car man. You just spend every day tearin' them apart. How many ladies need a big block to haul groceries and rug rats?"

"Don't make sense."

"So these boys souped up a station wagon before they took out the glass."

Brady's face twitched. He shook his head back and forth. "No, sheriff. No, sir. I see where you're going here."

He moved sideways, past the workbench. I followed.

"This how you found them?"

"Just so. I opened the door and the exhaust was thick as, well, it was thick. I came in, saw them, and made the phone call."

"From which phone?"

He pointed to the section of garage that had existed before the add-on. "Right around the corner. On the wall."

"You called from inside, in all the exhaust?"

"Uh, yessir, Sheriff."

I stood closer to him. "Why didn't you take off? Coulda been half way across the state before you was missed."

"Yeah, well, but I'd a had everybody thinking I killed Stu and Mars. And I didn't. Kill them, that is. No, sir."

I grabbed his neck and shoved him into the wall. Knocked a Craftsman wrench from a nail. Brady choked and his eyes flared like a horse seen a rattler.

Odum entered behind me. "Got the fingerprint kit—" His footsteps stopped.

"I'm not going to fuck with you all afternoon, Brady. I say the word and you spend the rest of your life jacking off to a concrete wall. You need to convince me you ain't bein' cute. Nod your head."

I nodded his head for him. Bounced his skull on cement blocks.

"You know the thing about a shop phone? It's got a lot of grease on it. You know what makes a fingerprint?"

"Gggghhht."

"Speak up."

"GGGGHHHTTT."

"When I dust that phone for prints, am I going to find yours?"

I eased up so he got his wind. He shook, said nothing.

"I asked you a question."

He shook his head.

"Where'd you call from?"

His eyeballs twisted toward the house.

"So you killed these boys and went to the house and called from there?"

I let him go. He stooped, hands on knees, and breathed raspy breaths. "No, Sheriff! I didn't kill 'em! I found 'em!"

"Odum, go look around the house. You remember how to dust a print?"

"Yes. Yes, Sheriff."

"Then do it. I need to talk with Brady another minute."

I circled Brady and slapped him into handcuffs before he heard them jingle.

"Aw, shit, Sheriff. I didn't do these boys. They was good to me."

I stood him up and walked him toward the bay door, and glanced inside Marshall's side of the station wagon. The floor caught my eye. Rusty and flat, not contoured like you'd expect.

"Stand here," I said, releasing his elbow. "You run, I shoot. Crime solved. Savvy?"

He nodded jerkily.

The Pounder boys had welded a sheet of half-inch steel under the seats that extended all the way up the foot well. The inside panel of the door was loose. Pulling it back, I saw they'd welded half-inch steel inside.

"Brady," I said. I pulled my piece. Cocked it. "I think you're trying to escape right now."

"No, sir. Shit!"

"What were they doing with this car?"

"Oh, Jesus Christ, have mercy!"

"He can't hear you. Don't want to listen. You better answer my goddamn question."

"They called it a war-car, is all I know. That's all. I swear."

"Well, your word's good with me. Just one more thing—and if I think you're lying I'm going to blow your fuckin' head off. Where'd you stash what you took from the house?"

Brady trembled and a wet spot swelled between his legs and down the inside of his right thigh.

"Blue mustang, below the spruce. Couple guns. Little cash. Fifty bucks. That's all."

"Keep talkin'."

"That's it. I came here and found them just like that. Went to the house, scrounged a bit. Got scared. I only took a couple things for safekeeping. Then I called."

"I'm havin' trouble with that." I pointed my piece at his head. Closed one eye and greeted him over the sights with the other.

"Look at them!" Brady said. "You saw them. Their faces wouldn't turn dark in just a couple hours, would they?"

Odum came out of the Pounder house shaking his head. Stowed the print case in the Bronco and joined Brady and me. As he approached, Odum watched my suspect, and his eyes followed Brady's arm to the cuffs. "He do it?"

"There's no work release on Sunday!" Brady said. "Couldn't have been me."

"How long can a car idle on sixteen gallons of gas?" I say.

"Not that long!"

"Half-gallon an hour," Odum said.

"Thirty-two hours," I said. "Was you here Saturday?"

"No work release on Saturday either."

I faced Odum. "He didn't do it. But he robbed them."

"Didn't see anything missing in the house."

"I didn't expect you would."

When we got the Pounder brothers out of the vehicle, neither had a mark—almost as if they'd made a suicide pact but forgot to leave a note. They'd been dead since the night before. Their faces were black and their eyes bulged. The gas tank was empty and the ignition was on. The car had idled until it ran out of gas, filling the air with a cloud of carbon monoxide that didn't dissipate until Brady opened all three garage doors. Engine must have run all night and only stalled shortly before Brady arrived.

I uncuffed Brady. Told him to fetch whatever he'd taken and put it back in the house. He watched me and walked backward the first few yards, jumpy as a fart on a griddle. Like facing me would stop a bullet, midair.

"Go ahead," I said. "But you remember this. I want you out of this state the day you get released. Y'hear?"

He picked up his pace.

After the Pounder boys killed themselves, things were different at the Lodge. The same suck-asses brought me beer and talked mindless shit, but the group's militiamen kept away. They stayed away from Burt, too.

It bothered me a little, the Pounders dying without any holes or bruises, until one day I overheard talk of the Militia losing track of a couple items. A gas mask, among other things. Burt lifted his brows at that. It wasn't hard to guess from there. I figure he held the Pounders at gunpoint and watched through half-fogged lenses while they got dizzy and passed out. Then he left.

Something about the way Burt done them kind of tickled me. If I'd have turned out bad and not good, I'd have been one of the cleverest killers ever. Like Burt. But there's nothing clever about Gale G'Wain. His blood is cold and he's got the brains of a cement block.

Councilmen I'd kept loyal for thirty years made new friends, new alignments. By the time Deputy Travis's daddy, the Mason, predicted the town council would find the money to fund another slot, so long as it went to Travis, I knew the fix was around the bend.

I'm accustomed to folks knowing who wears the brass ring. They don't have to kiss it, but they damn well need to know who wears it. My family's been prominent since my great granddaddy named Bittersmith after himself. Then these yahoos get gumption.

Odum's been with the Masons a few years now, and three of the four on the town council are brothers in the Masonic sense. And Travis's daddy was one of the crew that aligned against Burt after the Pounders died.

Long story short, I don't trust nobody.

* * *

Full of dread, I crest the knoll. Ahead, between trunks and bowed, snow-covered limbs, Cooper kneels.

He's in a bowl beside an ice-age boulder, and with no trees immediately above, the snow falls straight on him. His back is to me, but the wind goes out of me as I study his posture. His shoulders are curved, and from this angle, he looks like a man who has taken a fist to the gut.

Chapter Nineteen

I had a knot on my head and a three-inch ache beneath it. If anything, I bet Cal walloped me with a rolling pin. But I wasn't thinking about that with Burt dragging me by my boots, getting snow up my back. The cover was only a couple inches and plenty of rocks poked through. My time spent blacked-out let my temper cool, so I wasn't inspired to rip Burt's head from his shoulders any more. I figured he'd tire and drop my legs, and if I skedaddled, there was no way he'd have the strength to chase me.

It was funny, letting him drag me without a fight. Every minute, him wearing himself out and me getting stronger. I'd have let him drag me all night, but having spent the fall working in those fields, I knew my location almost from the slope of the terrain. His direction would have me at the edge of the woods soon. Burt was big, not huge, but a life of farm work will make an average fellow's muscles tough as steel. Burt must have already dragged me a half mile, and I took that as the measure of jealous fury.

There were a dozen ways he could have gotten me from his house to the woods. He could have thrown me over his shoulder and carried me, and it would have been less work. Or even tied me to a tractor. I think he wanted to drag me.

He mixed guttural sounds with curses. It took a lot of strength to lift my head high enough to see exactly where he was taking me. He hadn't bothered with a coat or hat. He had my ankles in the crook of one arm, and used the other to lock his elbow. He dragged me through a depression. Coming out the other side, he slowed and his grunts were strained.

We'd be at the woods in a few seconds, and I bet he'd rest before trying the scrap wood and briars. A few years ago, he'd cut the timber at the edge of the field and let it lay, and came by when he had spare time to saw the half-dried trees into firewood. In a moment we'd arrive where there was a lot of brush and short branches lying around. He'd have to switch to carrying me, or brain me there.

Burt dropped my legs and bent over, supported his weight with his hands on his knees. His breath came out like from a blacksmith's bellow.

I reared back and kicked. Caught his behind and sent him face-first into the snow. I flipped to my belly and jumped to my feet. The knot on my head made me woozy and it took five or six steps to the right just to get my balance. In that time Burt rolled to his feet, and my advantage was gone.

He gulped air, and I thought if I could sprint thirty yards, there was no way he'd have the lungs to catch me. But I stood there. If I took off, he'd have a few steps to grab me, but with my balance off and all my blood in my head from being upside down for fifteen minutes, my legs didn't have any confidence.

He lunged and I sidestepped. Lost my balance again while he came at me. I was at the edge of the woods. We squared off. His arms hung like a knuckle-dragger's and though his eyes were feral, his mouth curved in a smile. It was a frozen moment, him looking at me, me looking at him, and I figured the longer I waited the better shot I had at feeling normal, but I couldn't wait too long because he'd get his strength back too.

"Does Missus Haudesert mind you fucking Gwen?" I said. "Or does Cal visit his mother while you're with your daughter?"

His eyes remained glazed but the corners of his mouth were like a wave that had crested and now sought the other extreme. He hadn't shaved for Christmas. He crept sideways, still stooped, arms spread wide, like those National Geographic tribesmen who can catch rabbits by leaping to one side and it's fifty-fifty whether they guess right. Burt and I moved partway in a circle, only five feet apart.

"You know there's a special place in hell for men like you," I said.

He smiled.

I swooped to a maple shaft sticking through the snow, the end of a branch cleaned from a limb, but it was frozen to the ground. Burt didn't move, only grinned, and his eyes worked sideways.

"I'm going to leave you for the wild dogs," he said. "The coyotes."

I bolted into the woods. The first couple steps were awkward, on someone else's legs, but I got my stride, and after twenty steps, I hadn't heard a sound but my footfalls on snow-covered leaves, and I glanced backward quick. Burt was still there at the edge of the field, hunched, grinning.

"I'm going to find you at Haynes's, boy! An' run you through a grinder!"

I ran until my lungs burned and I had to stop to get my bearings. I'd never been in that neck of the woods before, and though I knew there was a lake somewhere, and I was headed roughly toward town when I set out, the woods jumbled my cardinal directions and I stopped to find the sun. There was no sound save my breathing and I thought about Burt's threat to find me at Haynes's and all the havoc a madman could wreak with a meat-cutting bandsaw and a couple of cleavers—but in the end, if two men go at it in the butcher shop, you just want to avoid being the one who dies first. Same as anyplace else.

The other thing I thought while I caught my breath was that Burt would take his frustrations out on Gwen. Maybe that afternoon, maybe that night. He'd tell her I was gone forever; he might hint I was dead.

Sometimes a man has to trust that the person he can't communicate with knows his heart, and that he'll come through. She'd already told me to leave once, and instead, I came for her with a ring. She was cool enough to keep her mouth shut and weather whatever storm came her way. I just hoped her heart was strong enough to remember that I wouldn't abandon her. I don't know how it works when a girl is abused, whether she gets stronger or weaker. I bet some go stark raving mad. I had to trust that for Gwen, her trials had made her tougher.

After I had my wind and a good sense of location, I made a line for Haynes's. If Burt was there waiting, I'd face him, but meantime there was no sense in thinking about it. I had to consider my next move: rescuing Gwen.

I decided I'd gather what little I owned, carry it back to the woods, and wait for nightfall. Then I'd rouse her at her window, and if she wanted to take off, we'd leave right then. If not, I'd do what she asked. If winter was too forbidding and she didn't want to head to town and catch a bus with barely enough money to cross a couple states in style, we'd wait. But it was going to be her choice. She was the one that was suffering because I'd felt obliged to ask Burt's permission.

Haynes's shed used to be for tools and general mechanical repair purposes. It came furnished with a workbench I'd cleared off for a hotplate and some things I'd accumulated. Below was a canvas bag stuffed with wrenches that smelled of old oil, rust, dirt, and some kind of hardy mildew. I emptied the corroded tools and turned the bag inside out and knocked the dirt from it. I had a couple extra sets of underclothes, and a copy of Bartleby that I'd picked up for a nickel a few weeks before. I rolled them into a blanket and stuffed it into the bag. If Gwen was desperate enough to run under these circumstances, then I was desperate enough to go with her, and even steal a satchel, but it wouldn't be me doing the providing. You can't put yourself in a situation that bad and not bank on a little help from the Almighty.

Whether He'll ante up is the thing you never know.

I cooked some side meat and filled up on that and a can of pork and beans. Everybody knows there's no pork with the beans. I thought afterward maybe I should have thought of a different meal. If Gwen went with me, she'd soon second-guess herself on account of my smell. But deep down I figured she wouldn't go with me into the cold. She wouldn't want to leave everything she knew, bad as it was.

Leaving was more difficult than I'd have imagined just a year ago. Of course, when I learned about my father, I was ready to go find him.

I was nineteen years old. Mister Sharps told me he'd been waiting for me to go. He wasn't quite so blunt. I'd been helping out around the Youth Home, and Mister Sharps had become my father like he was father to fifty or sixty other boys. Though he took interest in my welfare, his love was assailed every day by dozens of greedy boys who would improvise attention-getting tricks. Toby habitually killed frogs and planted them throughout the schoolhouse where their stink would generate the most frustration and remain longest hidden—heating vents, or behind a teacher's desk drawers, so that every time she sought a pencil or tape, she about gagged. That was Toby. George, a small fellow, started fights. His motto was to attack, and while he started out getting licked all the time, he became a dangerous foe, from sheer practice and meanness. Another boy, Eddy, was a master nose-picker. The rumor was that the *Guinness Book of World Records* had a two-inch booger in it, and Eddy sought fame as the mucous mining boy who could top it. Dried evidence of his dedication decorated the bottoms of several school desks, the restroom, and the chain link fence outside the play area. He kept a pint Ball jar on hand to preserve any boogers he thought might earn a place in Guinness's hallowed pages.

Rarely would a family come to Mister Sharps and request a boy, and when they did, it was the youngest that went. Most of us grew up without hope and without needing it but nonetheless hungry to feel something we'd only been able to imagine. It was toughest for the boys who arrived after family misfortune. One, Henry, arrived shortly before I left. He'd lost his arm and his parents in an automobile accident when he was ten and lived with his grandmother until she died. At twelve, he joined us. He sat in the play yard and brooded over an open book. I watched. He never turned the pages. Being older and somewhat in-charge, I sat beside him, and eventually, since I didn't say anything, he said to me, "How old were you when you came here?"

"Zero," I said. "My mother gave me to Mister Sharps directly."

"If someone cut your arm off, you'd know it." I thought he was getting fresh but before I put him in check, he continued. "You don't know what to miss."

"I got an idea," I said.

"That isn't the same."

He turned the page of his book. I patted his shoulder and left, but what he'd said stayed with me.

Mister Sharps gave me the idea of what I'd missed.

He taught me to shoot a twenty-two-caliber rifle and showed me how to bag a gray squirrel or rabbit every time I drew a bead. He relied on me to bring in game, and graduated me to hunting deer with a .308. But I only hunted what was in season and meticulously stayed within the bag limits. Mister Sharps didn't have a shotgun, so he taught me to hunt grouse and ringneck with the .22 short. I was never so proficient that I took a bird on the wing with every shot. But one out of three? Maybe.

Not entirely bad, Sharps said.

He also taught me to drive his car, but never in an official capacity, or with a license. Since I was useful around the Youth Home, bringing in a steady stream of game and doing other chores, and being a cooling influence on the younger boys, and also because I kept out of trouble, Sharps let me linger long after the usual age for boys to go. At seventeen, many joined the military. By eighteen, most every one had finished school and wanted a job, and a few even went to college by way of scholarships. Sharps encouraged me to apply to the finest universities, said it would be the greatest waste of a brain he'd ever seen to have me hunt animals and read library books the rest of my life—and besides, there wasn't a book left in the orphanage I hadn't read other than that blessed *Moby Dick*. He said a man owed his best achievements to himself first, and if he didn't have any personal ambition, ought to be productive to improve society—and if neither compelled him, he was useless as goose poop on a pump handle, and there was nothing to be done for him.

Finally, Sharps sat me down in his office one day last summer and said, "Gale, it's time for you to make your life. It's time for you to go."

"I want to know about my mother," I said.

Sharps removed his glasses. Pinched the bridge of his nose, but I saw the frown behind his hand. “Is that really important, Gale? When you have your whole life ahead of you?”

“I want to know why I’m here. Someone made a decision.”

“The circumstances? Is that it? You want to know why?”

“That’s right.”

“If you would have made the same decision your mother made, would your life have more value?”

I shook my head. “I want to know. That’s all.”

“I’ve seen it go both ways,” Sharps said. “No matter what I tell you, you came from the same place, and you have the same bright future. Why does it matter? In my years here, many young men have asked for their stories. I’ve always believed in telling them, because a man’s history belongs to him. But if you can, I’d like for you to forget that you want to know. Does the bear cub care that his father wandered in from another county? These things are immaterial.”

“Did you know your mother? Your father?” I said.

“I did.”

“Were they immaterial?”

He looked out the window for a long time. I didn’t let up on gazing at him, knowing that if I turned away, he’d feel less pressure. But as long as I stared, he was on the spot. No matter how he wriggled, I wouldn’t let him off without confessing my past.

He finally met my eye.

“I will tell you what I know, Gale. But I fear you will take an incomplete story and fill in the blanks with your imagination, and you will invariably guess wrong. You will fill in the blanks with everything that could hurt you instead of everything that adds meaning and promise. We remember the bad, and if we don’t remember, we invent. So before I tell you, promise me you will always favor yourself with absolution for wrongs which were not yours and for which no one holds you accountable."

"I promise."

"You are bound to this promise. It is your word. Even if your spirits are down, even if you are tired, you are bound to your word."

"My origin must be a very bad story."

He waved his hand. Looked away. Paused.

"An unsubstantiated story. Your mother was a good woman who didn't cause the trouble she found herself in…and did her best to be responsible. She was a good woman."

"Tell me."

"I'll tell you some."

"Tell me all."

"You tell me when to stop."

"Please…"

"She came to me with a baby swaddled in her arms. She passed this child to me. I was surprised, thinking she only wanted to ask questions, and here a baby brayed in my arms. You were a noisy one. A hellion, Missus Sharps said. Blue-faced from yelling. Some children are quiet for years, and when they learn to talk, they are never again quiet. You were the opposite. Always irritated and ever-willing to make sure we knew. But when you learned to talk, you ceased communicating. You were indrawn and—"

"Who was she?"

"I can't tell you her name. I don't recall."

"Gary," I said. "You have to know her name. It has to be on a form or something."

He studied me. I'd never said his first name in nineteen years. No boy ever said his first name, even behind his back.

"The laws are clear, Gale. I cannot tell you her name. And she doesn't live around here anymore. She placed you in my arms and disappeared."

"Who was she?"

"I don't know anything but what she told me. She was poor, and alone, and from the East. She was passing through on her way to California, where she hoped family would help her get established in life."

"Passing through and decided to drop off her baby?"

"Not exactly. She was passing through when she got pregnant and stayed in the area until she delivered you."

"And then she moved on."

"Right."

"Why would she do that?"

"She had no intention of getting pregnant, and the family that awaited her...they wouldn't have understood."

"What family doesn't understand being in a family way?"

"I can't describe them. I don't know. I'm telling you what she told me. It wouldn't have been fair to you as a baby for me to argue with your mother when she'd come to find a better future for you. Her actions...were an unselfish act of love."

I nodded. "Who was my father?"

"Your mother didn't tell me. She only said she was passing through a neighboring town and was hauled into jail for being a tramp. And it was there, she said, that a man...took advantage of her."

"Rape?"

His eyes flashed to the wall, then the window.

"I'm the son of a rapist?"

"I don't know that. She might have been trying to save face. The social pressures on an unwed mother—"

"She said she was raped?"

"That's what she said."

"Who?"

"I don't recall."

"She told you a name!"

"I don't know."

"WHO?"

"Gale, dammit, I can't tell you. Why? What will you do? Revenge? It doesn't matter. You're here. You're talented and smart and will have whatever success in life you choose. You can start a business. Learn a trade. Be a teacher. You can do anything. The man who made you isn't you."

"But I'm him!" I said, and stood. "I'm him. Who am I?"

Sharps pushed back on his chair and leaned forward so that his elbows found support on his knees. Shaking his head, he said, "Who runs a jail, Gale?"

"What town?"

"Bittersmith."

* * *

I waited in the woods where Burt had planned to brain me with a log. When dark came I had a little fire going under a rock overhang in a hollow. Pine trees muted the wind. The stone wall reflected the heat and by the time the smoke bent up around the four-foot-wide rock roof and drifted through the grove, it was so diffuse no one would ever suspect where it came from. Not that anyone would be out after dark on Christmas night into the woods, miles from any home but the Haudesert's and the Sunday's. Everyone was with family, eating ham baked with nutmeg cloves, and mashed potatoes drowning in sweet ham gravy.

It would be several hours before the Haudeserts bedded down, when it'd be safe to approach the house. I scavenged wood to keep the fire bright and hot and sat on a rock with my feet close to the coals, drying my boot leather. You can go a while with good leather before the ice and snow work through the polish, but once your feet are wet they're cold.

I'd hiked back and forth so many times in the past twenty-four hours, each time in the snow, that my boots were soaked. At one point I built the fire to a roar and removed my boots and set them close. I wrung my socks and the water fell like cow whiz on a flat rock. Then I suspended them on sprigs propped between rocks. The smell of baking wet leather and drying wool was potent, but every few minutes an easy breeze came through the hollow and replaced the stink with pine and snow.

I watched the moon from when it first appeared between tree limbs, sometimes no more than a flash of silver behind drooping branches dressed in icing, until it rose high into the sky. Sometimes I nodded off, but the dying fire always brought me back because my bare feet got cold until I threw on more wood. Eventually I slipped on my dry socks and toasty, but damp boots, and stretched the aches from my back and behind.

Somewhere nearby, I sensed eyes watching me. Had Burt stood on his porch and seen firelight through a dozen acres of trees? Couldn't be.

I shoveled snow onto the fire and stopped after a couple scoops, thinking it might be fortuitous to have cherry-red coals waiting for me if I met failure at the house. I put the remaining wood on the fire, trusting the three or four inches of snow covering the forest floor, and headed for the farm.

A shadow flitted across the corner of my eye; I stopped. My hands were empty. I cast about the ground for a rock or limb, but all was covered in snow. Finally, a coyote darted from trunk to trunk. He slunk with his head deviously low, pacing me, offering friendship on a lonely night. If I fell and broke my leg, he'd eat me.

The terrain was up and down, slippery. I stumbled on an iced-over log and fell. Landed with my elbow jammed in my ribs. I was two-thirds to the field, and rested a moment before standing. My lonely friend sat concerned on his haunches thirty feet away, tongue lolling, watching.

My pant legs rustled, ice crinkled underfoot, and my breath burst out in clouds of frost. The coyote pressed closer, as if unable to determine if I was old and infirm or young and stupid. The smell of my flesh in the dry frozen air must have been maddening. He grinned and revealed that of his twenty pounds, five were teeth.

I was alone, but my companion reminded me I was never so alone that there weren't others in the same plight, and though we were not cooperative, neither did we have to fear each other so long as we were strong. I talked to myself, entertaining him. He leaped along, content waiting for me to trip again and hoping when I did I would break something.

The forest gave way to heaping mounds of snow-covered brush where Burt had cut trees and let them dry. Piles of dead limbs, where rabbits huddled in warmth and safety. I flopped over logs, skirted stumps. Tripped on an unseen hazard. Regaining my feet, I saw my comrade had stalked within spitting distance. His head drooped, but his agile front paws lifted out of the snow one at a time, and his shoulders swayed each time.

I stepped into the field and he gave me a sorrowful glance, and bounded off.

From the edge of the field I saw the house was dark. I linked up with the trail Burt had forged by dragging me, and found his boot prints on top of the path my body had made. A man like Burt Haudesert would have found joy in so simple an act as that. It would have reinforced his sense of dominion.

I followed his footsteps, scrunching my toes every so often to confirm they were still dry.

I stood on the outskirts of the house a minute, like the knight Gawain, looking on the Green Knight's castle, knowing death waited within.

Between the barn and house, there were so many footprints in the snow I didn't worry about creating a new pair as they wouldn't have given me away. I wondered, though, if Burt or Cal—Cal had always been the loonier one—might be waiting for me in the dark with a rifle. The hair on my neck rose. Cal could have been in the barn; each loft had a side that faced the house with plenty of knotholes larger than a rifle barrel.

God gave me the imagination to gin up all kinds of abstract terrors, but he also provided the wits to hold them at bay. Realizing that I most feared Gwen would say, "Let's run tonight," I checked my other fears.

What if she said, "I'm ready, let's go."

What would I do but take her, and suffer a never-ending fear that she was hungry or cold and that I wasn't doing my duty by her, that I wasn't man enough to support her, that for all my hubris I was yet a mere orphan who'd read a lot of books and worked a lot of farms, but had yet to prove himself a worthwhile man?

At the same time I couldn't bear the thought of leaving her to suffer. This is what the mythologies called the Scylla and Charybdis.

I crept to her window. Stood to the side and listened. Sure she was alone, I tapped the glass with gloved fingers, issuing a tiny drumbeat until her bedsprings creaked. In a moment the curtain moved and her ghostlike face appeared in the dark. She wore no expression and the thought flashed through me that I shouldn't have come. That she had chosen her plight and would choose to remain in it.

While I dithered she opened the window and leaned from it into the cold and pulled me to her and swept her skinny bare arms around me. She shivered and squeezed, and I said, "I'm here."

"He said you'd never be back."

"Shhhh…"

"He made it sound as if he'd left you for dead."

"I got away. Everything I own is waiting in the woods. I'll take you away tonight, if you want."

She clung to me. "Tonight?"

"It has to be you that decides. If I steal you away, it's a tough life you're stealing to."

She put her fingers to my lips and kissed my cheek and said, "Give me a couple minutes to get some clothes."

Gwen disappeared into the room and I realized nothing could be more obvious than my footprints to anyone who came around the side of the house. I'd been in such a morass of worry the night before when I gave her the ring that I hadn't even considered the liability. Now I was doing it again.

The next time Burt came after me it could very well be with a rifle and a deer-hunter's aim. From the look in his eye that morning, he wouldn't know how to prevent himself from murdering me. I taunted him pretty good about Cal nailing his missus.

Gwen was at the window in a coat and I helped her outside. She pulled the window most of the way closed and said, "Let's go to the barn and talk."

Chapter Twenty

Gwen Haudesert is dead, murdered by Gale G'Wain. And I'm going to kill the son of a bitch.

Looking at Gwen, I see her grandmother's face. The faintest blush in the cheeks, the way her closed eyes sit under arched brows—as if in her final moment she was happy. Red hair so rich you can almost taste it. Skin so smooth you'd like to touch it.

There's blood on her belly and breast. Her blouse is open at the middle buttons, enough to expose a stab wound. Cooper must have checked, looking for a way to save her. But he had to have known he was too late.

Where I expected to find a bare-stockinged foot, I find she—or Gale—fashioned a moccasin from corduroy cloth. Not enough to protect a foot from the elements. I squat, and though Cooper has made tracks around her and has already done all of this, I check for a pulse at her neck. Her skin is hard, like a peach too close to the refrigerator cold air vent. She's been like this for hours. She's been like this since before I set out after her. Probably from before the time I got the call.

Who else is already dead?

I lay over her the coat and the sweater I carried and spend a moment staring into the trees.

Cooper stands a few feet away. Middle-aged dog breeder. Owns a five and dime in town.

"You find her like this, Coop?"

"I checked the wound."

"Was there a knife in her?"

"No. I undid two buttons and that was it."

I dig the photo Fay Haudesert gave me from my pocket and hand it to Coop. Watch his face.

"You ever hear of a boy named Gale G'Wain?"

"Gale?"

"That's right."

"Accourse. He works at Haynes's." He looks at the photo, passes it back. "That's him."

"What can you tell me?" I say.

"Did he do this?"

"Gwen's mother thinks he did."

"Nah. Boy don't have the gumption to slaughter a cow, let alone a girl as pretty as her."

"He's the one we're after. Did you stop by the barn or come right out?"

"I looked for you at the barn. Coroner and Deputy Sager was there."

"Any women?"

"Margot was visiting with Missus Haudesert, but I didn't talk with her. I was looking for you, and when Sager said you was out in this, I figured I'd best get a start."

"Yeah," I say. "So you saw Burt?"

Coop nods.

I look at the sky. Above the boulder the trees are hardwoods and look like skeletons. The clouds are mostly purple, what I can see of them. We stand in the lee of a giant rock that angles out like the prow of a ship. Where the rock meets ground, brown leaves poke up. A few feet away is a fire circle. I touch the cold ashes. Smells fresh. I check Gwen's foot, undo the knot at her toes. The snow and ice are worked all through the cloth. She didn't have the chance to warm her feet at the fire—so the fire was maybe from the night before.

This was all the lodge Gale had for her.

I swear I'm going to kill him.

The snow is thin where Gwen lies. Blood shows pink, since a few flakes have blown in. To the side of her body, ten feet away, is a mess of footprints and pink spatter. A circle is trampled, and the path that leads to Gwen's body is like you'd see if a log was dragged.

A single pair of wide-spaced footprints leads from the fire.

Gale ran.

"I know what you're thinking," Coop says, "and you're stark raving mad if you try."

"He's out there."

Coop is quiet. I tamp tobacco into my pipe.

"I saw you lying in the field," Coop says. "I thought you was dead and started toward you, but when you got up, I got back on the girl's trail. What was you doing in the snow, Sheriff?"

"He's out there ready to cut someone else up. There's caves in these woods. Rock overhangs. He could have a shelter made already. He could be sitting next to a fire right now, snappin' off while he thinks about this poor girl. I'll be goddamned if I let him."

"Maybe. But this storm? We ain't seen the start of it. There's a front coming through from Canada liable to bury us in ten feet, for chrissakes. If it does like back'n fifty-eight you can kiss your senile ass goodbye. We won't find you 'til March or April, and only what the wolves leave."

"Look at her!"

A black squirrel chatters at my outburst. Coop's eyes lock on mine.

"Look at her! You see what that snake did?"

Coop points beyond a lightning-scarred beech at the sky. "You see clouds that look like midnight, dumping snow by the truckload? You don't got to worry about Gale G'Wain. If he's got shelter out here, he's smarter than us. If he don't, we'll find him after the thaw. The girl's gone, Sheriff."

I step a few yards. Kick snow. Coop's bluetick stands a dozen feet away, tied to an oak sapling. He's dug a nest down to the leaves, but stands on it, maybe too cold to curl up.

"I'm sure Burt has a tractor that can get across the field," I say.

"Use one of his snowmobiles. We lash her to a toboggan and drag her out. We just got to get her to the field."

"Let's go," I say, and stoop to her feet.

Coop unties his dog from the tree, unclips the leash and stuffs it into his pocket. The dog watches with mournful eyes. Coop stands beside me.

"Let's put her on top of the coat," he says.

In the distance, the sound of a half dozen snowmobiles rises to a bare whisper and with a quick turn of the breeze vanishes.

* * *

After Mister Sharps told me about the circumstances surrounding my birth, and before I departed the Youth Home to fend for myself, I visited the Monroe County courthouse. Mister Sharps had named me Gale G'Wain after a medieval story about a particularly honorable knight—and had always claimed he didn't know the name my mother had given me. I would not find my birth record at the courthouse.

I climbed the courthouse steps and found a solid block wall at the top. I thought the doors might have been recessed between mighty columns. I had seen the courthouse a dozen times, always from the same angle, but never had occasion to enter the sacred building. It stood taller than four flagpoles and wide as thirty of the businesses located on the opposite side of the street. Each of its four sides was a facade. Up close, the pale weathered walls resembled an old textbook illustration of the House of Usher: rust colored stains near the roof and black decay between the giant blocks.

But the courthouse only appeared macabre up close. I wondered why those steps led to a wall with no entry, almost as if a hubristic architect had invited me to judge the fitness of the structure, and the institution it housed, and at the exact moment I accepted his invitation he proved a trickster.

I climbed down the steps and with appropriate distance, the temple appeared ghostly and spiritual, a truly hallowed house of justice.

If Bittersmith had arrested my mother, the record ought to have been archived there. Not that an arrest for being a drifter legitimized rape. At that time I wasn't looking for a confrontation with Bittersmith. I was investigating facts. The historical record was a starting place.

I entered from the north side, through giant doors constructed to make men feel insignificant. Lawyers with briefcases and chiseled frowns hurried here and there. I looked up the stairway, which started out at least twelve feet wide, and I got a foggy notion that the people who worship the Law will use any available edifice, or snag any circumstance, to make their god appear competent. The granite architecture, the big square looming shape, signified the court's conclusions were permanent and the institution was impregnable. I was happy to accept that. Should I uncover misdeeds as foul as Mister Sharps related had occurred to my mother, this courthouse would sustain justice.

I climbed the echoing stairwell to the third floor. Each step led to warmer and warmer air until I was sweating and nervous entering the records keeper's office. The woman behind the high counter remained seated. She looked like a barrel of mud wearing reading glasses.

"Good morning, ma'am. You look sunshiny today. I need to investigate arrests in Bittersmith. This courthouse has the records?"

"Who are you?"

"Gale."

She frowned. "Who you with?"

I turned partly to the side. "I'm alone."

"I guess I confused you. Who do you represent? Awful young for a lawyer. You with a newspaper?"

I felt my face flush because she was a poor communicator and I wasn't easily confused. A wooden item on her desk said Henrietta Gibbons. I said, "I represent myself, Miss Gibbons. Or if that isn't good enough, my mother."

"What's her name?"

"I don't know."

Henrietta inhaled and slumped at the same time. "I'm busy now. Sit over there."

"I'm not busy now, and if you'll just show me where to look, I apologize for the interruption."

"Sit over there and I'll be with you when I can."

I sat on a stiff wooden bench with no back, but situated close to the wall. I fought to remain square-shouldered and stiff-backed in case she chanced a look over the counter, but as the wall clock's minute hand passed the quarter-hour mark, and then the half-hour mark, I leaned. After an hour, I slouched like a no-good lazy dullard.

She sat been behind her counter, invisible, the whole time. I imagined her filing her nails.

I approached again and saw her reading what appeared to be the same paperwork as an hour before.

"Please, ma'am. It's very important. I apologize for my rudeness. Is there no way you could spare a minute to point me in the right direction?"

"What are you looking for?"

"My mother's arrest record."

"Why?"

"I don't believe she was arrested."

Her eyes narrowed.

"The sheriff in 1951 was Bittersmith, right?"

Her eyes began to widen.

I continued, "You heard any rumors about Bittersmith?"

Her eyebrows knotted and her cheeks flushed rosy and she pushed back her chair. The wood legs squawked until she lifted her girth on thighs hidden by a brownish floral pattern.

"What's your mother's name?"

"I don't know. She gave me up. But she'll have been arrested in Bittersmith in June, 1951"

Henrietta Gibbons led me to an ominous room with Documents and Records stenciled on the tilted glass above the door. The closer we got the stuffier my nose became, and I thought I was near a sneeze fit.

"There couldn't have been that many arrests in Bittersmith," I said.

She looked at me curiously, then turned sideways and sidestepped through the narrow doorway. She hit a switch and the room illuminated. It was full of file cabinets and dust. Each drawer had a year or two on the tab marker. I followed her. Going back in history, each file drawer contained more years, as if people in the past were less liable to run afoul the law.

She stopped, and I bumped against her. I'd thought she was a granite mountain, but she was soft like a cut of rare meat. She smelled sharp like crystalline sweat.

"Here you are. Nineteen fifty-one. What month you say?"

"June."

"Look from May to July. Every baby don't go nine months."

She unlocked the drawer, slid it open until the metal rails clicked. All of the records for Monroe County in 1951 took the width of a tackle box. Fifty-three, however, was a particularly pestilential year and was half-again as thick. I wondered how Sheriff Bittersmith fared.

I thumbed through each arrest card, reading the typed and often smeared name in the top left corner. Most arrestees were men, and I made rapid progress. Between May and July, only three women in all of Monroe County had been arrested. One was for drunk and disorderly conduct, another was accused of robbery, and the last arrest was for prostitution. This sparked my curiosity. I could imagine a corrupt sheriff maneuvering an itinerant woman into his jail cell by claiming she was a prostitute. But she was arrested in Monroe.

I carried the card to Henrietta. "Is it possible that a woman would be arrested in Bittersmith but the card would say Monroe?"

She shook her head, and I returned to the files.

Sheriff Bittersmith didn't arrest anyone during those three months. I went through all of the cards again. I checked 1950 and 1952 as well. Bittersmith never arrested anyone.

I thanked Henrietta Gibbons and shook my head when she inquired to the result of my search. Morose, I trudged down the steps. I stopped at the second floor. The courtroom doors were open. A dozen suit-clad men sat inside. A uniformed man stared out of the witness box, robust as an oak stump. He wore a silver mustache and hair that was neat and oiled, combed from a perfectly straight part.

"Now, Sheriff Bittersmith, is it your recollection that the defendant was at all nervous in his disposition, or in any way not forthcoming with relevant facts?"

My heart stopped beating and my blood halted in my veins.

Bittersmith grunted an answer I didn't even hear. I sat in a pew in the back and watched, fearing he would recognize me and know my purpose. Bittersmith's eyes remained fixed on the wall, and his voice carried a whisper of contempt, a man of action forced to suffer men of thought.

"No further questions, your Honor."

Ramrod straight, Bittersmith stepped down from the box. He made a point of staring at the defendant as he walked by. I hadn't even noticed the man, a short fellow with squirrelly hunched shoulders. Bittersmith walked past me.

I followed him into the hall, and down the stairs. At the bottom floor, Bittersmith whirled. I was higher by two steps, but our heights were equal.

I saw my face in his.

"You following me, boy?"

"I am."

He glanced me up and down. "What the goddamn hell for?"

"Do you remember an arrest from the summer of nineteen fifty-one? A woman…a drifter on her way to California?"

He shook his head, turned, and walked away.

"Sheriff! You arrested her in fifty-one, and I can't find a record upstairs."

He stopped. "Then how do you know?" He waited. He spread his arms partway to the sides, a merry gesture as if to initiate a gentleman's wager. But his face held no joviality, just the candor of his challenge. "How do you know, boy?"

My throat froze.

He walked away.

I stood looking at the polished floor, the granite walls, the fancy woodwork. I listened to the echo of his footsteps and registered the finality of the giant door swinging closed. They hadn't built this place for my mother, or me.

* * *

It used to be that even women would stop and stare at Margot Swann Haudesert.

When you saw her naked, you would give your life to touch one breast. You'd barter your soul to bury your face at her thighs. She used to squeal and giggle, and you knew you'd be a beast if you didn't give her more. She could call the goat out of any man. The first time I was with Margot, I spilled early. Anticipating her firmness, her sweetness…having tasted her. Smelled her. Breathed and consumed her. I kept going like a rock-ribbed son of a bitch and only lasted a few minutes before it happened again. I waited. Only on my third did she cry out.

Her husband was a salesman who took out-of-town trips. I'd made her acquaintance making a deposit at the bank while she was making a withdrawal.

Until you see beauty like hers, you can't conceive it. When you finally taste it, you're a slave.

I loved her many times, until one day she met me at her door with flushed cheeks and wet eyes, saying she was a terrible woman, a rapacious, irredeemable sinner, and that I'd taken advantage of her, and she'd rather be consumed by the flames of hell than ever feel my touch again.

Over the months that followed, on the rare occasions I saw her about town, she seemed to be gaining weight.

Chapter Twenty-one

Gwen was so close to being mine that I wanted to take her to the loft in spite of the hair standing stiff at the back of my neck and the nervous sweat on my brow.

"Is there anybody outside?" I said. "Is everyone in the house?"

"I don't think anyone came outside," she whispered.

"It's nothing. Just a feeling," I said.

She smiled, and I knew she figured I was afraid.

"Come on." She took my hand and I pulled it back from her and took my glove off so I could weave her fingers in mine. She put her thumb on top of my thumb, until I put mine over hers and she let me.

We entered the barn from the door beside the main bay, tiptoeing as if our footfalls might be audible above the gusts and groaning boards. An arctic front had moved in.

"The loft?" she said.

"Uh—is that smart? I mean—"

She pulled me to the ladder.

I said, "Do you know what time it is?"

"After midnight. Maybe one."

I didn't think there was much chance Burt would be wandering around at that hour. Unless...

"Did Burt...Did he visit you, tonight?"

She was partway up the ladder and I didn't want to raise my voice. Her pant legs brushed as she climbed; her hands smacked the rungs—all amplified by my mind, and my nerves. When I reached the top and found her already supine on a hay mattress, I kept my mouth closed and snuggled beside her.

I pressed my cold nose to her cheek and she pressed her cold nose to mine and next thing, her mouth covered my mouth. She was hungry. She tossed me back to the night months before when I woke up with her hand in my pants. I answered her moans with grunts. She squeezed my shoulder and I pressed her coat and unbuttoned it, slipped my hand around her back and then back to her front and then over her breast, as if I'd planned on touching her neck and her breast happened to be in the way and I'd no choice but to grab a hold.

I fought two battles. Since the first time she'd visited me in the barn, neither of us had ventured this close to erotic behavior. When we'd snuggled, it was only compassion, because I'd grown up questioning not just my place in the world, but my right to have a place at all. She was on metaphysical eggshells too. The first battle I fought was against Gale G'Wain, and whether I ought to enjoy her the way she wanted me to.

The other battle was in the back of my mind, all the time wondering when staying in the barn became a mortal liability. I rolled in the hay with a girl whose three defenders were crack rifle shots, militia-minded, and ready to kill. Not one of them was more than fifty yards away. Part of me thought I can't believe breasts are so soft, and the other part thought, how would it feel to have a bullet cut through me? Is this nipple worth it? The pair of them?

Before long she stripped off her coat and I did mine, and since hers was a full-body parka, we spread mine like a bottom blanket and pulled hers on top, and we just kissed and touched.

It oftentimes happens that you know what's going to destroy you ahead of time, and you're perfectly right.

* * *

The deputy's car is a few hundred yards from the house, catty-corner through the woods. I don't bother laying a set of circuitous tracks, or walking backwards like they do in the westerns. My leg hurts too much from the knife wound and the Lysol. Besides, the deputy found me at Coates' house, and probably made a radio call, and if not, whatever logic brought him will bring someone else.

Maybe Sheriff Bittersmith.

Part of the reason I wanted to work at Haynes's was to see how an artisan butchered. Another part of me wanted to make money to take Gwen away from her troubles. I denied the last reason. After being around Gwen and seeing the product of her father's abuse, and thinking of my mother in that context, I wanted to be closer to Bittersmith.

I wanted to know my enemy.

One morning, Haynes turned off a band saw and called, "I need salt. Twenty pounds."

"I think you have plenty of salt. I'll go look." I thought he meant the pound-and-a-half Morton canisters out front, for sale to his customers. He didn't sell much and didn't stock much, but he was far from out.

"No, for the hides. We slaughter tomorrow morning—you salt the hides. I didn't make it to the depot. I'll explain when I don't have a saw full of meat. Go buy twenty pounds." He retrieved his wallet and handed me a ten-dollar bill with a red thumbprint. "You can carry twenty pounds, right?"

I walked to the grocery. The morning sun hadn't warmed the air and my lungs ached. Two blocks away I saw a brown Bronco parked on the sidewalk out front.

I stopped outside the door. Many times I'd relived my feeble courthouse confrontation with Bittersmith, how he said I couldn't prove anything about him arresting my mother. In my visions I had a stronger riposte, that God could prove it, and if Bittersmith was lucky, it would be God and not me that addressed his sins, because my wrath was bigger, and I was not constrained by forgiveness.

But knowing the perfect rejoinder didn't give me the courage to utter it, and I felt guilty for blasphemy.

Bittersmith sat on the counter and leaned partly across so that he was above the woman ringing up his purchases.

I opened the door. Bittersmith twisted at the chime, sized me up, and spoke to the woman. His unintelligible words sounded like Burt Haudesert seducing a hog he was about to scramble with a twenty-two. The woman flashed a look at me. She was younger than I thought at first, and pretty as a three-eyed potato. I walked past them both. Her pupils were big and her mouth was narrow. I walked down an empty aisle, past the sugar and salt and flour and yeast, and loitered at the end cap. My fingers felt swollen and my legs itched from the exercise in the cold air. My face burned and my heart raced. I knew what Bittersmith was doing. The girl was prey.

I affected interest in the many varieties of kidney beans. Bittersmith didn't move, and for a long time I watched his back. Finally I spotted his eyes in a mirror on the wall, set up high. Fear shot through me like I'd been caught wrong, like I'd lost an advantage and was suddenly tossed headlong into a battle I'd been observing a moment before. He'd been watching me watching him. He had the eyes of a hunter. Did he remember me from the courthouse? I wanted to bolt without trying out my pert response, but the only thing between that girl and her fate was me.

Damned if I was going to turn my back on her.

Bittersmith rested his hand on the girl's shoulder and spoke to her. She nodded slowly, like the motion drove a nail into her skin. I held a can of beans. He turned and approached. I glanced at him. He grew taller and taller. I wondered how he was my father.

I wondered if I could brain him with beans.

"You passing through?"

"I work at Haynes's."

"That so?"

"Yes."

"You here for beans?"

"A couple items."

"I don't like you."

I squeezed the can. Held my tongue.

"I don't like the way you've been watching me, like you're set to rob the place."

"I'm no thief."

"You ought to move along, 'fore I decide you and me need to have a more thorough conversation."

"I'm here to buy a couple of things." I placed the beans back on the shelf.

The door chime sounded.

An elderly man and woman entered the store and took a pushcart. They walked slowly. Bittersmith scowled. "I see you again, it's royal goddamn trouble."

Bittersmith walked away. He made a click-sound with his mouth while he pointed at the girl, like he was calling a horse. I fetched the salt Haynes had sent me for. I didn't talk to the girl, other than to ask if she was okay and how her day was going. Her nametag said Judy. She was tightlipped and shy, but more relaxed than when Bittersmith was hovering over her.

Haynes sent me to the same store a couple weeks later. This time a bald angry man with a stiff waxed mustache sat behind the register.

"Where's Judy? Does she work today?"

"Judy, huh? She went to school."

"In Bittersmith?"

"College. San Francisco. What do I care? Now I'm here all day and all night too."

I was happy for Judy. She ran when she could.

* * *

During the fall I worked for Burt Haudesert, Sheriff Bittersmith was the source of at least two angry rants from Burt. He occasionally drank whiskey from a mason jar. It coarsened his manners and speech, and accented his drawl with a barbeque twang, impressing upon me that he chose moonshine because he was proud of being country, just as a rich man might choose an aged bottle of wine and say old chap in homage to his aristocratic forbears.

We sat on the porch. Like most nights after supper, Burt brooded, at once melancholy and tired from the day's work and eager to make me an acolyte of his views on the militia, the gold standard, and Nixon. But this night he held my look longer than normal and seemed unconvinced of what he was about to say.

In my fear I believed we each knew everything. Would he confront me about my relations with Gwen, or worse, attempt to justify his frequent visits to her bedroom?

Burt offered me the Mason jar; I sniffed it and gave it back. Cal was inside the house, in bed, as it was still early fall, and Jordan was inside too. Burt didn't launch into the militia being the only crew of honest Americans left, the last defenders of the Constitution. Instead, he told me of his schoolboy days. I sensed he was trying to bridge his growing up with a single mother and then a stepfather to my life at the orphanage. He told a story about hollowing the center of a history text and hiding a water pistol inside. Each time Mr. So-and-so turned, Burt squirted the back of his head. The teacher knew it had to be Burt and went so far as to stand him up and pat him down. Failing to find the water gun, he instructed Burt to open his textbook and read aloud the assigned chapter.

Burt hemmed and hawed. Mr. So-and-so flipped open the book, and found the squirt gun in the cut-out pages. He seized the book and smashed it to Burt's crown.

Burt giggled like a four-year-old girl. He filled the story with so many embellishments that he finished a pint of moonshine telling it.

"That's a great story," I said.

"That's the truth. Not a story."

"That's a great truth," I said.

"Goddamn right."

I winced.

"What? You got a problem?"

"No problem, Mister Haudesert. Did you go to school in Bittersmith?"

"Bittersmith. Hunh? Goddamn Bittersmith. There's a rotten son of a bitch, there."

He must have been thinking about Sheriff Bittersmith earlier, and the liquor loosed his frustration.

"You ever walk down the street and see him comin'. You see him walkin' down the street and you're on his side, you just cross. Don't even look and see if there's cars."

"You two have history?"

"History? Goddamn future too."

"Future?"

"You ask too many questions."

"How is it the town's named after him?"

"Named after his granddaddy—Walt Bittersmith, a rancher. Held a huge tract o' land and sold a right of way to the Burlington railway. They put a depot at the crick and Walt built the first saloon. So the great sheriff's roots go straight to the brothel. His grandmum was a hoo—ooo—oor." His voice scattered into laughter.

I was quiet while Burt tried to drink shine. He coughed booze across the porch.

"How long has Sheriff Bittersmith been the sheriff?"

"Shit. Longer'n you been alive. Longer'n me."

"Seems like a quiet town."

"Yeah. You make some noise and he'll see you quiet again. Slapped my ass in jail for a bar fight. That sombitch had it in for me my whole life. He used to come around and visit ma. Give her the willies. He'd watch me and I'd know why she was so goddamn disgusted with him."

"You said he made you quiet?"

"I was in a fight. Stupid thing, shooting nine ball. I was good back in the day and got in a pissing contest. I went to bust the other fella's head and Bittersmith shows up, like he was waiting, and hauls my ass in. He threw me in the tank overnight and the next morning came in and sat on the plank beside me and said, 'I'm not citing you for the disturbance, last night. But you ever fuck up in my town again, I'll kill ya, son.'"

“Bittersmith said that?”

“Them exact fuckin’ words.”

“He called you ‘son’?”

Burt inhaled deep. He exhaled, then gulped long from his shine.

“This is crazy. But I like you Gale, and I’ll steer you straight. This is how I put it together. I was a boy. Shit. Five or so. I found a baby. A baby rabbit, sitting under a pine tree. Just sitting there. He saw me and froze. He was easy to catch. I remember that day…Clear blue sky.”

Burt reached to his left boot and unlaced it. Bent over and half-grunting, he said, “I came running into the house with the rabbit in my hands. Didn’t know Bittersmith was there. Didn’t hear his truck.”

He untied his other boot, then sat up, kicked out his legs, and drank from his bottle. He pulled a half-burned cigar from his pocket. Lit it. I had never seen him smoke, and the stink of it blended perfectly with his mood.

“Bittersmith had my mother pressed up against the kitchen counter.” Burt grimaced. “Pressed against the counter with his pants at his knees and her wrists pinned to the cabinets. I dropped the rabbit.”

He was silent a long minute. His chin touched his chest.

“So that’s why he threw me in jail,” Burt said. “The son of a bitch had the paternal instinct. I saw that Mutual of Omaha show. The lion killing his young. That’s what the paternal instinct feels like with Bittersmith.” He drank from his bottle. “But he’ll get what’s coming. He’ll get what’s due.”

“What do you mean?”

His sleepy eyes danced inside shadows cast by the sixty-watt bulb.

“You look awful coy, Mister Haudesert. Like you’ve got a plan.”

He winked. "Board decides who's sheriff. Other places, the people vote. But Bittersmith's granddaddy made it the board so the law wouldn't be above him and his boys. Give him a layer of money insulation. Pesky voters and all. In these many years, it's never changed. But the board has. The board's made of militiamen. Masons, too."

"You've got some pull with the Masons?"

"I am a traveling man."

I studied him, tried to parse the secret language.

"I guess you're not. Shit. I got Bittersmith into the Masons." He leaned back until his head hit the wall, and he stared into the darkness. "He asked if I'd sponsor him. I figured sure, all I had to do was vote against him. The ballot was secret."

"But you didn't."

"At a certain age, a man wants to know his father. Pure-ass evil or not. A man wants to put it all to rest." Burt leaned forward and placed his elbows on his knees. His face was dark. "Have a drink of shine, Gale. You ask too many fuckin' questions."

I liked him, for a moment.

* * *

I cut through the snow at the best vector I can figure to return to Doctor Coates's house and stop at a cow fence. It'd be bad to see blood where I dragged the deputy across the porch from a hundred yards off. The steps are white, and I keep on.

I look across the field to where the deputy left his car, expecting to see a second vehicle. A pickup truck with six extra headlights on the roof, like the Militia uses. Or another police car, coming fast with swirling blue and red lights. I am happy in my disappointment.

I shield my eyes from the glare off the snow and take in the lake, a morbidly sullen expanse of pure white.

Firewood.

The deputy's face still melts snow, but ice crystals rest on his hands. Soon, drifts will cover him. I didn't start the day looking to see so many people die. Maybe I'm like the butcher Haynes. A man can only kill a dozen doe-eyed animals a week for so long before his heart grows hard.

I fill my arms at the woodpile and carry the logs past the deputy. I make two more trips so I won't need to get bundled up again until dark. Inside, I go to the list of food items I've taken and update it with each article of clothing I wear from the doctor's bureau and closet. Upstairs, I locate a duffel of World War II vintage and stuff it with several sets of underwear and socks, pants, shirts, a second pair of sloppy-fitting boots, another wool sweater. A toilet kit. A blanket. A tarp from the basement that, with enough twine and ingenuity, might become a tent. I lean the packed duffel against the wall by the front door.

In the room where I found the duffel is a bookshelf. I'd normally devour the titles for works I've read or volumes I've always wanted to read. This time I seek something that caught my eye when I searched out the duffel: a stack of folded roadmaps.

When Guinevere and I snuggled those fall nights, we traded dreamy runaway destinations. Hers was Mexico. I said Chicago because it came to mind. She wanted Mexico because it was warm and she could live beside the ocean.

"Which ocean?" I said.

"I don't care," she said. "Don't be specific with a dream. You'll be disappointed."

I check the front flaps of each map and one is for the southwestern United States. I stretch it flat on the bed. At the bottom, outside the double boldface line, its territories dull gray, is Mexico. The map shows no Mexican cities, no roads, no rivers, as if everything known ends at the border. As if the person who crosses that double line will be forgotten. I eyeball the distance between Wyoming and the word, "Mexico." Glance at the legend.

A thousand miles?

The closest road south from Wyoming comes out of Monroe.

Chapter Twenty-two

Margot Haudesert's car is in the center of the driveway. The coroner's GMC is parked beside my Bronco at the barn. I'm fresh out of jerked venison, and my stomach is like a fist squeezing a handful of sand.

Coop said Haudesert had plenty of snowmobiles, but I look in the barn and an ancillary shed and find only one. Eighteen-inch-wide sled tracks lead away, breaking sharply from the gate and shooting across the field, opposite where I trekked. Under snow, the tracks could be a few hours old or a few days.

Coop releases the hood spring on each side of the green Skiroule, checks the fuel tank up front. Straddles the sled and rocks it side to side, mixing the oil and gasoline. Turns the key, pulls the cord taut, releases, heaves. The motor sputters. His hand flashes to the choke and back to the throttle on the handlebar. The motor dies. Another quick pull and it sounds like a bored-out chainsaw. The shed fills with white smoke. Coop throttles up and the sled jumps forward. He allows the machine to idle on the snow, gets off, and we step a few yards away, our backs to the racket.

"Why don't you send me and Sager after the girl?"

"Sager and Fields," I say. "Appreciate your help."

"What are you going to do?"

"Find Gale G'Wain."

"You ought to find a doctor."

I straddle the snowmobile and cruise to the barn, where Coroner Fields and Deputy Sager wrap up. Burt's body is gone. Sager's pile of vomit is buried in snow. But Burt Haudesert's blood spatter still gleams like precious stones.

I feel eyes on me. Back at the house, Fay Haudesert holds the kitchen window curtain to the side. Margo stands behind her, a shadow.

"Just finishing," Fields says.

I turn. "Photos?"

Sager nods. "And we got the boy's prints on the fork.

"That so? You recognize them?"

Fields is silent. Looks at the floor.

"So far as I've heard, no one saw what happened here. The missus inside, there, don't know. And Gwen won't be saying anything. We got a coat that may belong to the killer. We got a few tracks in the woods. That's what we got."

"Blood samples," Fields says. "If there's two types, I'll find them."

I nod. "I'm sure you will. We do this by the book."

"Right."

"We found the girl. Coop found her. Sager, I want you to go out with Fields and bring her in."

"Now?"

I study his face.

"It's just that I ain't had lunch."

"And since you lost your breakfast—"

"It won't take long to pick her up," Fields says. "We've got to retrieve her before she's buried in the blizzard."

Sager sighs, the kind that says he'll be glad when he ain't taking orders from a geezer bastard every day. Fields tilts his head toward the barn door, and the snowmobile.

"You'll want to find a toboggan or something to drag her out. Take your camera and follow our tracks into the woods 'til they stop at a giant rock. I want a shot of every angle." I leave him with that. From this moment, he's Odum's problem.

Fay Haudesert is still in the window. I look at Margot's car. I never imagined Margot becoming a mother-in-law. Never foresaw her being a mother.

I was thirty-six and she was nineteen, an angel with a beauty that produced a purple aura. She walked in it; she was something different. Fresh out of high school and full of dreams. She talked about everything without talking too much.

In the summer, the fields are green and the air is sweet with corn. Tramping through the woods, dried leaves rustle under foot and smell rich with decay. Take a woman to a brook where the water's so clear you see trout twenty feet off and have her pose in the shadows with the sunshine breaking through the leaves, forming little golden stars on her flesh. Listen to her voice mingle with the stream; see her perfect ass disappear as she wades into the water. She'll turn sideways and you'll see nipples like acorns.

Margot was nineteen when I took her on a three-foot-wide oak stump—three times. She wasn't yet used to her powers. Hadn't learned how to *stop* attracting a man. You know sometimes when she says "no, please, no" she means give me everything, hurry. And you do it enough, she gets real honest. She'll tell you she was looking for the man could tame her.

That was Margot, and how she conceived Burt Haudesert. She was married to a salesman no one ever heard of and stayed hitched for two years. Later, Margot latched onto a farmer named Otis Haudesert. He died, and Burt took his name and his farm. Margot moved out when Burt married Fay.

It's going to be interesting, saying hello.

Fay meets me at the door. Her eyes are wide, lifted in

expectation—but she's a woman and I don't have to say a word. Don't even have to think her baby girl is gone. She reads it, and hope slips her face. She retreats to the hutch, wraps her arms around her shoulders and hugs herself.

Margot is in the other room, back to me, staring through the picture window into the cold. Fay pivots and rushes to me. Pulls Gwen's shoe from my front pocket and presses it to her cheek, and weeps.

"We found her," I say.

Her eyes blaze. "How? The cold?"

I shake my head.

"How?"

"She was stabbed. One time."

Fay staggers back. Her hands are fists. Her cheeks flushed. "My boys are going to handle this. You get the hell gone."

"They took off on the sleds before I got here," I say.

She stares at me. In the dining room, Margot turns. "You can go now, Josephus." Her voice warbles like a bird's.

"I appreciate you saying that, Margot." I hold her look until she turns. "But I think we all know I'm not going away. Missus Haudesert, where are your sons?"

"You've got no further call in my house."

"Was you the one found Burt? Or was it the boys?"

Silence.

"I'm betting Cal or Jordan found him, and it was a long shot earlier than you called. I think they went out looking to recruit Burt's friends. I'm betting you told them to—and none of you knew Gwen was out there with Gale. And now that the deed is done, you got a lot of blame on your shoulders, and you're wanting to cast some off."

"You've done enough," Margot says.

She's a curious interlocutor. Hasn't said nary a word to me

in all these years Burt was alive. On the day of his death, we're reunited.

"I tried, but it wasn't enough," I say. "I was late to the woods. Late to the farm. Late to get the call maybe. Fay?"

"What."

Outside, the snowmobile engine runs fast and Sager and Fields must be setting out after Guinevere.

"You sent them boys to get Burt's lieutenants," I say.

"What of it? What're you going to do? Didn't they vote your sorry ass out? Burt was right about you. Always was."

Margot looks at a picture of Burt on the wall.

I remove my pipe, pack the bowl, tamp it just so. Light the tobacco and blow a cloud toward Margot. "You cry for a strong man, and cry when you get him." I nod. "I'll leave you to your crying. Ladies."

* * *

No sooner than a set of tires stamp out a trail, snow blows in and covers it. I ease down the driveway in the Bronco and another vehicle's blocking the way, slipping sideways and straight. I swallow back a taste of bile, and the side of my chest gets tight.

Odum's come back.

I stamp the brake and the Bronco slides. I jump out. "What the fuck are you doing here?"

He's gunning the engine and can't hear. The vehicle lurches out of a rut. Odum puts it in neutral and rolls down the window.

"What the goddamn holy fuck are you doing here? I told you to go to Coates's place!"

"I sent Roosevelt to Coates's."

"You sent— why are you here?"

Odum kills the engine. Opens the car door and steps out.

Spits, and spends a moment with his gaze pointed at the snow, studying the brown spit hole. He raises his eyes like he's found his resolve. "I'm taking over."

"The hell—"

He holds up his hand. "Go talk to the council. They feel the investigation will last more than one day. We've got two bodies and a fugitive, and the worst storm in thirty years coming through. Town leadership wants continuity."

"I'll shove continuity up their asses. Up all your asses!"

"You had any decency, you'd have stepped aside on your own. Not make other things an issue."

"Other things…"

"Yeah, Bittersmith. Other things. You going to shove them up my ass too?"

He folds his arms and leans against the doorframe.

Don't this beat all? Odum's found his sack.

"You've had a good run. But that little episode out in the field…Coroner saw you drop like a sack of meal and not get up. He was a hundred yards after you when you finally wobbled to your feet. Didn't take three minutes for Coop to give up the details, 'cause he thought we'd be fetching two bodies across the field. You had a heart attack, and you're still too stupid to call it quits."

"Real damn nice, that concern in your voice." I pull my Smith & Wesson by the top of the grip, like to hand it over, and then snap the pistol into place in my hand. Point at his belly. "But it's bullshit. All this is bullshit. I'm sheriff of this town."

"You're an ex-sheriff about to get his ass thrown in the can." He spits tobacco juice. "There's other things you don't want drawn into this, out in the light any more than they are. You want me to say it? Bring out your philandering ways? Half the town knows your connections to the Haudeserts."

I get a tingle in my arm and feel my pulse in the side of my head. Squeeze my teeth so hard I could bust them.

"You got your stuff packed, Bittersmith. All that's left is to take off that badge. So take the Bronco back to the station and do whatever the hell you planned to do after you retire. Leave the badge on the desk. You ain't sheriff no more."

He climbs back inside his vehicle. "You want to move that fuckin' Bronco off the drive?"

I get an idea. I'll bet a sow's rear tits Odum ain't going to like it.

I lower my gun and stare until the pressure in my chest backs off a notch. "Yeah, I see things your way, Odum. You handle the lawin'."

I get back inside the Bronco and reverse to the farm. You handle the fuckin' law side.

* * *

I've spent today like a man on death row, believing I had a certain number of hours before the end. Now I feel like they're marching me to the chamber eight hours early.

"Fenny—you get word from Roosevelt?" I un-thumb the radio. The road bounces me and Fenny comes through broken with static.

I'll wait.

I arrive at the station and first thing see Travis's car is gone. Could be nothing. Could be Marge Whitmore wouldn't stop calling until someone came and cleaned her steps. Travis is the kind of boy who'd volunteer on the first call. But I know it wasn't Marge that called him. It was Odum.

Inside, Fenny jumps from her seat and races to me. "Good Lord!"

"Don't call me that," I say.

She touches my cheek with her hand, pushes them old tits against my belly. I give one a squeeze.

"You look like hell, you old fool," she says.

"I liked 'Lord' better."

"Sager said what you was up to, marching out into the storm, and you wouldn't let him go instead. Then have yourself a heart attack. Lincoln County's got sixteen inches and it's coming our way. And you out there, in it."

"Sixteen?"

"That's so."

"Been a little while since you had sixteen inches."

"You're confusing your metric system again." She pours coffee and I sit on the corner of her desk.

"What's word from Odum?"

Fenny hesitates, like she's wondering if I'm allowed to know what the new Sheriff is up to. "No word, other than Roosevelt called in that there's smoke at the Coates farm. It's in the log, there."

"In the log? Where was you?"

"Across the street. Lunch time. Travis took the call."

"Where's Travis?"

"He said Mrs. Whitmore phoned."

Fenny depresses the switch and speaks into the microphone. "Travis, you there?"

Static.

"Travis?"

His voice comes through. "Roosevelt's not at his car, Fen. You better tell Sheriff Bittersmith to boogey on up here."

"We'll get somebody up there. Bittersmith don't boogey."

Chapter Twenty-three

I stand at the window and ponder spending the night at Doctor Coates's house. Ice has frozen to the pane in a pattern like a thousand snowflakes holding hands.

Behind the pattern—through it—black dots move on the lake.

I press my palm to the glass and melt the ice. Wipe it aside with my sweater sleeve.

Those spots could be deer. Loose cattle. A posse of men from town. They could be anything, but they are not. I open the window six inches and reach for the .308 leaning against the sill. Drop to my knees and find a good picture through the scope.

Six snowmobiles. Cal, Jordan, and a few of the Wyoming Militia, if I'm right.

They'll arrive in minutes.

Cal is crazy as a rabid dog. Some of his talk around the supper table, once he could get around on a cane, would've had a man hanged for sedition in earlier times. He said if one true patriot just had the onions, he'd go put a bullet in Nixon's head and spare us from the fascists. The oligarchs. The polygarchs. The petrogarchs. I didn't know half his words because he minted so many. But he was all for shooting politicians, and in general, anybody else. When I approached the house on

Christmas night and felt a rifle trained between my shoulder blades, I imagined Cal's face behind the sights.

The snowmobiles come.

Jordan held the same opinion of Cal. I spent the better part of a month walking alongside a hay wagon throwing bales up to him. My arms got tore up like I'd slap-boxed a cat and got the worst of it, and in the sun, sweat glazed my skin and it wouldn't have been any worse if I'd have gone to the kitchen and rubbed a handful of salt into the cuts. The only part of the whole process I enjoyed was climbing on top of the wagon for the ride home. The work didn't permit much jawing, but up on top in the wind, bouncing along like we were riding stilts, by and by we'd strike a conversation.

One day we got on the subject of the toughest people we knew, and I mentioned Dan Burkett, a boy from the Youth Home who was part Irish and part ox. He had shoulders like twenty-pound rump roasts and his neck was wider than his head. He wasn't afraid to tuck anyone in his arm, holler "Noogies!" and beat his skull.

"He'd chuck bales like these all day long, and all night too."

"Well," Jordan said, "before Cal busted every bone in his body, he could toss a bale clean over. You could stand on top and jump as it come over, and still miss."

"I don't know. Sounds like a wasted effort. Like maybe he's a bit touched."

"Oh, he's sharp as a tack. Wily-sharp."

"How'd he manage to fall off that beam, then? And get himself in a body cast? That's crazy. Not smart."

"Crazy? You don't have a clue."

"What's that mean?"

"He'll do it someday. All his talk about killin' politicians."

"He's got a ten-gallon mouth."

"Windier than a bag of assholes. But he'll do it. He will. All he wants is to prove he's the toughest, meanest, whatever. You heard the story about him chasing a gutshot deer around a hill thirty times?"

"Right?"

"You know what he did when he found it?"

"You were there?"

"Of course I was there."

"What'd he do?"

"It was still alive. I said I was going to finish him, and had my .30-30 at the base of his neck, so I wouldn't bust his skull and cave his rack. Cal said 'hold up,' and kicked him in the teeth."

"So someday," I said, "when he's squeezing the trigger and there's a fat cat politician at the business end of the barrel, where'll you be?"

"Maybe sitting in the getaway car, listening to the radio."

"You're batshit crazy too," I said.

"Yeah. I suppose. But I'm crazy loyal, see?"

They're all batshit. Burt was, and Cal, and Jordan. Jordan talked up his brother, but it wasn't because he thought Cal was better, or smarter, or crazier. Cal might have been more daring, more needy of the spotlight. But Jordan was cunning. If someday Cal shoots a politician, he'll have gotten the idea of which one to shoot from Jordan, and if either of the two is ever caught and electrocuted, it won't be Jordan.

I shift the riflescope from one snowmobile to the other and in the minutes that have elapsed, colors have begun to resolve. Two of the sleds are green.

The Haudeserts had a shed to the left side of the barn where they stored things; a push lawnmower they never used, a chainsaw, and three green Skiroule snowmobiles.

Two of the six approaching riders must be Cal and Jordan. If they sought me at Haynes's Meats after gathering their posse and then took the fastest route back to Haudesert's, they'd have crossed my tracks on a neck of field between the forest and the lake. Or, as long as it's been, they might have gone back to the farm and followed me all the way here, in which case they'll blame me for Burt and Gwen both. There won't be any explaining to do. Not with Cal already wanting to kill and Jordan urging him on.

The snowmobiles advance across the lake. I aim the scope high, then pull my eye away and focus without the lens. Eight hundred yards? I don't know. I've never shot eight hundred yards, and don't know if a bullet will drop a foot or ten.

They've got murder in their hearts but I've got to give them the opportunity to prove it.

Besides, Sergeant York faced a line of attacking Huns and shot the last one first, and then the next so the closest wouldn't see his comrades fall and lose heart, stop the attack.

I wait.

Three hundred yards is my guess. Two-cycle engine noise comes muffled through the falling snow. The sleds are green and red, like Christmas.

Two hundred yards. The noise separates into the distinct sounds of different engines. I see individual riders on the sleds, each man with a scarf across his face and goggles over his eyes.

Where's the safety? I haven't checked the rifle. I didn't dry fire it. Nervous, I crack the bolt and confirm a chambered round. The safety is forward, but does that mean it's on? I push it back, and hope it operates as Mister Sharps' did.

At one hundred yards the snowmobiles fan and one of the green sleds follows my tracks to where I dropped through the ice. It splashes ahead, throwing water ten feet to each side. The sled bounces over the bank. Another is at the corner where the stream feeds the lake. They're only thirty yards away, maybe, coming from six angles, and I can't see each at the same time. I glance from one to the next and the middle rider waves a pistol in the air with his left hand. His right is on the throttle.

They're coming full speed, but without closing in, as if they intend to pass the house and keep going. I hunker lower.

The man with the pistol aims it toward the window as he zooms closer. He fires and I duck but I don't move a quarter-inch before the window shatters above me and there's a thwack at the other side of the room.

The snowmobiles roar around the house, both sides.

I had a feeling from the beginning that there was no way this would end good.

* * *

Gwen and I spent the night in her father's barn wrapped in coats and each other's arms, tangled in kisses.

We should have left—but we'd gone there to talk, and touch. As the wind outside grew shriller, it was like the air was rarefied and intoxicating.

I couldn't think.

Life is a harsh sport. The memory of rugged things improves the memory of soft things. The barn was frozen and outside, the harvest season had long ago faded into winter, the season of death. The air was winter-clean. The sky was brittle with stars and moonlight. But in our nest of hay, cozied between two winter coats, our talk drew away from escape, and we were warm giggles and sweet breath and perfumed hair, trapped in the forever green scent of hay and body heat.

Hours had passed. I expected at any moment to poke my head above the coat and find dawn upon us. We drifted in and out of sleep. Sometimes I would wake and realize I was kissing her, and she too was waking—so that both of us were roused by the other's kisses. As if something bigger than both of us had commanded us to forget saving our futures and love in the present. Our passion seemed beyond our wills. My hands over her body, hers across mine. My fingers probing. Hers grasping and guiding. My hips thrusting. Hers receiving.

W hen I finished she held me against her, and locked her legs around mine. I propped my weight on my elbows and let my forehead rest in a tangle of her hair. Before long I slipped to the side a little so I could ease the weight off my arms, and we fell asleep again, all the while me inside her.

"GUINEVERE!"

I jumped. It was light out and the hay over us was frosty with our condensed breath. I was stuck in her, dried to her. I grunted. She inhaled. I eased back, and she bucked, saying, "Fast, just pull!"

"Gwen! I know you're in there…"

"Oh shit!" I said. "Oh shit."

"Quick!" she said, hand on my hips, pushing.

I jerked away, rolled aside. She scrambled for her bottoms and I struggled into my underwear, still on one leg, and realized I'd slipped my boot back on after taking my underwear down and now couldn't fit my booted foot through the leg hole, and I'd have to take the boot off again. She searched on top of the coat and then under the coat for her underclothes and quit looking.

"Guinevere! Come out! You too, Gale. I goddamn warned you."

I shoved my boot through my underwear and the heel caught. I ripped it through.

The barn door creaked open and a shaft of morning light spilled inside. I slipped my boot off and wove my foot through a pant leg cold as the snow outside, then shoved my foot back into the boot. I had to face him dressed.

Lord, my heart pounded.

I cinched my belt and tied my shoe. I took Gwen's face in my hands and pressed my forehead to hers and with my eyes open and her eyes open I said, "I love you, Guinevere Haudesert, and don't you ever forget how much."

I pulled away to the edge of the loft.

"Don't!" she said.

I looked back and she crawled closer. I went over the side and found the ladder rungs and while I climbed down, Burt started talking.

"Just what I figured. An alley cat."

Burt worked sideways, his stance like a football player's. Arms wide. Knees bent. Low center of gravity. Legs ready to pounce. A man who'd decided his opponent was more likely to run than throw a punch. A man who'd decided there was no way in hell someone was going to get past him. He shifted closer and closer to the workbench, and I figured he planned to grab a pipe wrench or a hammer.

I stood at the base of the ladder with one hand on it.

"Burt, you got to let us get married. It's the right thing to do."

"What do you know about right!"

"Are you going to try to kill me again? Because I love your daughter and want to take care of her? What's wrong with you?"

He hefted a crescent wrench; in one motion he wound up like a baseball player and whipped it at me. The wrench spun end over end in a whirling silver circle and missed me by a few inches.

I moved sideways. I wanted him outside, away from all those tools. Eventually he'd hit me with one and then I'd be in trouble.

I kept stepping to my left, and he sorted through tools, lifting and dropping them with frustrated jerky movements.

"Burt, you can't do what you been doing with her forever. It ain't the way of things."

He chucked a screwdriver at me, but with too much follow-through. It bounced off the floor a couple feet past me. He looked up and I lifted my eyes to what he saw—a two-by-four suspended by a rope where we'd hung the hogs to cool after slaughter.

Burt lit up.

"Gale, I always liked you. You worked good on the farm..." He held his eyes on mine and talked slow like he was charming a snake while he gradually made his way to the end of the workbench, to an electric grinding wheel.

I crept toward the entrance, still open, and met him with the same tone. "I liked working for you, and I appreciated having a place to sleep and make my living..."

"Then how's come you went trying to steal a sixteen-year-old girl?"

"Well how did you figure it was right to poke your sixteen-year-old daughter?"

Burt was a flash of motion; he reached to the bench and grabbed something dark and hurled it. Pain shot through me. A deer knife stuck from my leg. It had brown and white hair sticking to the handle and clumps of deer fat dried to the finger guard. The blade had found my leg bone and the pain was so sharp I couldn't see straight and could barely stand.

Burt strode toward me with another knife in his hand.

I pulled the knife in my leg—but the point was buried in bone.

Burt trod closer, easily. "What'd you think, boy? You'd come here and have your way with my family? Do as you damn well please and no one'd do anything about it? In my house? With my little girl?"

I fell. Landed on my ass and kicked back a couple feet. He towered above, switched the knife from one hand to the other, as if debating whether he was going to slice my throat from the left or the right.

"Daddy! No!" Gwen teetered at the loft edge, fifteen feet away, twelve feet high. She'd donned her pants and top.

Burt looked to her, and I tugged again at the handle sticking from my leg.

"You just go back a couple feet and turn away," Burt said. "You don't need to see this."

"Can't you give me this one thing?" Gwen said. "Can't you let me go with him? I did what you said. I kept my mouth—"

"You shut up!" He pointed at her with the blade. "Shut your damn mouth."

She wiped her eyes and backed from the edge of the loft. I looked away. On my own again, like every other day. All night I'd been tangled in her limbs and hair and it was a feeling like no other. Pairing up was a metaphysical thing. An illusory thing.

I couldn't run. Couldn't fight him.

"You know the devil's waiting for you, Burt. You can't do that to your own blood and not go to hell for it. No amount of church on Sunday will absolve you. You'll be seventy years old with white hair and quaking hands and you'll be on your knees saying Lord! Lord! And He'll say He doesn't know you."

"Then I won't waste my time on church." He stepped closer. I kicked back. He lunged behind me, wrapped one arm under my armpit and across my chest, and lifted me. I felt his belly behind my head, and I knew what was coming. He wanted to feel my blood on his forearms. He squeezed his arm so tight I couldn't breathe, and raised the blade. "You see that? See the dried blood and hair?"

Gwen ran to the loft edge with a pitchfork in her outstretched arm. She halted, teetered at the edge.

Burt whispered, "I don't know if you're worth this knife, since it split a trophy buck's gut and sawed his meat to cubes. But what am I going to do?"

He drew the knife to my throat.

I opened my mouth but couldn't speak.

"You got anything smart to say now?" His mouth was at my ear. He hadn't seen Gwen. He pressed the blade into my skin.

Gwen stepped back from the edge. Pleaded silently, as if I could save myself. Then she closed her eyes and seemed to burgeon with light and confidence as if drawing from her source of visions and music. She opened her eyes, a preternatural calm flowing from her.

I relaxed.

She nodded.

I blinked an affirmation.

She stepped back two steps, lunged forward, and hurled the pitchfork with magnificent speed and flawless aim.

I threw my head to the side. My knees buckled. The blade scraped over my jaw. Burt froze—maybe he didn't see Gwen at all—and in a split second the pitchfork tines parted my hair. The fork struck Burt's neck and the force knocked both of us backward.

The tines hummed.

I rolled sideways and Burt bucked and wiggled. His arm slapped the barn floor and his throat gurgled but no words came. He kept backhanding the planks and his head flopped, rapping the pitchfork handle to the boards.

He grabbed the handle as if to pull it free and go on with killing me, but his strength failed. He smacked the floor with his other hand. His eyes bulged.

I wheezed and Gwen raced down the ladder. The pain in my leg was like every nerve in my body was scrunched into a ball and lit on fire. And the boys, Cal and Jordan, had to be coming. They had to have heard the commotion. They'd be on us with guns any second.

"Gwen!"

She ran to me and I said, "We got to go before your brothers come!"

"I'm sorry!" she said.

"What?"

"I'm sorry!"

"You saved me."

"Oh God!" She hugged me. Her eyes were wild. "What do we do?"

I grabbed her hand and struggled to the barn door.

Chapter Twenty-four

The men on snowmobiles circle the house.

With the .308 scope, I track the pistol-waving rider on the green Skiroule. I could blow his head off—just like a squirrel on the run, or a bird on the fly—except when I stand before the Lord having to admit responsibility for a man's death, I want it to be a matter of not having had a choice. It's incumbent on the moral man to bend as much as he can while the idiot avails himself of the facts. I don't want the fellow I shot to be up there with the Lord filling His ear with nonsense.

But is a clean conscience a luxury?

I let the man on the Skiroule pass through my sights because he wears a ski mask and I don't know if it is Cal or Jordan or someone else I'll be killing. But this whole situation is starting to torque my sense of right and wrong. This whole setup is about intimidation. Swarming over the house on growling sleds, waving guns, firing a shot into the window…

Who the hell do they think they are?

Engines mutter on the other side of the house. The sound drifts from all around, and one by one the motors go silent until a final snowmobile engine runs and it too sputters to a stop.

All is silent. Crouching beside the lake-facing, shot-out window, I smell sweet exhaust fumes. In my mind's eye, I see them hiding behind trees. Low-crawling to the house, pushing rifles through snow.

A window crashes and a rifle sounds. I scrunch lower. Glass tinkles to the kitchen counter—on the other side of the house. I peek to the window; no one's on this side. I leave the rifle and scramble across the living room, slipping in the deputy's jellied blood. Scramble up the stairs and enter the first room on the right. I stand beside the window and peer steeply to the ground.

Thirty feet from the house, a man hides behind a tree. From the angle of his rifle, he's the one who shot into the house. Ready to take my life when he doesn't know what he knows? So self-sure he's ready to kill? Wrong and all? Why doesn't he call me out, if he intends to take me into custody?

Fuck him.

I cross the room, down the hall and slip into the last room. At the window, the angle gives me a clear field to the man's head. A ski-masked orb that, darker, might resemble a growth on the tree trunk. Without raising the window, I lift the rifle, check the load, and rest the muzzle against the glass.

How much will the angle throw off my picture? I don't know.

I'll shoot twice.

The man swings his rifle to another window, to his right, and fires. I pull the trigger, but the safety is on. I flip the lever. Another villain, somewhere, fires into the house.

One at a time, boys.

Half his head is above my front sight post. Safety off. Exhale nice and easy. Lungs empty, I squeeze.

The rifle bucks. The window shatters. I slam the bolt open and closed and aim again. The man's body is prone and jiggling and it looks like a water balloon of red paint broke in the snow. I fire again into his torso and duck from the window. A bullet shatters the top pane and glass shards pepper my cheek. The shot came from my left. I look again—must have been a shotgun to have taken so much glass. I leave the rifle, and limp down the hall to the bedroom I visited first.

New rifle in hand, I swoop below the window and scan the snowy lawn for my enemy with the shotgun from the other side. He stands behind a tree, barely exposed. Looks like a shadow, an obscene six-foot cancer on the side of the tree trunk.

I'll chip him out. I aim for the tree edge, head-high, and fire.

The window crashes and the man lurches away. He dances with his hand at his face, rifle at his side, while I cycle another shell. I aim again while he moves. His keeps finding the same right limit, like a birthday candle on a spinning cake, only his motions are more erratic. I wait, and time my shot.

A bullet crashes into the room. Quick, I exhale. Fire.

He drops.

Fuck him too.

Shots sound from several weapons at once. I drop to the floor as the wall puffs plaster and the doorjamb splinters. I don't know where they're coming from—I didn't see anyone else hiding, but there are plenty of trees.

Downstairs, the front door bursts open. Clomping footsteps. I count shots outside, subtract dead men…there is only one inside. The rifle fire outside continues; lead chips at the walls. Glass breaks. Rifle resting on my outstretched arms, sweeping broken glass with my elbows, I slither across the floor and into the hallway. Five feet ahead is the stairs. Below, unseen, the invader is at the foot. Has his rifle trained on the space above me, no doubt. He knows the room from which I fired.

My advantage fades with each moment I allow my adversary's eyes to adjust. The Lord favors the bold? I shift forward, ever quiet, my rifle inches above the hardwood floor. I straighten the barrel before reaching the stairwell, and press close to the right wall.

"I know you're up there, Gale!"

It's Cal.

"Hey, asshole!" He fires and the ceiling showers dust and plaster chips. Before he cycles another round I squirm forward, point the barrel over the edge. No time for sights. I point. Fire. Cal staggers sideways. He's still got his rifle—he's lifting it. I winged him. I flip the lever action rifle open and closed as Cal draws his rifle to me.

He never cycled a fresh shell into the chamber. He doesn't know it.

"Put the rifle down, Cal."

"You killed my pap."

"I didn't kill anyone."

"You son of a bitch." He clings to the wall with one hand and points the rifle with the other.

His hand tightens, as if squeezing an unready trigger. He looks at his hand.

"I didn't kill your father, Cal. Go on. Call off your boys."

Cal slaps the bolt open.

I can't get a sight picture in the half-light, but my barrel points to his face.

Cal shoves the bolt home. Raises the rifle...

Fuck him.

Cal's head snaps back and red spatters the wall. He drops.

A fusillade opens. Sounds like every remaining window shatters. Bullets zing. I drop to my knees. The fire comes from all angles, but there's only three shooters, so which side of the house is unrepresented? I close my eyes. More shots ring out. Two come from the lake side and one from the front.

I shuffle to the last room on the opposite side of the hallway. From the floor, I glance out the broken window to frozen tree crowns. Sporadic shots splinter the wood. I approach from the side so that first the lake and then the drifted snow comes into view. Footprints betray where a man left the cover of one tree to find it behind another.

The other? Twenty yards away, working his way closer as he fumbles shells into his rifle's internal magazine.

I aim. Fuck him.

A near-instant response from the man on this side of the house zips past my ear. He's smarter than the rest. Maybe this is Jordan, the family genius. Another bullet rips through the window molding. He waits for me to show myself. I slip to the hallway, shove the rifle across the other bedroom floor and go to the stairwell. Slither down the steps face first.

I avoid Cal's corpse and cross the living room. The fire is low. I grab the rifle leaning against the wall and stand a dozen feet back from the window, studying the snow outside. The tracks. The shadows behind trees.

My adversary hides. Fine. From the sound of the rifle fire there's a man out front with nothing to protect him. I switch to the kitchen and peer from the window's bottom corner.

There's nothing out there but a red Bolens snowmobile. The sled's track cuts through unbroken snow, and no footprints lead away. The sled's rider must be crouching behind the seat.

The gas tank is under the hood, at the nose.

I glance out the window to my left, then right—to the living room window. Jordan's out there, somewhere.

I aim at the tip of the snowmobile and fire through the window. Glass sprays to the porch. Nothing happens—but what did I expect, shooting through fiberglass and plastic? I check the lake-facing window again. Cycle the spent shell from the chamber. Loaded and cocked, I take my time aligning my sights to the leaf spring on the closest ski.

I fire.

Lead clangs on steel—but why am I playing games, trying to start a fire?

I aim below the seat and fire. Through the track, and fire. Through the hood again, and fire. Through the track twice more. Whoever hid behind rubber and foam and bogey wheels is dead or bleeds from big, deep holes.

Fuck him. I eject the spent cartridge and cycle what should be the last round into the chamber.

"You killed my father."

I whirl. A ski-masked face peers from behind rifle sights, aimed through the window across the living room. He must stand on the deputy's corpse, or close to it.

"Jordan?"

"You killed him in cold blood—after he took you in. Gave you a job, 'cause he pitied you."

"That's not how it happened, Jordan."

Keeping the rifle aimed with his trigger hand and arm, he removes his ski mask. "That's a load of shit. You was pissed he wouldn't let you take Gwen away. Girl that age has no use marrying. Must be a pervert to think so. Is that you, Gale?"

"Your daddy was screwing her."

"What'd you say?"

"You heard me. And you knew it the whole time."

"Bullshit."

I glance at the entry to the kitchen and the country hutch standing flush to the jamb. In all, maybe enough to slow a bullet.

I've got one shot left in the chamber.

"Warn't enough that you left my father choking on blood. Where's Gwen? Where'd you leave her?"

His eyes flit across the room. He leans from the window and glances to his right, to the red Bolens snowmobile.

"Who rode the Bolens?" I say.

"You wouldn't know him."

"He needs your help, Jordan. He's bleeding."

"Where's Gwen? Only one set of tracks across the lake. You leave her in the woods?"

"Way the snow's blowing, I don't know. She'll be hard to find."

"Did you kill her?"

"No."

"Liar! Just like you didn't kill Pap?"

In the low firelight, he hasn't seen Cal's body at the foot of the stairwell.

I shift my weight from my bad knee to my good one. Press my strong foot against the wall. "There's a whole lot of killing today that isn't my fault. About the only way it could've been avoided is if I'd have said, 'Okay, Burt. Go ahead and cut me up.' Then things would've been ducky by you. That it?" I slip my hand forward on the stock, wrap my finger around the trigger.

Jordan glares into my eyes.

Rifle pointed at the ceiling, stock butt on the floor, I squeeze the trigger. The weapon bounces and roars. I shove off through the noise. I'm half across the opening and Jordan's rifle flashes. A bullet rips through my left arm, spinning me against the bottom cupboards.

Momentum carries me forward. I worm to the window on the far side of the kitchen, and a lever action .30-30. I try to reach with my wounded arm but it hangs. There's no pain, yet. I swipe the .30-30 with my good hand. Jordan's boots clomp on the front porch.

He saw me leave the other rifle—he thinks I'm unarmed.

I wiggle to the basement door and press my bloody arm to the paint so Jordan can make no mistake.

Downstairs, the air is a wall of winter, but it's the dead men around me that make me shiver. I killed the deputy after coming out of sleep and had no decision to make. Pulling the trigger wasn't the result of cause and effect, knowledge and action, so much as mere effect. Action.

But these other five on snowmobiles—their deaths resulted from volition. Will.

I move slowly, unable to see. Jordan's footsteps sound through the floor above and signal his progress into the kitchen. I ease another few steps. My arm is limp but I feel my fingers; I press to the banister. Sweat stands cold on my brow.

"You can't get away, Gale!"

A shadow crosses the doorway.

I cover the hammer with my entire hand and palm it back. Even still, the click rings. Half-cocked is no good. I press farther and it lodges all the way back. He must have heard.

"I didn't kill your father, Jordan. I didn't like him, but I didn't kill him."

"Liar!"

"No! He was raping your sister!"

"You goddamn liar!"

"I was trying to save her. What the hell were you doing, living in the same house with all that going on? You saw it like I did—at the dinner table! Too chickenshit to help your own *sister*."

Jordan stands in the light, a silhouette of an angry man, arms raised as if to fight a shadow that moves lightning fast.

"You knew, God damn you! God damn you! You saw him grab her legs at the kitchen table and you heard him walk the hallways at night. You damn sure saw the way she hid from him.

You'd rather raise hell about the evils goin' on half a country away than face the scourge in your own house."

"I didn't know."

"You made sure you didn't know. She needed you!"

I lift the rifle with one arm, nudge the stock tight to my shoulder. Press my cheek on the pad and align the rifle tube with the black orb that is Jordan's head.

Fuck him.

Chapter Twenty-five

Balls feel like two pounds of lead. I gotta squirt. Fenny scrunches her shoulders. She knows from my eyes that she's about to get bent over.

"Shouldn't you be trying to see the doctor before you hit the floor one last time? And if you're too stubborn for that, shouldn't you be up at Coates's place? I know Odum's playing like he's in charge, but couldn't he use your help? Travis said—"

"I heard Travis. I'll be along. I'm working a different angle."

I unbuckle, still sitting on the edge of her desk. From here I can see the lot through the front window. In twenty-five years with Fenny, only was interrupted once. 1951. Only had one deputy, and he was at a car wreck on Nineteen. We had all the time in the world, until a vagabond wandered in. She was pretty in a rough way, clean body inside dirty clothes. Hair as red as the inside of a rotten grapefruit—and I've always appreciated reds. I stood there drilling Fenny's backside while her face was against the desk. This young girl watched and came closer and swallowed like to clear her throat. Held her purse to her breast. Transfixed by meat. I reached to her and brought her in. Memories.

Fenny giggles. She's wearing a skirt that'll pull up easy enough. But that's in a minute. She's got oral work first.

"You sure got hay on your horns today," Fenny says.

I'm out of my drawers and she plants her hands on the corner of the desk and stoops forward. She likes to tease and nibble. I wrap my hand around the base of her skull and cinch her closer. Tight. "That's right. Breathe through your nose."

She makes a sound like clearing phlegm and that's the trigger. Some nerve fires and I gorge full and Fenny struggles to pull away.

"Through your nose."

She gags. In a moment it'll be teeth. I let her off and as she reels back, I take her by the upper arm to the side of the desk, where we'll both be pointed at the entrance. Toss that skirt up and snake around her old-woman panties. Dry on the outside, but a goddamn swimming pool inside. You got to go slow with an old girl. It's the only way she's got a grip.

Travis's voice on the radio busts my concentration. "Fenny? Fenny? Where's Odum?"

Fenny reaches to the microphone and presses the button. "Sheriff…He went back to the Haudesert's for a while."

"Well, how about Bittersmith? Can't he come out?"

"I'll send him soon as I see him."

From here it's steady, slow work. Eyes on the window. I think about falling on Fay Haudesert's porch. My back is stove up and that makes me wonder if that episode in the field when my arm hurt and things went hazy really was a prelude to the big one. I'd love to go stuck in a woman. But maybe not Fenny.

One more shot at Margot and I'd be ready to call it quits.

Fenny grunts like a sow as I finish. I wipe myself with a handkerchief she keeps in the desk. She takes it when I'm done and clamps it to her gizzy and runs to the bathroom.

"I'm going to Coates's," I call, but instead I sit and catch my breath. Out the window, the snow falls straight down and the sun is deep into afternoon. Shadows lengthen, almost as

I watch. Everything's a shadow. The fellow that stabbed my little Guinevere is out there. I hope he's braving the storm with nothing but corduroy pants and flannel. I hope the son of a bitch has ice in his eyebrows.

Fenny flushes the commode. I take the badge off my chest and drop it on her desk.

Slip out before she comes back and starts loving on me.

Chapter Twenty-six

Snow falls.

I've got corpses all over the place that'll be buried in a couple hours.

My arm doesn't work. My leg protests with each step. I'm coming down from the heady elation of surviving six men with guns.

I could take off right now and maybe I'd get away. But I'd be leaving unsettled business.

Doctor Coates's house could be my last stand. I don't know how I'd fare in the wild with a couple of holes in me, and I can't expect much friendliness from civilization. More men will come and I might as well face them here as anywhere.

Part of me thinks in terms of obedience. Mister Sharps said get a mop bucket and hit the cafeteria floor so it sparkles, and I did. Burt Haudesert said we'll be getting up early tomorrow because we got fifty acres of corn to get in, and I said okay, just wake me. And Mister Haynes said take this knife and press it to the cow's neck right here, where the swell of her shoulder ends and there's a little vale between muscle groups, and slit from the bottom to the top, fast and deep—and I did. My lot was doing as I was told.

But on my own, things are different. Months of working for Burt and then Haynes revealed that although Mister Sharps always did the right thing, other men are different. Most are like that old fool Schuckers who didn't know how to spell his name so it would make sense and thought he could take advantage of a bunch of boys just because no one wanted them. And Burt taught me the lesson, best of all.

Burt Haudesert showed me even family isn't a strong enough tie to keep a man straight and just. If a man wants something bad enough, he'll step on anyone at all to get it and then make up whatever justification he needs.

Burt also clarified thinking that Mr. Sharps had laid the foundation for. Though the lesson didn't apply to Burt's daughter, he said free citizens had rights granted by their very births that had to be jealously guarded. He said there was no authority so high that a man had to subject himself to it against his conscience.

I'd just add that God gave me my morals and if they run counter ten thousand men with guns, I'll stand alone.

The first I exercised this thinking was against Burt, when I tried to take Gwen away from him.

Hip deep in bodies and blood, the whole thing makes sense. Burt's ideas influenced me, and though I knew challenging him for Gwen was a crisis of obedience and expeditiousness versus moral reasoning and standing against a world gone mad, the latter ideas were comfortable like a truth I've always known, and following them gave me the thrill of being in for an honorable fight.

All that adds up to where I am right now, with a total of seven bodies, counting the deputy, cooling in the snow. Each dead from bullet holes I gave him. I don't expect Saint Peter will get his robes rumpled over it, but a judge surely will.

But I'll never explain this in a court of law.

At the last supper, Jesus turned to Judas and said, do what you have to do, and Satan entered Judas at that moment. But if

Jesus had held his tongue, would Judas have gone on like any other disciple? Did God give him a charge he could entrust to no other? When I missed my head with the carbine, was God sparing me, that I might accomplish some other task?

God has so many excellent ways of taking someone out, there's only one reason to have a man do it: to remind other men that in the case of protecting their little girls, they should have been culling the rapists all along.

The story of Judas always fascinated me.

Haynes told me about Sheriff Bittersmith, the sole arbiter of the law and truth and justice in town during the nine months before my birth. I know all about Bittersmith I need to know. Haynes related an incident with a niece of his that sounded quite like what Mister Sharps remembered about my mother.

I'm not going to leave knowing Sheriff Bittersmith is around to sow another bastard orphan. Coming full circle, I've only got one future. I'll stay here and fight until there are no more comers.

If there's more need killed after that, I'll find them.

Life sweeps along, full speed. I'm doing things so far beyond yesterday's imagination I don't know where they're coming from. When Jesus told Judas to go ahead and betray Him, maybe Judas thought the same thing. Maybe he said, "Are you fucking kidding? Lord?" And none of the disciples wrote down those words.

All these dead bodies tell a story, but the lawmen and townsfolk reading the pages are going to skip lines. Miss the justification.

I tend my arm. The bullet passed all the way through, just under the ball of my shoulder. I can't lift my limb horizontally. I can curl a little, with struggle. I smear the entrance and exit holes with ointment and stick a gauze pad to each, and propping my elbow on the sink while standing on my knees, wrap the whole thing with a bandage. When I lower my arm the wrappings cut my circulation and I have to redo everything.

Meanwhile the sky outside the window darkens. A heavy swath of snow-laden clouds is about to bury the bodies before I've had a chance to move them.

Sometimes the sparrow has to relax and know the food is going to be there.

I get my arm fixed so I can let it hang and the bandage isn't too tight. I take another shirt and sweater from the doctor's bureau. If he's watching, I bet it gives him indigestion, being a doctor, how many of his clothes are soaked in blood.

In all the excitement I'd forgotten that I'm wearing a revolver. The leather belt eats into my side and I loosen the buckle one notch, and adjust the way it rests on my hip. I put more wood on the fire, and fully dressed for winter, face the blizzard.

I want the exterior to look as much like it did before I came as possible. I don't want the sheriff to see a field of battle, strewn with corpses and dead machinery. I want him to wonder, aside from the smoke, if there's anyone here.

The red Bolens snowmobile is out front. A film of snow covers the seat. I glance left, across the field to where the deputy had parked his car. The snow falls so heavily I can only faintly see I am alone.

I reach the snowmobile. Slowly, almost afraid to see the corpse of the man I shot through the tracks, I lean over the seat.

There's no body.

Chapter Twenty-seven

Going easy, the Bronco tread holds. Word about the storm is out. No one's on the roads. I'll leave it in all four wheels for the duration. I turn onto 19 and head north. Wipers flapping, heater blasting. I drive with one hand at the bottom of the wheel. So easy to slide, you got to relax or you'll end up in a ditch. There's hardly a track, and after I pass Nordic Lumber, drifts from the bank force me into the opposing lane for a long stretch. If another vehicle approaches, one of us is short-term fucked. But I get through and back to my lane. No one's out. I'm two mile from Coates's.

"Uh, Josephus…Sheriff Bittersmith," Fenny calls on the radio.

"You don't have to call me 'sheriff,' Fenny."

"It's all so bad. Just awful."

"What's going on?"

"Odum swung by the station. Wanted to know where you were with the Bronco."

"What? He figured on taking it?"

"He's just stepped out to go to Coates's and wanted me to get on the horn and make damn sure you wasn't going there too."

"You tell him I won't be in his way."

"He's a damn fool—" Static cuts her off. "—a lot of shooting, and Travis is waiting a little past the driveway in the cover of the woods."

"You're breaking up, Fenny. I'll holler at you later."

So, Sheriff Odum's got a situation. He's got a killer holed up in a house that has more rifles than a National Guard armory—and not just any killer. A wild boy out of the Youth Home, brung up with no conscience or principles. A killer who'll do it with a pitchfork, or up close with a knife. Up so close he could've smelled Gwen's sweet breath.

Green sheriff is going to take a green deputy, Travis, and a useless deputy, Sager, against Gale G'Wain.

* * *

I press my knees to the Bolens' seat and hold the steering bar. Not only is there no body, there never was. The snow is unbroken.

The hair on the back of my neck stands.

Footprints—hazy with accumulated snow and wind—follow the wide snowmobile track toward the lake and diverge at a sizable hardwood that stands on the knoll, stark against the sky. A knob on the trunk doesn't seem right—it's a man with a rifle aimed at my heart.

I keep turning, like I hadn't noticed, while the man at the tree decides whether he has the conscience to be a murderer.

I head for the house at an angle that will quickly carry me beyond my adversary's sight. He'll have to adjust around the tree to track me, something he'll avoid if he's the coward I hope. Until today I wouldn't have known how easy it is to sit with your gun on someone and not have the courage to kill him. Still, each step I advance without another bullet in my body feels like a small miracle.

I imagine the spatial relationships of the house, my tangent, the tree, the rifle—to guess whether I've traveled far enough to hazard looking over my shoulder—giving away that I know his presence—

I glance.

The tree trunk is straight on both sides.

I draw the revolver from under my coat and pivot toward the tree, quickening my pace and pointing ahead, ready to blast at the first movement. Each step crunches the snow. My fingertips tingle. My socks have slipped and bunched at my toes. A nasal drip that normally I'd blast free with a quick exhalation tickles the tip of my nose. I draw closer and closer to the tree. Close enough to see the black-suited leg of a man on the slope, his toe dug into the snow. I approach from the right; his rifle points around the left. He'll have no way to swing it to me.

I step broadly around the tree and point at his chest.

"Who you waiting for?"

He says nothing. Slowly twists his head. "I couldn't do it."

The voice is falsely guttural. Female?

"Roll over."

"I had you in my sights and I couldn't pull the trigger," she says. "And now I'm going to die."

That voice is familiar. "Shut up and roll over. Who are you?"

She wears a full-body snowmobile suit and a balaclava with the flaps across her cheeks. I push her hip with my toe and she rolls away, jerks the rifle barrel into the tree.

"Hold up! I'm not shooting so there's no need to go crazy. Easy. Who are you?"

She's on her back. The balaclava covers her mouth but her eyes are black hot beads and her nostrils widen with each exhalation. She is not as young as Gwen, but young. Maybe as young as Gwen. I don't know.

"She loved you and you killed her for it."

"You're wrong. Who are you? What do you know of anything?" I glance across the lake and turn for a quick look at the road. Something in the trees doesn't look right.

"Well, who are you, dammit?"

"Go ahead and kill me if you're going to anyway. What do you care who I am?"

"Why'd you come with these guys? Get up." I nudge her with my toe. Her voice is way too familiar. "Get up, damn you!"

She rolls partly away from me but doesn't rise. "Get up!" I fire the revolver into the snow beside her. "Now!"

She braces her hands on her knees and stands. Her nylon snowmobile suit sounds like a symphony of zippers.

I remember being on Burt Haudesert's barn floor, kicking my feet to get away, knowing I was about to die. I don't know who this girl is but the anger in her eyes is made of the same stuff as the anger behind mine. Born of helplessness in the face of injustice—and dangerous because it only burns so hot before it eats away the crucible and spills out.

She's like me and if I can't make her see it, I'm going to have to kill her.

"Take your hat off." I lower my revolver. "Drop the rifle."

She does both. I holster my revolver and study her face.

Liz. The girl who tried to seduce me in Haynes's shed.

Thanks, Lord.

"I'm not going to hurt you. I only killed these guys because they came after me. And I didn't kill Burt Haudesert, like they thought. And I didn't kill Gwen, like you think."

"Then where is she?"

"She's dead. I had to leave her."

Liz stares straight ahead and I know she's wondering if she can drop to her rifle before I draw the pistol.

"I didn't kill her."

"But she's truly gone?"

"Yeah." I have to look away. "Yeah. Hey, you're not going stand around out here while I've got work to do. We're going to go to your sled, Liz Sunday, and you're going to start it. I shot the gas tank, so it isn't going to go very far. I want you to drive around the back of the house. If you take off, you'll have a long walk in a blizzard. Get to it."

"If I take off, you'll just kill me."

"Start the sled and move it to the back of the house."

"Why?"

"Damn! Do it." I march toward the sled as best I can on my wounded leg and realize I'm the only one moving. I turn, and Liz has the rifle pointed at my belly.

"Did she ever tell you about her father?" I say.

Liz nods.

"So you know why I had to take her away."

"I don't know why you killed her."

I shake my head and turn from her. Continue to the Bolens. Any instant a bullet could smash through my spine and I'll be in the snow readying a host of questions for the Almighty about Judas. But I'm not going to shoot the girl and I don't have the patience to answer her questions. Man's perennial quandary.

Her anger is my anger, and she needs a minute to sort it out. A minute with the rifle back in her hands so she isn't performing the calculus under the threat of my revolver. She'll come to the right conclusion. I'm betting it's why she didn't kill me when she had her first chance.

I straddle the sled and leaning makes my leg howl. I grit my teeth. It isn't the first time. I twist the key and look over the carburetor for a choke mechanism, but maybe I won't need the choke since the engine was running a short while ago. I twist to maneuver my bad left hand onto the throttle; once it is there I can squeeze the lever. The starter cord is directly below. I grab the toggle, yank it, and the motor sputters. Again, with less success. A third time, and the smell of gasoline is strong.

"It's ornery," Liz says, behind me.

"You start the damn thing."

"Here." She offers the rifle to me, stock first. I take it and step off the sideboards.

"I flooded it."

"You can't give it any gas at all."

Liz boards the snowmobile and eases the starter a half pull. Her rear end protrudes and her back arches; in an explosive move she whips her body and yanks the cord. Farm girl. The motor sputters; she nurses it to life. The engine catches and coughs. After a few seconds of being unable to smooth its tempo, she applies gas in a series of bursts, easing just before the engine bogs, and gradually turns the sled. Immediately shy of the house, the motor dies. Liz lifts the back end by a bar below the taillight, and swings the snowmobile ninety degrees so the entire machine is hidden from the road out front. She stands with her hands on her knees, breathing hard.

"I need to get each one of these snowmobiles behind the house," I say.

"Let me catch my breath."

"You're no more a killer than I am."

She studies me and her eyes have no sparkle whatsoever.

Four more snowmobiles wait on the road-facing side of the house. The last is at the back. Liz crosses in front of the porch on a tangent for the farthest, about thirty yards beyond the other sleds, parked closer to the windrow of trees where their riders died.

I prop Liz's rifle against the porch and head for the sled at the back. It starts on a single pull. The feisty snowmobile jumps with the slightest gas, easily spinning the track through a turn. I park next to the basement entrance, a sloped, six-foot door covered in snow like the surrounding yard. The engine rumbles to a stop and I look across the lake and back to the basement door and back to the lake.

I move to the corner of the house and look across the porch to the woods by the road. That darkness at the edge of the trees…it's still there. Bigger. A car joined by a second vehicle.

Liz approaches on one of the green Skiroules. Either Cal or Jordan rode it to his death. I think of Fay Haudesert and how alone she's going to feel come the end of the day—her solitude the reaping of what she sowed by knowing what her man was doing under her roof and never stopping it.

Liz kills the motor and says, "What are you looking at?"

"I was thinking. Who'd you come here with?"

"Link."

"Link…Sunday?"

"My brother. That's none of your concern."

She jumps from the snowmobile, circles the house. It's no use now, of course. They're out there waiting.

Which corpse is her brother? Her disregard spurs my imagination. Have I managed to execute another young man who thought his sister's welfare was none of his concern?

How did Liz wind up with this murderous posse?

I look at the basement entrance. Another snowmobile rumbles closer, this time from the rear of the house. Liz heads for the lake and at the last minute banks a semicircle turn. The headlight bounces and cuts through the flurries. Liz holds the motor wide-open as she races closer and at the last instant cuts left and then right and slides to a stop. The skis rest against the stone foundation. She jumps from the sled and strides around the house.

Liz retrieves the remaining machines and parks them. I dig through the snow on the sloped basement door. As she approaches on the last, I flag her and greet her with her rifle and prevent her from parking with the sled's nose to the wall.

"What?" she yells above the motor.

I draw a line across my throat. She hits the kill switch.

I offer the rifle to her. "Get out of here. Go home."

She crosses her arms.

"I don't want you here," I say. "There's going to be a lot of trouble soon, and if you stay you'll be part of it."

"Where's Gwen?"

"In the woods, straight back from the Haudesert house. Across the field. I'm sure the sheriff and his men have found her by now. We only made it a mile."

"What happened?"

I shove the rifle to her and this time she accepts. I step away. "Go! Get out of here."

She eyes me for a few seconds before placing the rifle lengthwise on the seat. She starts the engine again. I return to cleaning snow from the sloped door. All but uncovered, I brush snow from the latch, revealing a lock. I try it, quickly, though I can see it is secure. Behind me, the snowmobile idles. Half expecting her to have the rifle trained on my back, I turn.

She sits.

"Go!"

"I'm not leaving until I know what happened to her."

I pull the revolver from my holster and Liz's eyes widen. I kneel, place the barrel to the lock, sideways so the bullet will pass through to the dirt on the side of the basement entrance. I pull the trigger and the lock blows open. I flip the latch, holster my weapon, and open the basement.

"This is how it happened," I say, and begin with Burt dragging me across the field by my feet to kill me.

* * *

To my right, set back two hundred yards off the road, sits the Coates house.

My old friend Coates wouldn't mind that murderous bastard G'Wain squatting in his house, but Coates was a doctor and a churchman. A man of lifelong poor judgment.

The barn burned long ago, so now the estate is a dingy house looking like a piss spot in a blanket of snow. A two-story piss spot with smoke pouring out the chimney. Snowed-in footprints go from the driveway to the house.

I'm in the Bronco, parked in front of Travis's car. He gets out, fights through the snow to my window, and I wave him around to the passenger side and he gets in. He claps the snow from his feet and rubs his hands by the heater vent. To the right, trees obscure my view of the house.

"Roosevelt's in trouble," he says.

"How long you been here?"

Travis gives a sheepish look that doesn't fit his square face. "Twenty, thirty minutes. I cleaned Mrs. Whitmore's steps and came out on a quick patrol."

"Well, you don't have to worry about a thing. Sheriff Odum's on his way." I'm silent and he reads it like an invitation. His eyes shift. He's nervous.

"Fenny said Odum was tied up at Haudesert's," Travis says. "As for Roosevelt, I've heard quite a few shots, not counting that one right after you pulled up. And a man's been moving snowmobiles to the other side of the house. There's foot tracks up the driveway to the house—old tracks. Like Roosevelt parked at the drive and walked up. Smoke spouting out the chimney since I came. I scouted up the road and found Roosevelt's car run clear over the ditch and into the woods, like the pedal was pressed to the floor. The snow's tore up and the car's sunk in it like he spun the tires after he was stuck."

I nod.

"Then, a set of tracks go straight into the woods."

I tamp my pipe with tobacco. Wait for Travis. He says nothing more. "What's that tell you?"

"Roosevelt's in trouble. But that's not why. I got here and there were six snowmobiles out front and on the side, and a whole mess of shooting."

"Hard to see why Roosevelt parked at the drive, walked to the house, came back to wreck his car, and returned through the woods to help the bad guy in a shootout against the militia."

Travis shakes his head. "I think Roosevelt went up and got himself killed. The killer tried a getaway and wrecked the car. These others? Most likely they followed our killer's tracks across the lake."

"You'll be sheriff one day," I say. "If you put a plan together."

Chapter Twenty-eight

Gwen and I hurried across the field. I paid attention to the knife sticking from my leg and she rushed me forward. We'd crossed a quarter-mile and the agony was so bad I stopped. She came back to me and I noticed she favored one leg and was missing a shoe. It was hard to think. Her foot already had to be frost bitten, but she tramped along without complaint. I looked back the way we came and no one was coming after us. I had no coat, and she had no shoe.

"Pull this out," I said.

She came to me. I fell on the field and she put one knee on each side of the knife handle, and pulled it straight, but it wouldn't come. Finally she rocked side to side and the pain brought black borders tight on my field of vision. Torture came in dark waves and I leaned back into the snow, and I was unconscious for I don't know how long. When I came to, she was rubbing her foot between her hands.

"We've got to go back," I said.

"We can't. Cal and Jordan'll kill you."

She got to her feet and braced to help me up.

"Wait," I said. "Where's the knife?"

She had it in her front pocket, the blade out.

"You shouldn't carry it like that," I said.

I cut my pant leg above the knee, all the way around, and

pulled it over my foot. We were only a few miles from town. If we went as fast as possible, we could get her into shelter and her foot warm. I wiggled closer to Gwen. "Let me work on you for a minute."

I brushed the snow from her and found her socks were thin and almost worn through at the heel. I clasped her feet and for the first time since waking in the loft, shivered. We were in the open field with nothing to stop the wind. My hands were numb. I slipped my pant leg over her foot and then removed it, folded it on itself to double its thickness, and slipped it over again. Cloth covered beyond her ankle; all I could ask. I cut a strip from my pant leg and tied her toe closed, and another to cinch the makeshift boot at her ankle.

I rubbed her foot a moment.

"It's already warm," she said.

"Let's hurry."

* * *

As I tell Liz my story, I lead her into the basement through the sloped wall door and search in the dim light, for the inevitable boards that will be held in reserve. I've worked for enough farmers to know there isn't a single one that doesn't have a ramp to get his wheel barrow or lawn mower or antique motorcycle out of the basement. Doctor Coates is no different. He's got three two-by-tens stacked vertically on the side of the steps so they don't warp under their own weight. Liz helps me position them on the steps. I use a railroad tie—apparently kept by the doctor for the same purpose—to support the ends of the boards on the last step so the door can be closed with the ramp in place.

Liz finds a two-gallon metal fuel can in the basement and we use it to drain the gasoline-oil mixed fuel from one of the snowmobiles' tanks and fill the sled I parked next to the basement entrance. With the tank full, we fill the can again and strap it to the metal floor in the gap between the seat and the engine mounts. I reload a rifle from upstairs and slip it into a two-foot leather scabbard riveted to a box built below the seat and shove a box of bullets into a storage compartment behind the taillight. Last, I drag the duffel from the wall by the front door, down the stairwell to the basement, and leave it against the wall by the ramp.

In the phraseology of war novels, this might be an expeditionary assault snowmobile.

Liz starts the sled, drives toward the lake and back to the house, then eases into the basement. She putts down the ramp and kills the engine. Together we slide the nose back toward the exit.

The final touch is a few armloads of snow over the ramp. Liz will not leave, or let me, until I finish my story. Yet I sense that like the night she visited me at Haynes's, another motive lurks between her words and deeds.

Chapter Twenty-nine

"What are you thinking, Sheriff?" Travis says. His face is earnest, looking for answers.

"Did you follow the trail from Roosevelt's cruiser?"

"No. I radioed and waited for your call. That's when Fenny told me about Odum being sheriff now."

"So you did nothing."

"I wasn't supposed to be here… And I didn't know…"

"What?"

"Didn't know if you had something else in mind. Some other plan."

Travis is smart. Maybe learned in the Army to avoid leading his leader. But him thinking I'm working some kind of plan means everybody else'll think the same. I'm sitting here debating how to look like I'm doing right when all I want is to murder Gale G'Wain.

"Go back to Roosevelt's vehicle. Follow the tracks until you're sure they go to Coates's place. It's going to take a few minutes until your new sheriff gets here. He'll need to know beyond a shadow of a doubt whether Roosevelt's in that house, or whether he's one more body, out in that."

Travis opens the door. Wind blasts inside and snow scatters across the dash.

"One more thing, Travis. Things are in a flux now. You

might think on what kind of opportunity presents in situations like this."

He holds my look a long minute and nods like he's only barely aware.

He'll figure it out.

Travis closes the door and tramps to his car. Spins tires and swerves around the Bronco. In a moment, I'm alone with the trees and the empty cold between them. Alone with a killer two hundred yards away.

Twenty years ago, I'd have walked up to that house and come back with a prisoner or a body. But now, after a blowjob, heart attack, and a mediocre lay, all I got left is my wits. Seventy years of wiliness.

I lift the radio. "Fenny—"

"Sheriff?"

"Send Sager out here. Tell him to bring two ought-sixes."

"Odum's already issued that command."

"Brilliant."

Travis's taillights disappear ahead. I don't know if it's from snow obscuring visibility or if he's already at the bend.

I pull Fay Haudesert's photo of G'Wain from my pocket. It's gotten damp and the lower corner has a purple hue. His face is skinny now, Fay said. Skinny like mine. Skinny like I remember him a couple months back at the grocery, nebbing in my affairs, watching sly from the end of the aisle.

The red-haired vagabond—I don't know if I ever asked her name. Back then, I was like a rancher naming cattle. Why bother when there was so many and I had my brand on each ass?

Nineteen-fifty-one—and Gale is now twenty, and raised at the Monroe Youth Home.

I'll look any fact in the face. I got kids all over this town; some know me and some don't. Burt wasn't the first or the last.

It's why we're here: there's nothing before and nothing after, so why shouldn't I enjoy women? I've never skirted the truth, but I don't think Gale is mine. It's a damn sight different thing killing a man with a pitchfork—stabbing a sixteen-year-old girl—and womanizing. Totally different.

Hell.

The sun's close to the horizon. Already the shadows are like a carpet being pulled over the trees and fields. I grab binoculars, open the door, stand by the hood. Look through naked trees. Can't see much, but the house windows are dark. Now and again I taste wood smoke from the chimney.

It's good to stamp my feet and get the blood moving.

I slip to the edge where forest meets field and stand behind an ash. Rest against it and smell the bitter bark. The house is still, save the smoke rolling out the stone chimney. Wind lifts a swirl of snow from the roof. Light flickers through the kitchen window. I should announce the law with a bullet, but a pistol at two hundred yards in the wind—I'd be as likely to take him out with a stiff fart.

Other side of the house is a bank, and beyond, the lake. Sizable trees grow along the slope—enough to provide cover even on a moonlit night.

The ash I'm standing behind is at the corner of a stretch of woods that runs to a pasture. Tree cover will get a rifle within fifty yards of the house, and at a good angle to put bullets into both the living room and kitchen. And through the front door.

Still, this is going to come down to a face-to-face.

Static bursts through the Bronco's radio. Prob'ly Fenny. I head back. Should have gotten a bite to eat instead of bending Fenny. I've gone a day on two eggs and handful of jerky.

I pack my pipe as I walk. Reach inside the Bronco. "Fenny. That you a second ago?"

"Sager and Odum both is about there."

"All right."

I climb inside, turn the radio volume down, and kill the Bronco's engine. The wind whistles across the roof but sounds far off.

I locked the redheaded vagabond back up when I was done with her. Told the judge she was exemplary and asked him to go easy. She was a wild one, and I'd have liked to keep her around, maybe cultivate something regular. Low-class women can hump. But she disappeared after I cut her loose. The address she'd given was made up. The street was real but the numbers wasn't. One fine quinny, though.

She could have moved anywhere. Could have run off to Monroe, most likely. They got the population to absorb a trampy woman. I suppose a baby given up for the orphanage could find his way back to Bittersmith.

Ahead, lights cut through the falling snow and then blink out, leaving a black form slowly approaching. Travis parks a few yards ahead of the Bronco's nose and gets out. Comes to my window. I roll it down. He's flushed.

"The tracks go to the house," he says.

"You learn to shoot in the Army?"

"Before the Army."

"Never killed a man, though?"

He doesn't answer.

"Come in the Bronc, a minute." I start the engine and crank the heat. He climbs into the seat and claps his boots. Brings in his legs and the snow sticks all the way to his knees.

"How far'd you track him?"

"The woods end at a pasture closed off with barbed wire. From there it was only two hundred yards to the house."

"Get a good look? You'd have been facing the front porch?"

"That's right. It was dark inside. The tracks and the smoke says he's there."

"See anything else?"

Travis hesitates. "There's a mess of snowmobiles parked on the back slope, far side of the house."

"That so?" I think a minute. "How do we know it isn't Roosevelt in the house, roasting wieners? Maybe called a friend or six over to help him with the suspect?"

"We don't know. Either the men that rode the sleds are in the house, working Gale G'wain over, or they're dead."

"Why would they send one man outside to move all the sleds to the back of the house?"

The heater gets toasty and I crack my window. Travis removes his gloves and rubs his hands above the vent. He keeps his eyes straight ahead. "They wouldn't. But if it was just G'Wain, and he knew we were coming..."

"Uh-huh. So. You give any thought to your future?" I say. "Because you're about to face a man with a body count of what? Eight armed men ? In ten hours? You may as well be going up against god himself. Body count like that."

The question hangs. Finally Travis meets my stare. "What angle you workin', Sheriff?"

"No angle. I'm done. Odum's got the sheriff's badge."

"How's that going to work out?"

"Depends on facts we don't have. I'm curious. Your daddy could have pushed your name with the town council. You two didn't have a falling out?"

"It's a matter of experience. What town has a twenty-six-year-old sheriff?"

"How far you going to go in life only doing what's been done? Or what other folks say is okay?"

"That's been your guiding principle?"

"This is an easy town to sheriff. Crime wave is two cars with bad taillights in a single day. Only two suspicious deaths in forty years. Only one, really, seein' as how they died at the same time. Now, I've gotten square in a man's face and told him about life in Bittersmith. I've suggested different men might examine their hearts and think hard if they want to spend their time in a peace-loving town. And that's something like doing more than other folks say can be done."

"Where's this going, sheriff?"

"We don't know if Roosevelt's dead or alive."

"More'n likely dead, the longer we jaw."

"More'n likely dead since before either of us got out here. But supposing he's taken hostage in there. You think Odum's got the stones to get him out? Alive? Take a step back and look at the big picture. You think Odum's capable of looking a man in the eye that's bigger and stronger and faster and meaner, and telling him he ain't welcome? Capable of telling this big ornery son of a bitch he's liable to wind up swinging by his balls from an oak tree if he sticks around?"

"Maybe."

"No way in hell. Odum would book him. Judge would give him a fine, and he'd be right back doing what he was doing to begin with. Only now he knows nobody's going do a goddamn thing about it. Tough love takes toughness. A goddamn spine. A sheriff has to be able to call up a mean streak. Has to be able to turn off that little voice that only looks at short-term right and wrong, and take the long view. After the dust settles, this town's going to be better off with Gale G'Wain dead. So if I was sheriff, one way or the other, by the end of this evening, he'd be dead. You understand that kind of logic?"

He nods slowly, like I'm dealing a trick question.

"Well, Odum don't. So take him out of the picture. You think Sager could understand that kind of logic? And if he did, you think he'd have the nuts to say, 'I don't care if Gale gives himself up, he's as good as dead'?"

"Nah. Not Sager."

"Hell no. He puked his breakfast at Haudesert's after twenty minutes getting used to the corpse. Roosevelt's likely dead. Odum's going nowhere. Sager's about as useful as a steering wheel on a mule. That leaves you. The only one of the bunch that can do the job."

"They'd change their minds if Odum screwed this up."

"Town council?"

"They'd keep you on."

"Like hell."

It's time for a smoke. My pipe bowl is crusty with carbon and ash. I pull a pocketknife and, arms out the window, scrape it clean. "No, Travis; I'm done. Don't have the stamina." I pull my arms back inside and fish my tobacco bag. "The job's yours if you want it. Rules are a lot of words on a lot of paper. The town council will find the ones to back you. Only thing you got to think about is Odum."

Travis looks through the windshield again. Jaw locked, thoughtful. Come on, boy. You ain't that fuckin' dense. I shift my leg and groan like it pains me.

"How?" Travis says.

I shrug.

Travis keeps his own council a minute. His brow wrinkles and his jaw sets. "You must be hurting after a day tromping through that." He nods at the window. "How was she? The girl?"

"Stabbed right through her heart, I'm guessing. Her eyes were closed."

"That ain't normal, is it?"

"No."

"Why would a cold-blooded murderer close his victim's eyes?"

"Make it look like remorse set in," I say.

"How many men are clever after killing their lover?"

"Why did the snow on the road not get hung up in the tree limbs? Who the fuck knows? There's always things that don't fit."

Travis is silent. Finally he meets my eye. "If he starts shooting, there isn't a whole lot we can do but defend ourselves. Bullets flying all over the place, maybe."

Travis glances at me like a child testing his answer.

"All right. You go back to your car and wait on Odum and Sager. They'll be here in a couple of minutes."

"Where will you be?"

"I'm going up ahead, loop around. Take Election House Road back to town."

"You're going back to town?"

"I'm not sheriff any more. You think on all that. Good luck."

Chapter Thirty

"Did Gwen ever tell you about the music?" Liz says.

"She heard it when someone was about to die."

We're huddled beside the fireplace. The kitchen and stairwell are dark. Most of the windows are blasted out. We've kept the fire small and take heat from embers and tiny blue flames. Sitting close on the hearth, we're as grave as orphans telling ghost stories.

During our preparations, we cached candles and matches at the basement steps, and every rifle in the house is reloaded and repositioned by a window. We even dragged Cal and Jordan into the cellar.

Liz has been indispensable and I don't know a thing about her save she was Gwen's friend and she tried to seduce me at Haynes' that night I froze with the cows on death row. But all the help she's given has just been her playing along to find out what happened. If she doesn't like the way the story ends, our partnership will dissolve and she'll be my worst enemy.

Problem is, I don't know why Gwen died.

Liz says, "Gwen told me she saw faces with the music, and that's how she knew who was going to die."

*We can't go back...they'll kill you...*Gwen had said.

"She must have seen faces last night," I say.

"Maybe she didn't want you to know."

An ember pops and the fire sounds like crinkling foil. A flame issues from the butt of a half-burned log, and though Liz is beside me and the firelight makes her face about as gentle as Gwen's, I'm alone like that flame, and as weak.

"You're here to find out about Guinevere's death," I say. "But it won't be long until the Sheriff and his boys come for me. Every minute you stay risks your life."

"I don't have a life to go back to."

"You got family—other'n your brother?"

The question hangs.

"Suit yourself. Since you can walk easier than me, you mind taking a peek through the kitchen window? See what's going on outside?"

She rocks to her feet.

"Stand way back from the window. If there's people outside, you don't want them to make out your shape."

She regards me with a look that I interpret as meaning I'm less intelligent than she is. Or maybe it's the harsh shadows across her face. In her behavior there's a secondary melody that clashes with the main tune. It's like she wants to be a coquette but doesn't clearly remember the song and mixes lines from one instrument in with another and the whole thing sounds awful. This girl doesn't quite know how to be a girl.

She stands silently in the kitchen a few moments, and then her footsteps move more distant, and she is silent again.

Can I trust her?

I've told my story as if purging confusion with my words. Dying to have the truth out. There's only one person alive who knows what happened to Gwen, and it's me, and I don't know what went on inside her. I don't know Liz's story, either. I shot her brother and she hasn't said a word of complaint. Been too caught up in my drama to ask why she didn't mind me killing him and is all-fire concerned with understanding Gwen's last minutes.

In her heart, is she on my side, or is she ready to turn as soon as she knows? Is Liz the one who kills me? Or is she still looking for me to help her run away?

"I guess you went home that night after visiting me at the butcher's?"

She answers from the other room, "I had no choice."

"I was sorry about that—not being able to help."

Her feet shuffle across the kitchen and I squeeze the rifle's grip.

"There's no one outside," she says, rounding the corner into the living room. She stands to the side of the window overlooking the lake, where Jordan poked his rifle through, and watches. "Maybe no one will come. Why do you think they will?"

"The first man I killed was a deputy. I woke up on the couch and he had a gun to my temple. He was here for revenge, and I guess he figured he'd make it look like I resisted arrest and he had to kill me. He didn't know I had a revolver on my hip. If he figured out where I ran to, the whole mess of them can figure it out."

"Finish your story about Gwen."

"There's more than that. I've seen vehicles parked through the trees. They're out there."

"What happened with Gwen?"

"I'd prefer if you come over here, beside me."

She reaches to the rifle propped at the corner of the sofa and the wall, cocks the hammer and points at me. "I prefer staying over here."

"Oh, come on. Aren't you tired of this yet?"

"Tell me the story, Gale. I won't leave until I'm satisfied with what happened to Gwen."

"Satisfied? That's a hell of a word."

"Maybe if you'd tell the fucking story you'd be satisfied too. Maybe."

"Don't point the rifle at me while I'm talking. You'll have plenty of time to aim if you don't like what you hear."

She lowers the muzzle. "You left off when you and Gwen entered the woods."

"It was getting hard to walk. The shock of the whole thing with Burt and the knife wore off and I was starting to think better. I don't know if you've ever been really, really cold, but your mind gets cloudy and then clear. Tranquil, like everything's going to be fine. By then we were at the forest and had difficulty crossing all the brush Burt left when he cut firewood a couple years ago. Gwen had to help me move my leg high enough a couple times. Once we worked through twenty or thirty feet of brush and briars, the trees calmed the wind and it wasn't quite so cold.

"I kept thinking about her foot, and that there was no way she'd escape frostbite. I couldn't move fast enough. I swiped a few curls of bark from a paper birch tree and told her, 'hold up and we'll build a fire.' And she said, 'just a little ways farther so the smoke won't catch anyone's eye.' I said 'There's a grove of bull pine ahead.' Ponderosa is good for holding the smoke and spreading it out before letting it go. I'd built a fire there the night before while I waited to go see her."

Liz nods.

"Gwen took the lead. I watched her feet cut through the snow. Even in the woods it was deeper than her ankle. She didn't say a word about it. I saw through the tree limbs that we were getting close to the pine and I wanted to build a fire and press her feet to my belly and make them warm, and then trade out with her and let her wear one of my boots, even though it'd be too big. We'd been in the snow fifteen or twenty minutes, and I still hoped…she'd be able to stay healthy. If I could have gotten her warm.

"We got to a spot under a giant ponderosa where the snow was thin and Gwen said this looked good, and I said, 'in a little ways we can be where I spent half the night. There might still be some coals.' The night before I spent about eight hours drying my boots and socks. A rock overhang reflected heat from the fire. We kept going and it was only a couple minutes until we came up to the rock and the ashes were still warm."

I can hardly go on. Liz stares at the fireplace.

"There were so many things we could have done! She could have put on one of my boots and snuck back to the barn for her shoe. We could have built a fire long enough to get her foot warm and then gone to Haynes's, where at least we could lay low through the storm. She could have gone back to her mother and said I dragged her away and she escaped. Anything!"

"What did you do to her?"

I swallow. Exhale.

Chapter Thirty-one

It's taken Odum a half hour to talk things over and start deploying his men. I drove ahead to the bend beyond where Roosevelt's cruiser is parked half into the woods. Slipped back on foot, but on the other side of the road, behind it all. It'd be no good to have another unexplained set of tracks mingled with the rest.

I knock a thin layer of snow off a log lying under the protective wing of a pine. Park my tired ass on it. The air is still and silent and my view to the farm is unobstructed. I turn away and light a pipe bowl.

The line between dusk and night is never clear. The moon is already midway through the sky. It won't get truly bleak until around midnight.

That's better for Gale than it is for Odum and company.

Coates was a hunter and his house is an arsenal. He reloaded his ammo in the basement. Kept enough powder on hand to launch a brick house, let alone a wood one. G'Wain has access to all of it.

And that house…I helped Coates replace the front door years ago. The jamb was water-rotted and we pulled it out. The walls are boards, four-thick. Modern house, bullet hits a sheet of plywood, goes through some insulation, and then a little plaster. This house? Any bullet makes it through that wall is going to come out in ten pieces, and each one'll drop to the floor.

Suppression fire has to be direct, concentrated on the window Gale's shooting from. They'll have to expose themselves trying to keep him from shooting back—but they don't have the man power to cover all of Gale's options. If Odum has any smarts, he'll deploy two men on the same side of the house—the one with the fewest windows—and have a third covering escape out the back.

But Odum's got the brains of a frog fart, and G'Wain will pick off his deputies one by one.

The dome light in Odum's cruiser flashes yellow. Deputies spill out.

Travis gets in his vehicle and drives forward. Sager heads to the corner by the driveway, and keeps looking at the others as he moves closer to the house under the cover of trees. Once he gets to the pasture, he'll stop. Odum walks fifty yards along the road toward Roosevelt's ditched vehicle, and turns into the woods.

Travis drives to the opposite side of the field in front of the house and parks. He steals along a windrow. Looks like he's going to follow it to the slope by the lake and angle to the house.

Odum takes off into the woods, like to make a circle and come at the house from the orchard. So him and Travis will come in facing each other, the house between them.

Odum's already fucked this up.

I clean out my pipe and tuck it into my pocket. Step out from under the bull pine limb and start moving toward the house.

* * *

Liz's finger is on her trigger. "What did you do to Gwen?"

"I dropped the birch bark I'd picked off the tree onto the ashes and walked off to find wood. I'd burned up every last bit of what I'd had the night before, thinking it might keep the coals burning longer in case I had to come back. I brought a few pieces of brush and knocked the snow off them. They were too big to light with a few scraps of birch bark, so I had to find some pine scrub. I said, 'Hang on, Baby. I'll have your feet warm in no time, and you can take my boot.'

"Her eyes had been melancholy but they firmed. She stood and walked through the snow to me like she was walking across a ballroom floor in the middle of July. She took my face in both her hands and then slid them to my neck and pulled me to her, began kissing me with her eyes open. She said, 'I love you, Gale.'"

Liz comes forward a little and sits on the arm of the sofa. Her rifle points toward the stairway.

"I told her I loved her too and she should just hold tight a few more minutes and we'd figure out how to get out of the mess we were in. I hugged her. You know how a dismissal hug is different from an I-love-you hug? I gave her the quick kind because I was in a hurry to get a fire going. I was only a few feet away, reaching into a ponderosa branch, when I heard a whoomp! sound, and I turned around and Gwen was laying face down by the fire. I ran back to her, best I could, and rolled her over."

I wipe my eyes. I've avoided this picture all day. There's no explanation for what she did.

"What happened?" Liz says, on her knees before me. She tugs my sleeve. "What happened?"

"She had a knife sticking out of her chest, buried clean to the hilt. She'd fallen on the same knife she'd pulled out of my leg."

"No!"

"She did!"

"No. No."

Liz weeps and I wipe my eyes. There's only one more thing to tell her.

"She was alive for a minute, though the knife went right through her middle. I—I know where a person's heart is and she must have too. She smiled, though her eyes were wet and full of panic."

"Did she say anything? Did she say why?"

"She said something…"

"What?"

"I don't know what she meant. Maybe… I don't know."

"What?"

"I don't know."

"What did she say? Tell me!"

I look past Liz to the window overlooking the lake. "She chose for her very last words, 'I stole your music.' I held her eyes closed for five minutes after she was gone. To make sure they stayed that way."

Liz nods slowly, and then faster. Tears roll down her face like two columns of soldiers.

"She stole your music." Liz lifts the rifle in her hands and points it at the ceiling. "You know what she was telling you? You—"

"Music was like her soul, I think. Maybe she meant she'd take a part of me with her."

"You fool." She smiles and clears phlegm from her throat. She makes a face like she has a mouthful and looks at the fire, and then turns, heads for the window. She spits through it and as she turns to me the wood at the window splinters. A rifle shot explodes at almost the same time.

"Down!" I yell. "Are you hit?"

She leaps behind the sofa and scrambles to her rifle. I low crawl, more of a wriggle with a useless arm and half-dead leg, to the living-room window farther to the right.

More shots echo from outside—some close, some far away. There's rifles on two sides of the house, and something smaller. A gun that yips like a small dog. Three men? Counting the dead deputy, that makes four. One shy of the whole department. They're keeping things in-house, and one man in reserve.

I whisper to Liz, "Go upstairs. All the way down the hall. The window is shot out and there's a rifle. You might be able to see the shooter."

She nods and wriggles across the floor. Gunshots crash through the house, concentrated on the bottom floor. The fire is a steady patter, a shot every couple of seconds.

"I'm going to the kitchen," I say. "There's two shooters on that side."

"She stole your music!" Liz says.

She ascends the stairs in a quick burst and her footsteps echo from the hallway. I grab the rifle beside the window and with all the speed I can muster, cross to the kitchen. Bullets tear through the house, but only through the windows. I stop part way and listen. Lead rips through plaster in the middle of the house, and shatters picture frames.

I peer over the windowsill. I've got one shooter at the pasture alternating shots through each downstairs window. Sounds like a pistol. The other shots from out front are difficult to distinguish, but it seems they're not coming inside the house. Like the other fellow is shooting into the walls.

Upstairs, Liz fires a rifle. She follows up with several more and screams, "I missed and he's moving around the front!"

I shift, place my back to the fireplace, where the stones will protect me from fire originating on the other side of the house.

The pistol shots from out front seem to get closer. The patter is steady, and then the loud bangs stop and it is just the rifle from the pasture that keeps hitting the outside walls.

Maybe the one with the pistol is reloading. I shift to my right and see a muzzle flash in the pasture. Hear the bullet strike the side of the house to my left. Though the moonlight is strong I can't make out any people. I approach the window, rest the muzzle on the splintered wood and wait for the next flash.

There!

I zero on it, and when the next flash comes, it is perfectly aligned with my rifle barrel.

Fuck him.

I duck and a bullet zips by me. A pistol shot from twenty feet away. Upstairs, Liz fires again and after a quick pause, again. She rattles down the stairs.

"I got him," she says. "I'm sure I got him."

"Stand back!"

Another pistol shot comes through the window.

"Get back! He's right outside."

She drops to the floor and approaches me.

"There's time for you to go," I say. "You can make it now. Go downstairs. Take the snowmobile and blast through the door."

"You've been watching too many movies."

"What are movies?"

She punches my good arm and I make out a smile on her half-lit face.

"I'll stick around," she says.

I slide across the kitchen floor, pulling with one good arm, kicking with one good leg. At the steps I sit and then work my way into the darkness, taking the first few steps on my behind. I grab a candle and a book of matches and Liz Sunday is right behind me. She swings the door closed and we're in total darkness until I strike a match.

I hold the flame to the candle and she finds another and tilts its wick to my flame. I climb to my feet and descend. At the bottom I say, "Take the snowmobile. Blast through the door. He'll think we've both gone, and I'll surprise him from down here."

"Whatever you do is going to work," Liz says.

"Just do it for me!"

"You still don't understand about Gwen?"

"What?"

"She stole your music. She died for you."

"For me? What?"

"In your place."

Liz rests her candle on its side on a shelf and I see what she doesn't—a can of black powder a few inches away. I rush to her as the dust on the table ignites in a flash that leaves me half blind.

"Are you all right?"

"What was that?" she says, groping me. "I'm blind."

"Gunpowder. Can you see? Now?"

"It was the flash. Thank God. Gunpowder?"

"The man who lived here reloaded his rifle shells. You lit powder that must have spilled on the table."

I move the candle closer and she reads the label on the can of black powder. She looks at me, and then past me.

"Shit!" she says. "Put it out!"

She snuffs her candle and knocks mine from my hand. She shoves me aside. A bullet shatters through a window high on the basement wall and smashes into the reloading station. A second and third shot follows. I can barely see in the shadows.

Liz points her rifle at the window and blasts through it. Works the lever and fires again. I move to the end of the table and gather all my strength to topple it forward.

"Go now," I whisper. "Blast through the door. He'll think we're both gone. Go—while there's time!"

I hear her snowmobile suit zip-zip to me. She feels for my shoulders and my arms and places her rifle in my hand. "There's two shots left. One in the chamber. The safety is off. If I don't hear this gun go off within five minutes, I'm coming back."

She feels for my face and pecks her lips to my cheek.

* * *

Guinevere was beyond shivering. Her foot was numb and the cold that blew through her clothes had long ago frozen her goose pimples solid. Even her eyebrows were hard, and when she squinted against the arctic wind her face remained stiff until she pressed her cheeks back to normal with her palms.

Gale limped from the wound he'd received at her father's hand; she'd watched Burt hurl the knife, she'd seen it glint as it tumbled end over end until it stuck in Gale. So many times during the previous night she'd closed her eyes only to see Gale's face staring into death and to hear the bullfrog dirge—croaking tunes that recalled the smell of rotten earth.

She'd thought Gale's life would end and had closed her eyes. Then she'd seen her father's face on an azure field and immediately cast about the loft for a weapon. She found the pitchfork and somewhere deep within found the strength to hurl it. She hurried down the ladder, wearing only one shoe, and shivered at the sight of her tormenter's dead eyes, and the knowledge that at this moment heaven was rejecting him.

Gale would survive!

But on the long march across the field she stopped walking into the driving wind, and turned her back against the stinging ice pellets, and again she saw Gale's face. Somewhere within the shrieking storm was the plaintive moan of the frogs.

It was remarkable that he was beside her and didn't know another part of him was this very moment staring into the face of death...But his eyes angled upward, and Gwen realized this might be her only opportunity to see the face of God, because Gale might be the only man clean enough to deserve a place in heaven. She swiveled inside her mind's eye and the azure field brightened until it was no different than staring into a sunny blizzard.

Was that God?

She looked farther and the whiteness intensified, almost becoming heat she could feel through her bones; she dared farther and farther and the heat burned. She fell to her knees and the snow was warm and wet; she raised her hands to shield her eyes but it was no good; the light was within. She searched the glory until her heart juddered and her lungs refused to expand and contract, farther still until she couldn't hold a thought together, couldn't conceive of one word to follow another.

Where? She thought. Where? She continued and the brightness faded. Still moving, fading. The heat ended and she wanted to go back and explore the warmth, but she sensed the drawing of another face and she drove farther from the godhead until the bullfrogs started to groan and she saw, staring back through her, Guinevere Haudesert.

She saw herself and it was startling like electricity. She heard the notes, the bullfrogs. On another plane she contemplated death with certainty; indeed she stared into her maker. Gwen searched her other face for a sign and her heart quickened when she detected a trace of smile, a flinty mirth in the corner of her eye. Unlike her grandfather, grandmother, grocery man, and Burt—unlike all of them—she would go some place nice.

Only she and Gale.

Gwen tried to find the place in her mind where this very moment her other self beheld God. Someplace within her must burn from seeing Him, but no place was warm. Now that she had looked farther to the left and found her self, she was again aware of the driving snow and ice and that she stood ankle deep in coldness.

The disparity was that between black and a rainbow; between nil and love. This world was pain and confusion and embarrassment and sin, and the next was so pure it burned, so loving it attracted her deeper and deeper until she wanted to forget herself and dive in, and merge and finally be stolen from endless night.

"Gwen?" Gale said.

She left her eyes closed for another moment, and soaked in the truth. She may never see these things again.

"We have to hurry," Gale said. "If you can hang in there, we'll be to the forest soon. We'll find cover. I'll build a fire. Gwen, please, stay with me. Open your eyes, baby."

Gwen opened her eyes. Wind assailed her. Ice. Snow. Cold. Again she was numb, and tired.

"Come on, baby," Gale said. "I got you. I'll take care of you."

She righted herself with her arms and hands in the snow. Took Gale's hand, and faced the wind. The forest was ahead. Gale's voice faded. She'd seen God. On one side of Him was Gale, and on the other was she, and everything was clear. They would not be together long.

* * *

Gwen's gaze fell to Gale's boot print. Drifts had accumulated in the lee side of a windrow of brush. They had reached the edge of the field and now entered an obstacle course of ice-covered logs and stumps, half-buried in icy waves of snow. She dropped her foot into Gale's boot print the way she might drop a frozen fish into a bucket.

Gale plodded onward. His ruddy ears shone through locks of hair that seemed like frozen tufts of mud. If she closed her eyes, she would see Gale's other face, the one that communed with the Almighty. Looking beyond, she would glimpse purity—and on the other side she would see a version of herself in the same contemplative pose as Gale.

Earlier, she'd yanked the knife from Gale's leg and his eyes were full of water and when he'd regained his feet, he spun in circles like a rain dance, hopping and slipping, and she'd tucked the knife into her pocket with the blade up in the air.

Now she pulled out the knife and used one hand to wrap the other around the haft.

Gwen followed deeper into the woods. They neared a copse of ponderosa where the snow on the ground was lighter. Gwen stopped and Gale continued. She pressed the tip of the blade to her ribs until the point homed on a trough between bones. She angled the handle to point the blade at the center of her core, and inhaled. Closed her eyes.

The bullfrog song came. Gale looked through her into the deity beyond. She studied Gale's face and though he couldn't see her, she desperately wanted to communicate with *this* Gale, the one who would understand what she was about to do. She would tell him she hadn't loved him at first, but it was her fault. And that he was so pure she'd fallen in love with him in spite of the ugliness Burt had planted in her heart. This Gale would understand she was saving him and her choice wasn't merely selfish. That it was all good, that everything was white, that coldness and ice melted in the face of purity.

She had no voice for this Gale. He stayed where he was, imperturbable, looking into deity without needing to rush headlong into it. He was stronger than she. That was why he could stay a while longer, and why he would someday understand she had no strength to remain.

She opened her eyes and Gale was yards ahead. She dropped the knife to her side, hid it in her pocket. "Gale!"

He whirled to her, raced back. "Let me help," he said.

"I love you. I just wanted to say that."

"I love you," he said. "Soon we'll be at a rock ledge where I built a fire last night. I'll carry you." He stepped to her.

"No. I'm fine."

"You're shivering. Your lips are blue."

"So are yours. Hurry. I'll follow."

He nodded, holding her eye. "Okay. Hurry."

"And Gale? I love you. Remember."

She followed to where Gale had spent the night. He gathered wood.

She brought the blade to her ribs. Nestled the point below her breast where it would glide between the bones. Closed her eyes and looked into the other Gale's face one last time before slipping beyond him, around, toward the white heat and purity. She turned and as Godhead grew closer she wilted under the glare. It was agony and it was magnetic. Farther, farther. Hotter. Up and down were gone. Left and right didn't exist. Everything in all of time and space was inside her. Deity was a crucible, and she was within it, burned pure. Whiteness blinded every dimension of her being; she was agony and pleasure; she writhed and her skin leaped, her heart soared and in a vague way she knew she had fallen onto the knife. Some other part of her let go. Some other part was sticky and red and rapidly freezing—but not Guinevere Haudesert.

She saw Gale one last time and whispered.

* * *

I watched the firefight. I remember that much. Odum did like I thought—came in from three sides, totally exposed, like an idiot.

I rushed as best I could on old legs in deep snow. I remember that. Sager went down first, and I couldn't see Travis. Must have happened quick, because inside of two minutes it was just Odum firing into the basement, and then taking off around the back. I set off at a run, right up the driveway.

And next I know, my legs don't work and my chest is inside a table vice. Everything's black and my face is numb from snow. I'm thinking of Burt, and Gwen, and Margot, and the vagabond from 1951. I'm thinking of bullets and numb skin, wondering if this is the end of Sheriff Bittersmith—couldn't even drag his sorry ass to the fight.

I'll be damned.

But I can't move.

* * *

Everything is black. I look out the window for the last shootist, but it's dark outside, too. The pistol fire has stopped.

In a moment the snowmobile rocks as Liz mounts it and the springs adjust to her weight. The key clicks and there's a mild knocking sound as she sets the starter cord.

She yanks and the motor surges to life. The headlight fills the basement and in a second the air is smoky with exhaust. Liz revs high while holding the brake, getting the engine hot. I point the rifle at the window. The din is like holding a chainsaw to your ear; the metallic rattle penetrates skull bones and vibrates the brain. Finally—all this has taken two seconds—she releases the brake. The engine screams bloody murder and the snowmobile darts across the basement floor, up the ramp, and blasts through the sloped wall door.

A series of flashes appear as the snowmobile becomes a receding airborne shadow—flashes that carry sharp reports with them.

Our third adversary was waiting. The snowmobile flies

following the cant of the ramp, and smashes the man on the downward slope of the yard.

I struggle to the ramp and hold the rifle barrel before me as I climb out of the basement.

A man lies crumpled in the snowmobile's tracks. His pistol is pressed to his chest. He's breathing. On either side of him is the door, ripped in two by the sled's nose. Liz races across the lake without letting up and then turns left. As the headlight begins to point back to the house, her progress stops. She waits and her snowmobile engine idles.

I step to the man's feet and aim at his head.

"I'm Sheriff," he whispers.

I take the pistol from his hand. He bleeds from his mouth and his body begins to shake. I've seen enough death moments to recognize his. "Where's Bittersmith?"

"He's done. Last day."

"Yours too."

* * *

I sit at the edge of the basement entrance on the cement block wall. Liz races closer on the snowmobile.

She died in your place…

I should have been killed so many times. Which death did Gwen take for me?

Liz stops at the lake bank, just off the ice. The motor dies and she sits there, waiting.

Only now in the silence does everything make sense. Gwen saw my face with the music and convinced herself she could save me by dying. Only now does the uncertain feeling I've had all along—not knowing if I loved her because she needed my protection, or if I loved her because of her character—resolve. I've never known anyone so beautiful.

And only now do I fathom the depth of my hatred for Burt Haudesert. He thought invading Gwen's bed was an inconsequential thing, but he stole her entire life.

Liz walks toward me, rifle in hand. I wave. I'd like to redirect my thoughts back to Gwen, but Bittersmith is still out there. He'll come to me, or I'll go to him.

"This was the new sheriff. He's dead," I say. "You can go home."

When she is a few feet away she says, "Now let me tell you my story."

Chapter Thirty-two

Liz Sunday is a sprightly character, brimming with anger; she moves like a bowed whipsaw and her voice crackles like gunfire. She begins talking as we circle the house, me gimping and her gesticulating, more and more overcome by her own audacity.

"Gwen and I were the same," she says. "The same things happened to us, and some to me were worse. My mother ran off when I was three, and..."

I parse her excited language while she bends to her brother's corpse.

"You want to get his other foot?" she says.

I stoop and lift, fold his ankle in the crook of my elbow. Together we heave him toward the house.

"We were friends and all," Liz says. "Gwen told me about the music, and why it started."

Her brother is still warm, and a red trail marks the first few feet of his passage through the snow. It quickly fades and though we are dragging a bloody corpse the snow is virgin white, something so remarkable that I cannot get my mind around it. Liz is talking still, mincing around confessing that her father raped her and that is what bound her and Gwen together.

Am I losing my mind? Have I heard all this before?

Her brother's foot is in my arm and when I look at his ruddy, blood-speckled face, I see Jordan. Words avalanche from Liz's mouth but she says nothing of the corpse in her hands. This is the fellow that pulled her pigtails, according to the vernacular of family life—who taunted and teased, and told his buddies that no one save he got to pick on her. Liz's mouth foams as she describes the things her father did to her. We're lifting and dragging her brother like a sack of meal, and her coldness informs equally on her scars and her brother Link's apparent lifelong disregard.

His complicity supplies one more confirmation of the half-truth every orphan clings to, that he'd rather be alone after all.

"And my father sent me away to have the baby. They took him from me before I even nursed him," she says.

"Did you ever love your brother?"

She stops. "Him?"

I don't think words are going to penetrate her. Maybe they shouldn't. "Where did they take you to have your baby?"

"I was at my aunt's in Monroe. They took the baby to an orphanage there."

Something in her tone has changed.

"An orphanage in Monroe?" I drop her dead brother's foot. "Monroe?"

"Yeah," she says, and her eyes seem more focused than any time I've seen them except the night she surprised me at Haynes'. She says, "What? Pick up his foot. We don't have much time."

"What am I doing here?" I say. Did her brother molest her? Is she mad? Are there any untouched girls? Any who remain sane?

We are silent as we drag Link. I'm tired of this sport and I want to find my bunk at the Youth Home, where I spent winter evenings buried in books, imagining other men's troubles. I follow Liz to the front of the house.

"Who are these two?"

Liz drops to her knees, pulls the man's head to the side so I can see his face. "This is Tom Taylor. The boys called him T.T., or Titties."

I stoop, best I can, to his feet.

"Why?" she says. "You know him?"

"No. Did you?"

"Only that they all thought he was queer."

"Why did they take him into the group?"

"Needed members. It isn't easy throwing a revolution."

I recall Burt Haudesert's continual recruiting, and the man who gave me a lift to town when I went to see Haynes about a job. The militia always needed men.

I lift Taylor's feet and am momentarily disgusted by the vigilantism he chose to die for. "What about that guy over there?"

"Must be Wilbur Barnes. Just snuck home from Canada."

"So he wouldn't fight our country's war, but was willing to fight one against me."

"He got a job at the farm depot."

"Of course."

She hoists Taylor by the shoulders. He bows in the middle and we scoot him over the snow. We drop him at the back of the house and catch our breath.

I say, "How'd you join this gang?"

"I wasn't in the group. Link was."

"They took the son of the town communist?"

Her nostrils flare.

"I guess you hear a lot of that."

"They told me I could come if I stayed out of the way. And about my father… being a communist is far from the worst he's done." She grits through the moment. "The militia didn't want

Link. We heard things at school. We found our dog with his head sawed off. We went to bed every night wondering what was next. At school, Link started asking about the Militia. Finally him and my father had a knockdown drag-out. That night Link went away with his ought-six, and when he came back I could see from his eyes they'd let him in. He slept like a baby."

"He slept like a baby? Like, on the couch?"

She turns away. Her shoulders are still. "Don't judge me."

"I don't judge you. I can't say a damned thing right."

But did she sleep in the same bed as her brother? With her father?

She twists and her face is red. "I didn't choose any of this."

"We're almost done."

"They didn't like Link. When Cal and Jordan came to our house this morning, they didn't have a big enough posse. They said Link had to prove himself to the organization."

"And you came along."

"They said you killed their father and took Gwen."

"Why'd you care?"

"Gwen was my friend."

"Why put yourself in danger?"

"You came from the Youth Home."

The night she visited me at Haynes's, I wondered why she would seek me instead of the other boys in town.

I stumble away and circle to the porch steps. Inside the house, the fire has dwindled to coals. I cross a bloodstain from the deputy. Glance at ocher marks on the wall from Cal.

I hold my hands to the embers and they surprise me. Warmth in the cold. Like when I spent last night with Guinevere Haudesert in her father's loft, snuggled between two coats. After a bout of love she stood in the frigid air, her arms aloft, breasts and triangle leaping through moonlight at me. She said, look at me, and I said, I can't help it, and she said, love me. I can't help that either. Her smile radiated heat like these embers. She was happy and loved and unashamed.

Footsteps sound on the snow-softened porch. Liz, at the door.

"My father raped me. You helped Gwen make justice. That's why I had to know what happened to her. And that's why there's more to be done when we're finished here."

I understand where Liz has been and what makes her tick. Having killed so many, I find it easy to think about applying justice where the law has failed.

"There won't be any going back."

She nods. "Are you going to help me finish my story?"

* * *

Gale G'Wain has a partner. A girl I know.

They've been working together out front, not like she's a hostage. They've been dragging bodies. Give me a chance to get my strength—though what would help me best, a bowl of tobacco, would tip them off. So I've been a dark clump on the field. Going numb in my legs, not knowing if my heart's plum give out or if I'm buried in snow that comes down from above and blows in from the sides and doesn't look to ever let up.

They go around the house and a few minutes pass before I figure they aren't coming back. Getting from the ground to all fours is easy, but from all fours to upright takes reminding myself of Burt lying in a ruby pool with a fork run through his neck. Placing one foot in front of the next takes a vision of Gwen with an inch-and-a-half-wide slit in the side of her pert young breast.

That, by God, keeps me moving.

* * *

"I grew up at the orphanage where your son lives," I say.

We've worked in silence. When I get lightheaded from my wounds, she carries on dragging bodies, driving snowmobiles into the basement, leaving one more outside. I told her to leave the Sheriff outside as well, and she continued with other chores. She's packed a second bag with food and bullets. Stuffed a coarse wool blanket inside. She's raided desk drawers for dollars and bureaus for valuables. She's stolen anything she's fancied and loaded another sled. It waits outside.

Who made her what she is? Gwen wasn't like that.

"I'm going to get my son back," she says.

I sense this is her long-running motive. "How are you going to take care of him?"

"I'll find work. I do what I have to."

I open the hood of a Skiroule, uncap the half-full gas tank. The sled is heavy in the front. I can't rock it.

"Give me a hand."

She joins me and we roll the snowmobile on its side. The fiberglass hood bends and the gasoline and oil mix splashes onto the concrete. Together we flip another sled. The scent of fuel burns my throat.

"Is the door at the top of the stairs open?"

"I'll see," she says, and circles the pool. She climbs the stairs.

I grab a can of gunpowder from Coates's reloading station and place it by the exit. "Bring matches from the fireplace, and meet me outside."

I track her upstairs by her footsteps. A few minutes ago I explained what we're doing. This isn't about getting rid of evidence, as if converting bodies to ashes will absolve me of killing them in the eyes of the law. Nothing since this morning has anything to do with the law. I'm not above it. I'm ignoring it, the way it ignored Gwen. My mother. Liz.

I'm going to fire this place and these bodies because when a mortgage is paid, the only thing to do is burn it.

I slip down the slope to the Sheriff who replaced Bittersmith. Liz stands a few feet away.

"Help me drag him inside," I say.

She grabs a foot and I take the other. He's heavy, and going upslope quickly consumes my strength. We flop him over the edge of the stairs, and his body angles downward..

"Wait for me outside," I say.

I stand over the new sheriff. His feet are in snowmobile fuel. I uncap the gunpowder and spill a line from the pool, over his crotch, and up the ramp. The can remains quarter-full when I'm done. I toss it inside.

"Take this sled down to the other, on the lake. I'll be there in a minute."

She passes me a box of matches. In a moment she's a hundred yards away, sitting on an idling sled. I strike a match and touch it to the powder. It burns quickly, a shooting line of orange and sparks. I duck and the basement whooshes with flames. There's no explosion.

This isn't meant to be dramatic.

* * *

I'm twenty feet away when I see orange flames. Powder from downstairs. The little bastard's burning the Coates house and everything in it, as if the law won't find bones. It would be contemptible, if the orphan wasn't so good at killing people.

Time I get beside the house, two snowmobiles race across the lake. I pull out my Smith & Wesson and aim at the second sled.

Fire one off, then another. My arm gets heavy and I can't hold it steady, but I pull the trigger until the pistol is empty. G'Wain probably thinks the noise is reloaded cartridges exploding in the basement, if he hears at all.

That's fine as frog hair, Gale G'Wain. It's dark, and we got roads all over this fuckin' state, let a man keep track of a pair of sleds' headlamps in the woods. I've got more jerky in the truck. I'm coming for you. The longer I walk, the stronger I get. The blinder I get to everything save my part in your miserable goddamned fate.

I turn back for the Bronco. Follow the trail I broke coming in. My legs are dead but slowly coming back to life. They sting, but the pain is strength. Almost got a normal gait. Only takes a few minutes to move a hundred yards.

Odum's left his car unlocked. I slip inside, but he kept the keys. Of course he kept the keys, but I curse him for it and relax on the seat to catch my breath. Not too long. Gale and his partner must be most of the way across the lake.

I'm not going to end my forty-year run as sheriff on Gale G'Wain's escape.

I spot a lunch box in the passenger foot well. Open it and pull out a peanut butter and jelly, leaving two more inside. I bite into stiff bread. Crunchy peanut butter and cherry jelly. I shake Odum's half-full thermos. Pour a cup of piss-warm coffee and gulp it.

Now I feel alive. I keep the sandwich with the bite marks and repack the pail. Return my feet to the snow. I'll eat the rest on the road.

The Bronco's only another two hundred yards.

Yes sir, Gale. Two can get lucky. I bet your luck runs out first.

* * *

If I had done a dozen things differently, Gwen would be alive. We'd be together, heading south.

I know what Doctor Coates was talking about in his letter, when he said he was giving his time to the urchins who didn't know God's gift and hadn't even begun to regret being born unknowing. He was answering what I said to Mister Sharps—I didn't want to be bad—and he was saying it's okay. That's what we've got a God for. He's there when you finally wake to regret. When you know you are bad no matter how hard you try to live by rules that make sense.

Nothing is quite as clear as the cold air that's setting my lungs on fire. Steering a snowmobile with one arm is a challenge, and leaning into a turn on a leg that's earned an appointment with a surgical saw is close to crippling. I steer by applying steady pressure to one side of the bar or the other, aiming for the distant edge of the lake. Staying in Liz's track helps.

She has an edge I'm not at home with.

The sky is black. The snow is white. Our headlights cut a yellow swath through both. Before today, I would have never thought of turning a firearm on a man, even in self-defense. I don't know if I can remember all of them, but today's dead men share one commonality. When I account for their deaths, I'll look God in the eye.

But the deed that Liz and I race toward is different. It says the law isn't good enough. Men—not institutions—must mete out justice, or it won't be done. This is judicial in the most literal sense. If I could spend the rest of my life avenging girls like Guinevere, if I could do nothing but murder men like Burt, I'd do it. I bear wounds in my arm and leg, but the deepest is in my heart. From Burt and his ilk, child-fuckers, sex-thieves, perverts.

Snowflakes swarm to me through the headlight.

It is appropriate that this march of assassins is in the winter. It is the natural order that things wither and are reaped in the fall—and if any that deserved to meet their end survive, winter ensures they do not escape.

These are my thoughts as Liz leads across the lake. She slows as we approach the frozen shore, and stands as the sled plows over a small bank. Her track strips snow from tufts of dead grass; the golden blades reflect my headlamp and then I too navigate the bump. An icy lump knocks the skis hard right and the sled lurches. I press the steering bar with my shot arm, but the snow is deep. I am weak. My leg is too stiff to counterbalance a blastoff to the left. The sled plows into unbroken snow and I fight to get back to Liz's path.

Liz's taillight flashes red. She looks back, perhaps alarmed that my headlight cut so wildly. Two-cycle exhaust fills my nose. I ease behind her. She leaves her machine running; gray exhaust clouds her skis. Liz dismounts.

The headlight on her snowmobile dims and the swath it illuminates looks ghastly; jagged corn stalks protrude through the snow like skinny Arlington headstones. To the right, a field bends like an oxbow lake around the hill on our left. A pair of eyes, probably from a deer, reflect our headlights.

Liz wades through the snow and stands beside me. My sled's Sachs engine vibrates heavily at idle. She leans to me and says, "Can you steer? Why are we on separate machines?"

"I don't know."

Joining her is not marriage, but I sense other things will follow.

Monroe.

"Are you cold enough to do this?" I say. "Your father, I mean."

"I said 'never again' a month ago," she says. "But never happened last night."

"Saying it isn't good enough." I look into the darkness beyond my headlight. "It's like telling a wolf not to hunt. Just shoot it."

I switch the key off; the engine rattles through death throes until it stops with a ragged valve-tapping decrescendo.

She stares like something profound is behind me. She says, "You ever get the feeling things have changed? The rules you've followed your whole life don't count?"

I don't say it, but she's describing my last three seconds before shooting the deputy. A French fellow said rebels weather abuse until one moment they understand any future—no matter how risky—is better than more of the present. They take action that hurtles them away from pain, even if it promises more of a different kind. "You get to decide your own rules today."

She has a crafty look, like Mister Sharps playing chess. A chill descends my spine. She is moves and moves ahead. Did she help her brother and the militia boys lay siege to the house so she could learn about Gwen? Or was she pushing her knight ahead and around, on a path she conceived three moves ago, knowing all twenty-eight to come?

We're stopped at a meadow. Thirty yards ahead, a trail cuts through the woods and passes behind the hill where Guinevere Haudesert died. The trail eventually leads to the Sunday farm, adjacent the Haudesert estate. I won't be able to make the turns.

I shoulder my duffel with my good arm and grab my rifle, a .30-40 Krag-Jorgensen with a beastly heavy barrel. We get to Liz's house, what's she going to do?

"Your father associated with the Wyoming Militia, by chance?"

She snorts. "You know he's a communist. Why? You stop feeling reckless?"

It's like a slap to my face. "I've spent the day curled up in God's hands. I was worried about you. We're not going to have a quick getaway on just one sled."

"We won't need to be quick."

* * *

All these dead deputies—town council might see the wisdom of inviting me to stay another year or two. Rebuild the force. Or a few months until they find a replacement.

But times are changing, and survivors get old. I've seen enough. I find Gale G'Wain and kill him, I'm quits. It'll be good enough that they beg me to stay on.

Half way to town, I tramp the brakes and kill the headlights. Grab a pair of binoculars and pore over a stretch of field. On an upslope at the end of the lake, a pair of piss-yellow lights cut into the dark.

Gale and his partner are dark masses moving against the dim glow. Even with a .30-06 I couldn't reach them. But once a hunter knows an animal's location he can figure where it's going and get there first.

G'Wain and his friend have to choose between a trail that branches down to the Haudesert farm or continues on to Sunday's and beyond that, joins the power lines to Monroe. Or they can ride the fields to roughly the same places. If they don't cut around the lake, or cross the road on this side, they stay within my sights.

It happens often enough that a killer returns to the scene. But I don't think that's what G'Wain's up to. I think he's going to the Sunday place.

I've been mulling over Burt and Gwen. Watching pictures flash through my mind, sometimes so clear I can smell the day like I'm sitting in it. Taste the Budweiser I drank with Burt while we memorized Masonic catechisms. Smell the perfume Liz Sunday wore that day I caught her and Gwen skipping school.

She had long brown hair, like the girl helping G'Wain back at the house, and up there on the side hill.

She was big boned, a farm girl, and G'Wain's partner had a certain workhorse heft to her movements, dragging men's corpses through the snow. This girl's got thighs. Strong back.

The mind wanders. Some thoughts are like briars, you get a few feet in, and find so many snags, it's best to set the mind to staying while you pick them out one by one. Thinking on that Sunday girl is like that. She meets the physical description. Would she have the wherewithal to get over to Coates's place? Some girl did. May as well be a tough farm girl with a brother the same age as the dead girl's brothers. A brother who, against his father's obvious inclinations, flirted with joining the militia and had a cordial relationship with Burt Haudesert and his sons.

Those jaggers scrape but they don't hold. For the real tangle, let's speculate Gwen and Liz were bosom friends. Shared their secrets—like you'd expect out of girls that hold hands. Maybe there was more. Could that situation launch the Sunday girl onto a snowmobile to track down the boy that killed Gwen? I can see it.

G'Wain and his partner look to be helping each other—and that opens up another set of brambles. Gale G'Wain lived and worked at Haudesert's, but boys sniff tail all over. Sunday farm only sits a mile beyond Haudesert's—scrappy boy like G'Wain could trot that distance in five minutes. Some kind of free-love between the two? The three? Maybe he turned over one field, ran over and planted seed in the other. It ain't unusual. And it ain't hard to imagine Liz Sunday's been involved from sunup 'til now.

Thoughts turn every which way, trying to find a route out of the briar patch. What if Gale was set to run with Sunday and Gwen found out? Called him on it and involved Burt?

Maybe I'll never know. None of it matters. I'll guaran-goddamn-tee one thing. When we meet up, it won't be to tell G'Wain how a Bittersmith man needs to comport himself. This isn't a tough love mission to turn the wayward back to the straight and narrow.

No, that conversation implies the recipient has a future.

Chapter Thirty-three

Liz mounts her rumbling snowmobile. I slip behind her, grateful for the seat back that supports the weight of the duffel and presses my pelvis snug into Liz. She nestles against me. I position the Krag across her legs and do my best to hold both it and her as she lays her duffel of booty across her lap and the heavy Bolens grumbles forward.

Between killings—I know I'm about to do another—I yearn for some metaphysical banister, because the heights get dizzying. Yearn for something stronger than the Golden Rule or Murphy's Law. I'm on a course that defies everything I've ever learned yet this course came *out of* everything I've ever learned. I don't see how I've erred, and I don't see how I can fail to complete what I've started.

I whiff Liz's hair. She must use the same shampoo as Gwen. I first smelled it in the barn loft at the end of summer. The heat was heavy and the hay was scratchy. Humidity kept our skin flush and with the dust in the air and salt in our sweat—it was as if the barn itself chastened us. I smelled her hair then and through the fall when she would nose against me. As the season got colder the perfume became more fragile, so that last night Gwen smelled the same as Liz does now. Flowers. In the icy air, a whiff brings with it the worry the smell will freeze like a petal and crumble, and nothing will remain save snowmobile exhaust.

We're on top of the hill. The valley is like a ghost seen through dead twigs and trees. Burt Haudesert's barn stands against the fields and its darkness merges with the swampy forest below the garden. From this vantage the surrounding hills look less imposing. Somewhere beyond a fold and around another bend waits the Sunday farm. Liz's father maybe wonders about his son and daughter.

Liz jockeys back and forth, throws her weight twice as far as normal to offset my mass. She is alive under my arms; her thighs continually shift below my hands; the rifle is wobbly like a pole lashed across the top of a buoy.

We blaze across an open field. Liz steers diagonally and every second a twelve-inch cornstalk thwacks the sled's underbelly. We crest a knoll and there's a house and barn. The porch light beckons. The barn seeps yellow through gaps in the wallboards and knotholes.

A farmer works in a harsh economy; must tend the animals before he can tend his family. Her father will be working with the cows; he'll hear the noise and come out. He'll see two of us on one sled and imagine his son has returned with his daughter. Will he be angry about the missing snowmobile?

Liz trembles below my hands.

She slows the snowmobile. We reach the farm at a scant crawl. The trail leads across a flat to the barn. The sled drifts to a stop. Liz kills the engine. The headlight beam vanishes and I smell her hair again.

"You or me," I say.

"Me."

I press my good hand to her shoulder and dismount the machine. The Krag is loaded and I face the barn. The bay light is on and the tractor-door is partly open. A butchered hog hangs from his hind legs. Liz retrieves her rifle from the scabbard on the side of the seat, and standing on the opposite side of the sled, turns to the barn.

"In there?" I say.

She plods forward. Though her first step is short, the next are longer. I clamber around the back of the sled and follow, already ten paces behind. She carries the rifle at port arms, the stock at her right hip, barrel across her chest.

A door thuds closed behind us. I turn, but Liz keeps walking. Her old man stands on the porch under a light and looks like a yellow dog in flannel and overalls. He holds a pistol in his right hand, loose at his side. He's got hog blood on his arms.

"Whole county lookin' for you, boy."

Behind me, the sound of Liz's boots on the packed snow ceases.

I say, "What does a fellow say to that?"

"Liz, come on back here." He watches me. "What, boy? You figure to kill one girl's daddy, and when that don't work, you come looking for another? That it?" He taps his leg with the pistol barrel. "Come here to take me out?"

How many years of playing the game? Of acknowledging another man's strength only because he is willing to break the rules? How many victims are stronger than the men who subjugate them? How many could rise against the bastards holding the chains that shackle their ankles? How many of those bastards owe their seats of hubris and animosity and greed to the tolerance of their betters, the men and women and daughters who do the toiling and the sweating and the grunting, but equate morality with meekness?

He raises the pistol toward me. "Well, boy?"

"Nah, it's not like that," I say. "There was an accident at the Haudesert's and I flipped out. I ran away, and Liz here's the only one that knows the truth of it."

"What's the truth of it, Liz?"

"Truth is, I'm freezing. Let's go inside."

"Where's Link?"

"I don't know. He took off on the other sled and I haven't seen him."

"He better bring it back in one piece."

"That's what's important," I say.

Sunday lowers his gun as Liz steps beside me. She's dropped the rifle to one hand. "Inside," she whispers. I follow. Sunday stands aside on the porch and hair rises on the back of my neck as I hear his footsteps behind me.

The kitchen air hits me like a wall. Blood rushes to my cheeks and the warm air gives me vertigo. I reach to a countertop and my hand brushes an upside down copy of a tattered newspaper that is no less strident looking for all its wear. *The Daily Worker*. It's old. Torn edges, yellowed, folded and opened so many times the paper seems to have peach fuzz.

Liz lays her rifle on the kitchen table.

God knows how long Sunday's been a Red encircled by townsmen with a different take on injustice. They rail against the commies, and Sunday points to the capitalists manipulating the prices of corn and beef and oil and railcars. Except the others have the numbers, and Sunday has to turn his insufficient strength against something even more insignificant in the grand scheme, the girl growing into a woman under his roof. She isn't his daughter. She isn't sacred. She's a place to rub his dick.

I watch condensation form on the blued metal. Sunday steps inside and closes the door. Liz sits at the table, facing him. His eye whites are like busted egg yolks. His skin is creased and sunburned, though it's been months since he's done fieldwork.

"What you got in mind, coming here?" Sunday leans against the countertop by the stove. He crosses his arms and the pistol dangles. His thumb crosses the hammer.

I look at Liz. At some point she's going to decide what she wants to do. She's in the house where it all happened, the refuge that was the site of her terror, at the hands of the man whose politics maybe included her in the town's ostracism. She a cagey creature, this girl who doesn't know how to be a girl. She glances at me and suddenly I'm in Burt Haudesert's kitchen, at the table. Jordan's at my elbow and Gwen is opposite, and she's got that same stare as Liz does now. She's looking straight at the center of the table. Her jaw is set but her brow is soft. There's concentration in her eyes, but no anger or consternation. Her heart's probably beating like a rabbit flushed from the briar but outward, she's spaced out and for the life of me I'll never understand how a man can do that to a girl.

And there's Sunday. Speak of the Devil. The man at the head of the family, defending it…

He's three steps away but ten times stronger and faster than me. But there are more guns on my side of the battlefront. And frankly I don't give a shit.

"Liz, are you going to kill him, or what?"

I'm watching him but at my peripheral right I see her face swing to me. Sunday's eyebrows rumble with an earthquake of rage; his face splits at the jaw and he raises his pistol to me.

Liz says, "No!" and clutches the rifle on the table. She points at her father. "Don't," she says.

I'm the only one with a gun who isn't pointing it. I hold his withering gaze, and the barrel aimed at me is a dot below his right eye. He's bore-sighting me, but the muzzle is no more alarming than the knob on the cupboard behind him. His eyes flicker to Liz, and his rage tinges a different shade as he recognizes her treason.

My throat is raspy. "Your son is dead. Are you happy to know your daughter will make it out alive?"

"This how you do your old man?" He leers at Liz. With his shifting attention, the muzzle drifts. I look at Liz.

"I can't," she says.

I fall leftward, swing the Krag level. Sunday fires his pistol; the muzzle explodes into orange. The shot cracks past my head. Liz screams. I cock the Krag and fire. The rifle erupts and the cupboard behind Sunday must have been filled with dishes. I smell powder. Land on my bad arm. Missed Sunday and he lines his pistol to my face. The sight posts obscure his eye. He's being careful. Slow.

"Goodbye," Liz says. She fires from her hip and Sunday jerks back. He stares as if unhit, though the blood on the wall belies him. A red blot expands in the center of his chest.

His eyes flit from me to her and back. He musters his strength and lifts his weapon arm, fires again. The bullet crashes into the floor beyond me. He drops.

Liz lands her rifle on the table. Circles to her father and stands above him. She kneels and takes his hand.

Sunday chokes and each breath is choppy. Drowning in blood. Sucking up the fear. Standing on the edge of the unknown, yet with the absolute certitude his future won't be pleasant. Maybe that's the way Gwen felt the first time she heard her bedroom door open in the middle of the night. Maybe Liz. I watch and his chest rises. His hand flops. Leg spasms.

Die, will you?

I crawl to my knees then my feet and kick away the gun in his hand. Tears fall from Liz's eyes and I say, "You want to finish this?"

She shakes her head.

"Plug your ears."

She plugs the ear closest the rifle, and leaves her other hand on her father's. I place the Krag muzzle to his forehead.

"No," he grunts.

Fuck him.

* * *

I sit on the edge of the porch.

A pile of steaming vomit marks the snow between my feet. I scoop clean cold powder from the porch and rinse my mouth. Press another handful to the top of my head.

Inside, Liz moves about the kitchen like the woman of the house. I know at least one other role she inherited from her absent mother. She steps around her father, opens a cupboard, stuffs a small item I can't make out into a handbag. Circling the body again, a whimper escapes her. She crumples at her father's feet. The blood on the floor won't let her get any closer.

I think of what her life in that house must have been. He's been her tormenter and it would be a mistake for me to think her tears and shudders are grief. Her lips are tight with anger and her brow is mottled and ridged with frustration; in the slump of her shoulders and the way her derriere rests on a twisted ankle, I see profound relief—and shock—that he is finally gone.

Bittersmith is still out there. There's a link between his evil and Sunday, between his blood in my veins and Sunday's blood curdling in his clothes and soaking into the floor. But I am not his victim—not like Gwen and Liz have been victims. Good people dwell on every little sin. For Gwen and for Liz…for my mother…I have to deal with Bittersmith.

* * *

Liz comes to the open door. I'm watching the barn, the sky, the snow as it is born into existence right here in the light. I hear feet scuffle and look back at Liz. She's parked a suitcase at her feet. She has keys in her hands. "I'm taking the truck to Monroe, and then heading south."

"Monroe?"

"My baby. Do you need to burn this place to the ground?"

"I need very little at this point. Just one thing. Do you?"

She turns to the kitchen. Glances back at me.

She spends a moment near her father, studying him. She finds matches in a cupboard. Rolls *The Daily Worker*, strikes a match, and holds it to three separate places on the newspaper. The flames glow fiercely, and she thrusts the paper to the curtains.

I enter the house again. I'm hungry and won't have food for I don't know how long. It's absurd and comical—entering a burning house for a sandwich. Fire swells to our side. Smoke rolls above our heads. I open the refrigerator.

"You know how to drive that truck outside? In a blizzard?" I look to the refrigerator's shelves as the air thickens with smoke.

"Tires have chains and there's four bags of sand in the bed. I packed everything we need to treat your wounds." She stops cold. "What? What's that look?"

I step away from the refrigerator with a block of cheese wrapped in plastic. "I'm not going with you to Monroe."

Chapter Thirty-four

I see where Gale and his tramp girlfriend parked. I switch off my headlights and crawl closer in moonlight. Park on the road and approach on foot.

I know that filly, Liz Sunday. Brown mane thrown back, eyes bolt open, nostrils wide. Ran into her last fall a few days after she ditched school with Gwen. Couldn't help notice the size of them thighs, and imagine their strength. Got a rack on her, too. Wide and heavy—enough to make a man want to get familiar. I pulled beside her in the Bronco. Told her to get in. She had her shoulders hunched over a single textbook and took small steps. Any girl old enough for freckles knows how to fake the cotton pony.

"I'm not well."

"Sheriff tells you to get in the truck, that's a lawful command."

She climbed inside.

"You're the Sunday girl. That your daddy? The communist?"

She watched the glove box.

"Whoring around, skipping school. You're going nowhere fast. You want to break rules, you'd best learn to please the men who make them."

She swallowed.

"You got problems in school. I might smooth things over. Superintendent's a friend of mine. A good friend. But you miss two weeks of the year and skip days here and there like I saw you the other week…all that makes things difficult. Maybe you and me can work together."

She squinted.

"I might be inclined to help, if we was to get familiar with one another."

"Familiar."

"That's right. Come over here. You've done oral work, I take it?"

"What the hell does that mean?"

I judged her with a stern look. She judged me right back. I pulled her shoulder. She wrenched away. "You know how to use your mouth. Get the fuck over here."

"No—God help me!"

She swiped for the door handle. I grabbed her wrist and yanked 'til she stopped pulling.

"You're in real stiff trouble. I'm going to give you some tough love, so you might learn to get on in a town like Bittersmith. 'God help me.' How old are you?"

She wrinkled her brow. Jutted her chin. Looked out the windshield.

"Something you've got to learn, and I'm going to break this down simple, and only say it once. This is all you got to know the rest of your days. There is no higher law. You can't appeal to God, because nobody believes in him but you. *God help me.* You can't trust your neighbor's goodwill. You can't even trust your father. He's a fuckin' pervert. I know all about that pinko son of a bitch—raised an uppity girl for damn sure. The only way you're going to enjoy your wretched-assed life is to accept the rules. God don't have a goddamn thing to do with it. So fuck your attitude. Fuck god. Drag your ass over here and suck."

I gave her a chance. I let go her arm and she bolted. I watched her run down the sidewalk, period and all.

I'll enjoy getting reacquainted.

I walk up the Sunday drive. A snowmobile is parked in the stretch between the barn and the house. A truck sits nearby. Both the barn and house got a light on. I watch the glow in the kitchen window and before long, shadows move inside. Murderous thug like G'Wain wouldn't think twice about planting a bullet in a man's back. Twenty yards out I stop, waiting 'til I see both of them.

Instead Liz Sunday steps to the glass and holds a flaming wand to the curtain. I don't give a shit for the communist's house, but these kids have a habit of burning bodies. Three sandwiches and a half-thermos of coffee, I'm feeling my oats. I run. Maybe too fast, without thinking.

The door is open. I come straight at it and the picture resolves. The man on the floor is Sunday. Got a puddle of brain noodles all around his shoulders.

G'Wain's on the far side of the kitchen, turned to the side, got a pistol in his holster and his hand hanging loose. Gunslinger holds a lump of cheese while the house burns. Twenty feet out, I stop and line the sights on his head. I squeeze the trigger. My Smith & Wesson jumps and Liz Sunday steps into view. She drops the burning paper. She lifts her open hands to her chest. Panic pales her face. I shift left. Fire again.

G'Wain spins. Ducks away.

I shot the damned girl. I shot that big-titted Liz.

I follow my Smith & Wesson barrel to the door. The flames chew both curtains and lick at the ceiling. I see Liz's knees and wonder if she'd gotten down on them, would any of this have been any different?

"You don't have time for a gunfight, Gale! Put the rifle on the floor and come outside. This is the law speaking."

I fire again, into the flames.

* * *

Liz fell toward the hallway. The front door remains open. I glance at her father as if he lifted his dead pistol-arm and shot her, but the blast came from outside. I jump back. Another shot cracks by and I see the muzzle flash.

Bittersmith.

I reel back, lose my balance. He would have had me, but Liz stepped in his way. He's waiting. He's been after me all day, and I've been after him six months. His path is maddeningly direct and mine is woven between the lives of girls and perverts. He's biding his time until I check Liz. I choke on smoke. Flames curl from wall to ceiling and leap at the other wall. Orange spreads exponentially. Everywhere. I fire my pistol through the open doorway.

"I'm coming for you, boy!"

"You'll feel at home!"

I fire again and step closer to Liz. Fire again. I kneel beside her, take in the pool of blood, the glaze on her motionless eyes, the stillness of her chest. She's gone, and though I don't know if she's going to heaven or hell I wish for a moment I had time to eulogize her. She didn't choose to be bad.

Bittersmith fires through the door and the kitchen window shatters. "You're going to die in that fire, 'less you come out now!"

I can barely hear him above the roaring flames.

"I'll take you to the station. We'll talk!"

"You into boys too, you prick?"

I continue firing and lurch to the hallway where the fire hasn't yet ignited everything into a swirling orange maelstrom. The hallway feels like an august afternoon, but it will soon be hell. I point the pistol back toward the door, squeeze the trigger, feel an impotent click on my fingertip. I chuck the pistol and duck below heavy smoke.

Bittersmith would be a fool to wait at the front of the house. There are doors at end of the hall on the left and right, and one on each side. Each is closed. I don't know which is escape and which is Bittersmith.

I grab a broom leaning in the corner; hang my coat over the handle. Crouched low, I open the first door on my left and ease the silhouette-maker into the opening. Bittersmith does not shoot. Fire broils my back. I close the door, open the opposite, a bathroom, and flames lurch closer. I shift the broom and coat into the doorway. No response. I cough like to exhale three organs. I slam the door. At the end of the hallway, I throw open the door on the left. Mucous and spit hang from my jaw. My eyes burn and no amount of blinking soothes them. I shift the broom, but before it enters the opening a window shatters and a firearm barks.

"I got you covered! You're going to die, you murdering son of a whore!"

I swing the door closed. Grab my coat and rush back down the hall toward the kitchen. The fire halts my advance. The heat is unbearable. I reverse to the bathroom, burst through the door, crawl inside. Another shot zips above me. I toss my coat into the bathtub and turn on the water. It splashes for five seconds and my coat is soaked. I drape it over my head, toss water to my face, my pants.

I can't escape the premonition that I'm going to die in this fire. For the first time, I want to curse God. For putting me here, for giving me this mission and abandoning me in flames. I want to blaspheme; I want to say I'm on my own; I want to relinquish my faith as God has forsaken me. But biting my tongue brings clarity. I am not evil. I must not quit.

I'll continue on my own and meet up with God later.

The flames have overtaken the hallway. Smoke pours into the bathroom. A bullet smashes through the window—rips my coat, creases my skin—and flames advance in an orange-black tornado.

My heart thuds. I see Guinevere. Red-faced. Ashamed and broken. I see hair stuck to her temple with tears. I leap into the hallway and for a split second my face is cool from damp air. I feel relief. This isn't hot—

And then every inch of my body screams. I can't breathe. Each step is a battle. I crash into the table. Trip on Sunday's dead shoulders. My lungs are about to burst and my face feels about to ignite. I reach the front door and gulp brittle air. I'm steaming and dripping and expecting a bullet. The porch is dry. Breathing air is like biting ice. I hurry toward the barn over melted snow and mottled grass. I have to get cover before Bittersmith circles to the front of the house. How much time before he thinks of the barn?

The light is on in the top bay. I rush inside as a bullet smacks into a timber at my side. I have a minute. Maybe two.

In the center of the barn hangs a recently slaughtered hog. The carcass is hoisted high, as if Sunday feared roving animals. The blood that has dripped to the floor will surely bring coyotes. I glance at the workbench on the right side of the bay, below a hayloft, and thrill at recognizing the tools of slaughter—a bell scraper, hooks, knives—but they are useless. No small handgun like Burt Haudesert used, no grease pencil to draw the X.

I search the other tools. There's a scythe on nails, a rake, a pitchfork. I study it. A pry bar—I could pull up a floorboard. I spin, look around. Haylofts above. If I could climb I could topple a dozen bales on Bittersmith. But he'll arrive in a minute. There's a hay chute a dozen feet away for a quick drop to the lower level. Back to the bench. Ropes, a set of tire chains. Screwdrivers and even a rusted chisel. Vice grips.

I feel like Judas looking at a tree over a cliff, and wonder if the best way to meet up with God is to get it over with.

* * *

That fuckin' redheaded squirt jailbroke the house and made it to the barn. If he takes off through the snow, I'll hound him to hell.

The barn's got a yellow bulb shining sharp against darkness that covers the farm, the fields, the hill. The door is part open. I walk until I can see inside. G'Wain stands below the light. His face is pale. His hands hang at his sides and from the bottom of the slope, I can't see what's in them. He sees me and nods like he wants a palaver.

I stop and reload my Smith & Wesson. My fingers are cold. My arms are heavy. I drop a shell and leave it in the snow. Finished, I keep the pistol in my right hand. I face the barn and walk, but glance side to side. It wasn't a mile from here that Burt met his end, and Gwen too, back in the woods.

I climb the slope. Gale's hands are empty. As if reading my mind he rotates his wrists and shows me palms. Probably has a pistol tucked behind his back. His eyes are steady and the bulb overhead makes his brow sharp as a ploughshare.

I point my Smith & Wesson. It's over for Gale G'Wain.

"You raped my mother."

I pull back the hammer.

"Nineteen fifty one. She was just passing through."

"Oh, you want a conversation? Bodies all over. Gwen. Burt. Deputies and militiamen. Even shot the town commie. Now you're too chickenshit to face the music."

"You raped my mother."

He's too cool. "Turn around. Let me see your back."

Keeping his left foot planted and his arms away from his body, he pivots. He favors his leg and one arm shakes. No pistol stowed at his back; no knife. Nothing.

"Put your arms down. Turn around."

He drops his arms and faces me.

I ought to shoot him. Lord knows I ought to blow his head off. It'd be an abrogation of duty to let him live. I hold the gun on him and my hand wavers. My arm is lead. I squeeze slow and try to time it so the sights are on Gale when the pistol goes off.

Nothing doing. My Smith & Wesson jumps, but Gale G'Wain don't.

Closer. I won't miss with the barrel at his forehead. I cross the threshold into the barn and the sounds change but the air is still crisp. Between us is the hitch-end of a rusted harrow, a Frisbee-sized dribble of blood from a suspended hog, and a foot away, a long clump of hay from a busted bale.

He stares like a judge. I step closer. Glance up at the hog.

He's killed half of Bittersmith and thinks he's going to turn himself in? Something ain't right. G'Wain shifts and I look at his legs, his boots, and the rope below his left heel. He watches my eyes. The rope runs from his foot and disappears under the workbench. Seems to reemerge at the joist above, and stretches across the trusses, and concludes at the hog dangling in the air between us.

I snort, can't help it. He thinks he's my son, but any boy of mine would know better than to try to use a hog for a deadfall.

"I ain't your father."

He's silent.

"You said I had your mother and that's even odds. But you surely didn't come out of it."

G'Wain's a scrappy little son of a bitch, and the wounds…he's got a limp just standing there. Stiff like he's full of bullet holes and it's all he can do to keep from falling over. Yet he stands. He's tough—I'll hand him that—but he ain't clever enough to be my blood. Rope out in the open. A hog!

I keep the pistol sights steady on his head and a memory seizes me, cotton candy smells and all, in a single flash. I watch his feet. The rope. I want to prolong this for just a moment. I want to study his face.

"I remember as a boy my father took me to the fair in Monroe. I was walking in front of him, and another man was coming. There was plenty of room on both sides, see? But he was coming straight for me. I shifted out his way and he didn't even look down. I didn't see half of it, but my father didn't step aside. He knocked that man on his ass. And after the brouhaha, Dad cuffed the back of my head like to raise a knot a calf could suck on. Spun me around and grabbed my neck. He said, 'never step out of another man's way. Make him knock you aside. The day'll come when he can't.'"

G'Wain studies me. "So we've got shitty fathers in common."

I fire again. He stares. I miss.

G'Wain looks at the floor, then to his right, at a stack of bales. "How many have you raped? Did you count? Because I don't think it was just my mother."

I shift my pistol and step closer.

"I've been thinking what it must be like," he says. "You see something you want and you take it. Have you ever had to admit what you've done?"

"I've lawed this town forty goddamn years!"

"Whose laws?"

"Mine!"

"You're a ravager with a badge living in a town of cowards. None of them have the guts to meet your eye and you think their fear gives you impunity. But I'm calling you out. You raped my mother ."

I fire again. This one nicks his arm.

He lurches back but keeps his left foot planted on the rope.

I'm mad enough to piss blood. "There wasn't a single damn woman didn't want it. You wasn't there! Who the fuck are you to question me?"

"Your son."

"You're not!"

I'm going to put a bullet in his head. I lurch forward, stop inches shy of the hog. He was goading me. It was an act.

The harrow blocks me on the right. Looking up at the hog, I step around its path and into a mess of straw—and my leg drops. I fall and my legs wishbone—big snap in my thigh—one leg sideways on the barn floor and the other hangs down below. My gun-hand slaps a plank and my Smith & Wesson clatters away.

A full five seconds of shock pass and then my groin feels completely ripped out. Never such pain…There was no board… He pulled up the board and covered it with hay…

G'Wain smirks. He lifts his foot from the rope and the rope don't move. I follow his gaze to the hog, swinging above. They're not connected.

I strain for the pistol but I've got coffee and sandwiches wanting to scoot out the way they came in.

"You—"

He steps closer. "What?"

"You deceived me."

"Yeah."

I laugh. I can't help it. My nuts feel like the inside of a pin cushion and I swear my boot is filled with blood—but this skinny clothesline of a boy just put a hurt on me. Out-clevered me. I laugh. "You got me."

* * *

Bittersmith wriggles back and forth. Sweat beads on his brow and his breath comes out like steam from a train, each blast followed by a prolonged, regenerative pause. He reaches for his pistol. I lift it.

"So that story about your father. You blame him?"

Bittersmith emits a long, gritty sigh. With one hand he tries to shift his topside leg closer to the hole he's fallen into, but the bone is shattered. I can tell from the angle and blood.

"Ah, shit. That's homage. I don't blame my father. That's respect. You wouldn't know a thing about that."

"No, I wouldn't. You missed. Why didn't you hit me?"

He laughs. Pain—or hopelessness—makes him merry.

"Didn't want to." He snorts back a laugh, then groans. "You want to pull me out of this mess, or push my leg straight so I can drop it down with the other?"

I aim at his head. "Why didn't you shoot to hit me?"

He looks everywhere but at me. I believe I'm the first person to ever put his mind in a vice and twist the handle. I see the struggle in his eyes. The madness. Finally his gaze meets mine.

I say, "I'm your son."

He chuckles. Coughs. "Fuck this hurts."

"You raped my mother. In ten seconds you'll have to confess it to another."

"You got no fucking authority!"

"No, I have a gun. Confess?"

"Never."

I get down on both knees. I press the barrel to his temple.

"NEVER!"

I squeeze the trigger.

* * *

After a minute of looking at his dead face and not feeling any better about my life, his death, the day that has passed, or my prospects for the days that will follow, I kick his leg until it aligns and he drops through. The pressure from his ribs forces a final grunt from his mouth. It sounds lascivious. Horrific.

Maybe he'll fall all the way to hell.

I'm tempted to find a horse blanket and nap in the loft. Maybe I'll wake and find the day has been a nightmare and that Gwen and I escaped to Mexico.

I see Gwen with more clarity, now. And Liz.

Their situations made them consider self-preservation above all. Survival required them to use any available means to end their subjugation. Liz took it farther. She was ready to use her sex to trap me. It became a tool.

Gwen started down that path and turned from it.

Neither girl was bad, but only one was good. I loved her. How could Gwen have loved anybody? Or seen any man as anything other than a new instrument of oppression? The world presented Gwen a hard vision and she willed herself to see softness. Our romance began because of proximity, but she loved because she knew it was better than the hatred, anger and pain her father had visited upon her. She was strong enough to see beauty in an ugly world. She was an eminently lovable woman.

I better leave.

Sunday's truck is out front—but the keys burned with Liz. There's a snowmobile halfway to the house, but I won't be able to steer it.

And there is Bittersmith's vehicle, parked out there somewhere.

I find stairs. Bittersmith has fallen into a milking stall, and is bent harshly backward over one of the tubular steel dividers. The structure holds him with his head wound lower than his body. Blood trickles to the shit-trough at the end of the stall.

When I kicked his leg straight and he vanished through the floor, the image convinced me he might fall all the way to hell. That's what he earned; he sowed his seeds and how many women suffered the harvest? But looking at him with his head bled out on the cement, his eyes blank, and his crotch saturated with blood…

Now men will know fear.

I fish keys from his pocket.

Acknowledgements:

I'd like to thank Julie, my wife, for honest help and ongoing support. Sometimes it isn't easy to be interested in a new "greatest paragraph ever written"—especially an hour past bedtime—but you always were.

Thank you to my mother and father, Georgina and Donald, for the exact life you gave me. I wouldn't change a moment of it.

Thank you to Cameron McClure, my agent, for your belief in *Cold Quiet Country*, for really getting it, and for making it so much better with your insights. And thank you for the title!

To Guy Intoci, my editor, it's a thrill seeing you make this book more crisp, more clear, stronger. Thank You.

Thank you to Loren Fairman. This book wouldn't exist without your encouragement and surgical criticism. Truly, you're one in a million.

There are a thousand people whose encouragement has kept me writing. Dan Youatt, Fatima Sharif, thank you. Oh, and Michel Rau. You said, "This sounds like a real book." That was great.

And finally, thank you, Cathy. We all love and miss you.